CLOAKED

EASTHAVEN CREST, BOOK ONE

A. D. JUSTICE

Cloaked

USA TODAY BESTSELLING AUTHOR
A.D. JUSTICE

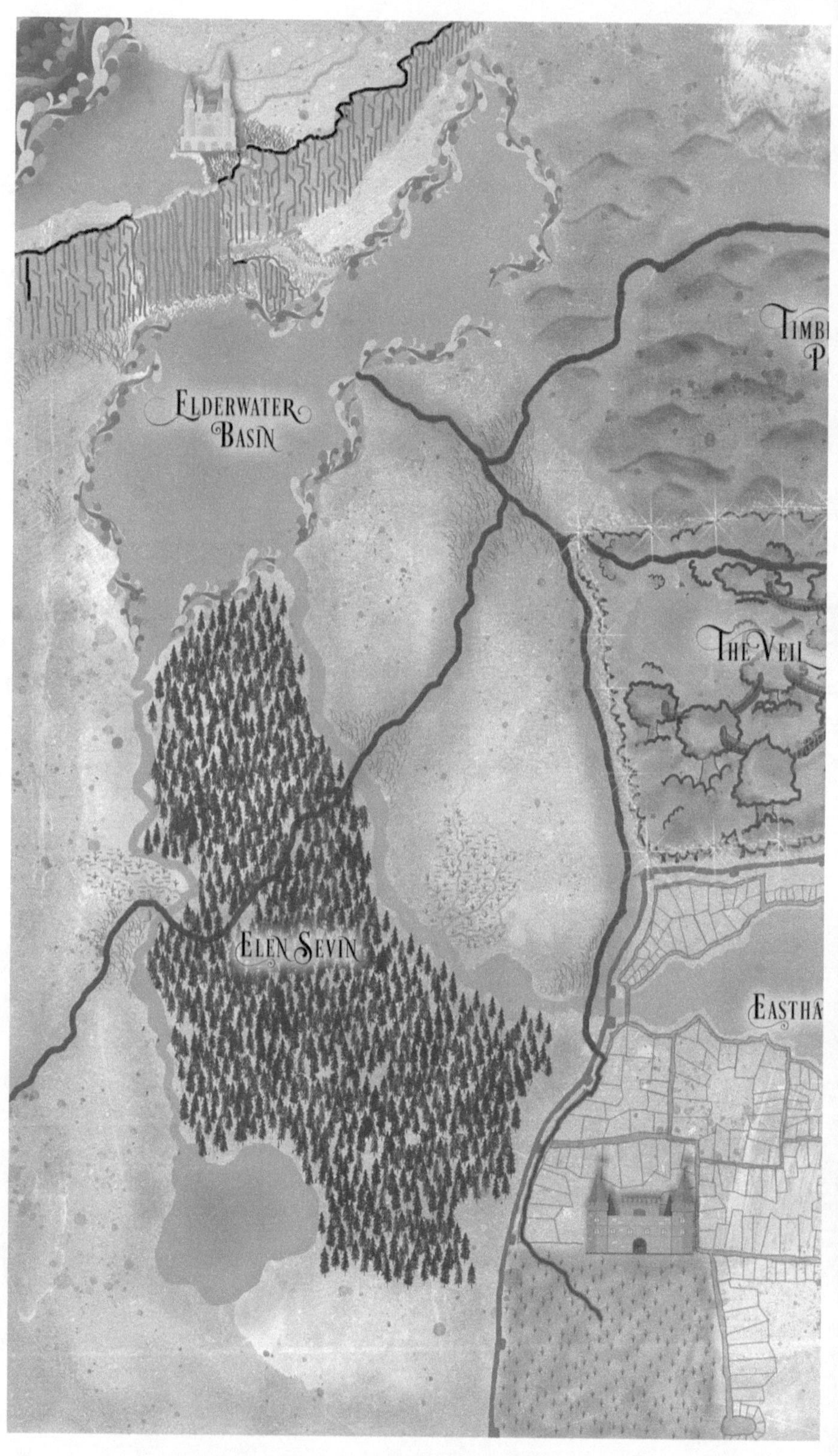

ELDERWATER BASIN
ELEN SEVIN
TIMBER P
THE VEIL
EASTHA

NIGHTSIDE MOUNTAINS
TIMBERGARDE POINTE
STHAVEN CREST
the COVIS realm
N

CHAPTER 1

Present Day

Confusion mixes with an inordinate amount of fear as I walk toward the front of my nana's store. The door looks like it has been kicked in, barely hanging on by the bottom hinge. The glass pane that displayed her store name and logo is shattered in a million pieces on the floor. The large picture window from the front of the store is smashed, mixed with the debris scattered throughout the front room. The usually safe and quiet streets of Aspen Springs, Montana, that I've known my whole life, and have walked without adult supervision for almost as long, suddenly feel very dangerous.

"Nana?" I call out into the dark room and pull my phone from my back pocket.

With no regard for my own safety, I rush inside, using the flashlight on my phone to peer into the store. The crunch of glass and mixed debris under my feet as I move room to room makes me sick. I search for her everywhere —behind the cash register, in the bathroom, the kitchen, and finally, the storeroom. But she's not here, and I instantly feel lost and alone.

This store has been her pride and joy my whole life. If she were aware of the break-in, she'd already be here, cleaning up before the police arrived to do their job.

Unless she was inside the store when the door was knocked in and the front window was shattered…

That thought sends chills down my spine, and I quickly call for help. When the dispatcher answers, I rattle off the address and ask her to tell the deputies to hurry. Not that it'll take the police long to get here in this small town, but hearing the dispatcher reassure me they are already on their way makes me feel so much better. When she begins to tell me to stay on the line until the police arrive, I hang up and call home instead. I have to reach Nana and make sure she's okay, then break the bad news to her.

The phone at home rings endlessly. We live on the edge of the forest, several miles outside of town, so we're one of the few places left in the world where landlines are a necessity in this modern age. Nana refused to get an answering machine or, God forbid, a digital answering service. With no way for me to leave a message telling her to call me as soon as she can, the level of anxiety building inside my chest feels as if it'll explode, leaving no trace of me behind.

She knew I was going out with my friends tonight, so she wouldn't have been far from the phone. Every troubling piece of this situation is so out of character for her. I can feel something is terribly wrong, like a sixth sense warning me of impending danger, breathing down my neck.

"Calm down, Sara. She could just be on her way home. They waited for her to leave the shop before breaking in." I try to talk some sense into myself—aloud because I'm still alone—but it's not helping at all. In fact, it sounds a lot like I'm lying to myself.

The wail of the police sirens grows closer, and a voice inside my head tells me they won't find her. I shake my head harshly as if that will dislodge the depressing whispers. When I turn toward the oncoming cars, I notice one is a regular patrol vehicle and the other is an unmarked car. They stop with their headlights shining into the front of the building before getting out and walking to me.

"Detective Ryan Miller. And you are?" He extends his hand to me, and I shake it absently.

"Sara Nemertes."

"Is this your family's business?" He pulls a small notebook and pen from the breast pocket of his jacket and starts taking notes.

"It's my grandmother's store. Her name is Sue Nemertes. She's usually still here at this hour, especially when she knows I'm going to the movies with my friends. But I just walked up and found it like this. I called our home phone, but she didn't answer. I need to try again."

When he doesn't say anything, I look up at him and see an empathetic expression in his eyes. He's thinking the same thing I did earlier. If she's not here and she's not at home, the alternatives are not good. He doesn't have to voice his thoughts for me to hear and feel them. It's something I've dealt with my entire life.

Nana always told me I was just more intuitive than others, that's why I could sense what everyone else was thinking before they spoke. I learned to filter through all the extraneous noise at an early age and focus on what was important. Detective Miller's thoughts flow freely to my mind because I'm so focused on him and he's standing so close to me.

"Have you been inside yet?" He quickly changes gears, getting back to business and refocusing his attention on his job.

"Yes. I know that's against the 'preserve the crime scene' rules, but I had to know if she was inside and unable to answer me because she was hurt. I tried to touch as little as possible, but I couldn't stand here and not look for her."

"Sounds like you know a bit about police procedure."

"I've watched way too many crime movies and episodes of *CSI*." I shrug one shoulder, knowing watching a few fictional shows doesn't make me an expert in anything.

"Wait here while we have a look around."

Another call home is fruitless. No answer, only endless

ringing on the other end. She's not there and she's not here.

After the detective finishes asking his final questions and assuring me he'll be in touch if anything turns up, I watch him get into his car and drive away, all while my feet remain glued to the floor. He offered me a ride to a friend's or family's house, but I lied and said I already had someone coming to get me. The last thing I need is to be away from home right now.

Nothing feels real when I turn my head and look around the store Nana loved so much. The once perfectly arranged displays of soils, herbs, and seasonal plants are now strewn across the floor in pieces. The shelves lie flat against the floor, leaving the stacks of paperback books and boxes of plant food bent and mangled.

The deputy is still here, boarding up the smashed window. Then he fixes the broken door as much as possible before he leaves. With a hammer and a few nails, he boards up the door enough to prevent anyone else from getting inside. He also offers me a ride home before exiting out the back, but I decline, choosing to wait for my best friend Kristi to pick me up instead.

Detective Miller said there was definitely a struggle, but he didn't find any sign of injury in the debris. No blood. No hair. No pieces of torn clothing. Nana couldn't have just disappeared, though. She wouldn't have left the shop in this state. The only explanation that makes any sense is someone took her against her will. A botched robbery, maybe? A store invasion that went wrong, possibly? So many scenarios fly through my mind, each worse than the last. Each with a more disturbing ending.

"What if they come back?" I ask myself aloud. The words tumble out of my mouth before my brain even has a chance to consider them.

In an instant, I'm across the room and standing in front of the back door with my hand on the top deadbolt lock. Everything is such a blur that I don't even remember crossing the room. With a flick of my wrist, I secure the door, my heart beating so hard it makes my shirt jump. Next, I rush to the remaining storefront windows and pull down the shades, hiding inside.

Now, I'm alone. All alone. Just me, in the middle of the broken pieces of Nana's livelihood.

And just like that, I can't breathe. All I can hear over the sound of my pounding heart is the blood rushing through my veins, swishing in my ears as violently as the Class III rapids on the Yellowstone River.

"Kristi, are you almost here?" I try to keep the terror building inside me out of my voice. I don't want to scare her any more than I already have.

"I'm about to pull into the parking spot now. Are you okay, Sara?"

"Yeah, just freaked out over all this. The front door can't be opened now because it's nailed shut until we can get someone out to fix it. I'll come out the back and around the building."

"I'm right here in front, waiting for you. Stay on the phone with me until you get to my car." This time, I listen to sound advice and keep talking while I lock up and sprint the entire way to her car.

I know Kristi talked to me on the ride out to my house, but I can't remember a single word of our conversation when we pull in my driveway. Our home is set among the trees, bordering the national forest behind us. When the house comes into view, all my hopes are quickly dashed when I see the completely dark windows and no car in the carport.

"I just realized Nana's car wasn't behind the building either. Someone really does have her, don't they?"

"I don't know what to say, Sara. I'm just so sorry about all of this. You should stay with me tonight. You really shouldn't be here alone." Kristi pleads with me, but one thing I have in common with Nana is my stubborn streak.

"No, I need to be here in case she calls or comes home. If she's not home by morning, I probably will stay with you tomorrow night. I just can't leave tonight."

"Do you want me to stay with you?"

"No, Kris. You're my best friend and I love you for offering, but I know you're taking the ACT in the morning. You need to focus on that instead. I'll talk to you tomorrow afternoon, and we'll go from there."

She doesn't like my answer, but she can't argue with my logic either. She gets out with me, insistent on checking the entire house before she leaves me alone. Now that we're both satisfied no one is waiting in the closets or behind the doors, we hug goodbye before she gets back into her car. I watch her drive away through the

front window with all the lights off so she can't see me...
and the river of tears flowing down my cheeks.

Nighttime feels as if it lasts forever. I toss and turn all
night, sleeping for a few minutes at a time before turning
over and looking at the clock yet again. When the sun
begins to rise, I decide to get up with it since getting any
sleep now is out of the question. I head straight for the
shower and get dressed before moving downstairs. As
much as I was awake last night, I would've known if Nana
had come in. Since I know she didn't, I'm in no hurry to
walk into the kitchen, look at her empty chair at the table,
and see her favorite coffee cup unused on the counter.

But that's precisely what happens...and it's all too
much for me to process.

TWO DAYS PASS IN A BLUR WITH ME WAITING FOR SOME
word from Nana or Detective Miller. I've called him too
many times to be socially acceptable, but he's shown
nothing but patience with me. He continues to reassure
me he's working every angle possible, but he doesn't have
any answers yet. That's a roundabout way of saying he
doesn't have a single shred of evidence more than he did a
couple days ago when he showed up on the scene. He has
no leads that point to where Nana may be. He has no idea
of who has her, where they are now, or what they could
possibly want. If that's even the case.

All I know is, I'm going crazy after two days of not

having any news of her whereabouts. I can't even entertain the horrible thoughts trying to invade my mind.

I wake up Monday morning with every intention of going to school, despite knowing I won't be able to focus on anything in class. I've debated with myself over the merits of staying home—or facing all the questions from my other friends at school. I decided being with others would be better than staying here alone for another day, with my mind dreaming up new and more inventive horrible scenarios with each passing minute. I've rejected Kristi's requests, and eventual demands, for me to stay with her family for the time being. I'm just not very good company right now, and I don't want to bring my burdens into their home.

When I step out of our house with my backpack in one hand and the other on the doorknob, my mind plays tricks on me. I see Nana everywhere and in everything—the flower beds waiting for spring planting, the garden that needs to be tilled and planted, and the forest she taught me to love so much. My future feels utterly uncertain without her guiding hand, the one I've tried to get out from under for the last seventeen years.

The weight of the world on my shoulders is too much to bear. Over the past couple of years, I've thought I was grown and didn't need my grandmother's constant watchful eye. I thought I was ready to take on the world as an adult, making my own decisions and plotting my escape to more exotic locales. Funny how quickly perspectives change.

On second thought, it's heartbreaking how quickly life has changed for me.

So much so, I can't stand the agony for one more second.

My book bag slips from my hand, crashing to the ground, and my legs move without conscious thought, as if they have a mind and a will of their own. When I finally slow down, I realize where my feet have carried me—deep into the interior of the forest that feels like home to me.

This is my happy place—the one that fills me with peace and clears my head of all the noise and clutter. Before my lungs have time to stop burning, I scale the biggest tree I've ever seen, climbing from limb to limb until my legs burn and shake, too fatigued to hold me up any longer. Feeling lost and afraid, I lean against the enormous trunk with my legs stretched out along the branch. I don't sense the bitter sting of February in Montana. The snow on the ground and on the boughs doesn't faze me. It's actually the oddest sensation I've ever felt. I'm simultaneously completely numb and a raw, exposed nerve that feels so many levels of the indescribable pain.

My last conversation with Nana replays in my head and how I complained about details that don't seem so important anymore. A couple days ago, those trivial desires were all I could think about. Today, they only crossed my mind because of her absence.

My world feels as if it's crashing down around me, and I can't contain the feelings threatening to strangle me from the inside. When the heartbreak inside my chest becomes too much to restrain, I sit up straight and scream out at the top of my lungs. Letting go of everything I've bottled up over the last few days, I release one long, sorrowful wail after another. With no one around to hear or judge me, I can wallow in my pain and get it out of my system to focus my attention on finding her instead.

With my throat sore and my supply of tears depleted, I release a defeated sigh. It's time to get back to real life and face the hard tasks the way Nana would expect me to. I reach to grab the limb above me to stand and begin the climb back down, but a loud pop underneath me makes me freeze in place. Before I can wrap my hand around the limb above, the one below me breaks in two, and I start to free-fall toward the thick branch ten feet below me.

This is really going to hurt.

Just before I reach the thick lower limb, a vast black hole appears from nowhere, pulling me in and closing behind me.

I land on a soft, thick cushion of moss with barely a thud.

The only problem is…this isn't *my* forest.

In fact, I have no clue where I am.

CHAPTER 2

Three Days Prior

"Sara, are you pouting again?" My grandmother puts her hand on her hip and cocks one eyebrow at me, her usual stance of disapproval.

"Nana, it's rude to read other people's minds, you know."

"I don't have to read your mind to know you're over there pouting about not going off to college at the end of summer instead of counting the inventory like you're supposed to do."

With a sullen sigh, I turn back to my to-do list and finish my current task. Maybe I am pouting, but I'm still only seventeen. There are so many things I want to do with my life. So many places I want to see that are far away from Aspen Springs.

Population 3,118.

"Did you know more than half of all high school grad-uates attend college?" It's a rhetorical question—one I've only asked her every day for the past several months since my senior year in high school started. She knows.

My eighteenth birthday is in May. It's currently February, so it's only a few months away. It's a day most teenagers view as our very own independence day. Our first step into adulthood.

But I don't feel liberated.

Instead of excitement over my birthday, I feel trapped in a mediocre life.

Maybe it's the small-town atmosphere that makes me struggle with these feelings, especially since I have no plans of ever leaving and no prospects for the fast-paced, exciting life I've watched others live out in movies and on TV. I know, I know—my comparisons are based on wildly unrealistic expectations. I've been told that sentiment enough times, the mantra should be laser engraved into my brain.

How could my life ever measure up to the glitz and glam I see online?

But I don't understand why I can't have a multicity college campus tour, like the ones so many other kids my age have been posting about for months now online. Where is my future headed, other than working for my grandmother in her store in our small town? I'm well aware that money doesn't grow on trees and we can't conjure it out of thin air, so Ivy League schools were never on my list. The truth is, I just never expected all my studying, maintaining straight As, and graduating as vale-dictorian of my class would mean so little in the end.

The grand plans I've dreamed of for years aren't part of my future—and never will be. I'm destined to live in a world of perpetual boredom and servitude.

"Sara, if you've finished sulking, can you bring me a glass of water?"

"I'll bring you one even though I still have at least another hour's worth of sulking in me."

Nana's amused chuckle makes me smile despite my morose attitude. When I hand her the glass of water, she pops two pills in her mouth and swallows them with a big gulp of water.

"Thank you, sweetheart."

"Another headache, Nana?" She nods and purses her lips but doesn't meet my questioning gaze. "You've had several migraines in a row now. Maybe you should go see Dr. Henry and let him check you out. I don't think it's a good idea to leave you alone today. I'll call Kristi and tell her I can't make it after all."

"I'm fine and still strong as an ox. No need to worry about me. Finish the inventory then you can go have fun with your friends. Kristi, Doug, and Phillip will be disap-pointed if you cancel on them now. It's only a movie—you won't be out that long. Besides, you're too young to worry about me like that."

"Are you sure you'll be okay?"

"Believe it or not, I'm fully capable of taking care of

myself, even at my old age." Nana raises both of her eyebrows at me, daring me to dispute her words.

Don't go, a voice in my head whispers. Or is it my over-active imagination? My conscience?

The first time I heard something like that, I thought I was going mad. But Nana explained that sometimes our thoughts and feelings take over, convincing us we've experienced things that weren't there. Other times, it could be divine intervention. Still others, it could be malevolent voices. She helped me work through them until I was able to discern them for myself—for the most part.

Since she has assured me she's okay, it's probably my tendency to worry about her health. She's the only family I have left in the world since my parents died when I was a baby. No brothers or sisters. No other family members still living on either side. Nana and I have faced the world together and made the best of what we've earned, through hard work, sweat, and tears. While the more logical part of my seventeen-year-old brain understands she just wants me to be proud of the business she's built and continue it long after she's retired, a bigger part of me only wants to leave here and live my life to the fullest.

Then I feel guilty, because that would leave her all alone.

I don't know of a way I can have her by my side and have the world at my feet at the same time. Each scenario boils down to an impossible choice—stay here with the only family member I have or leave her here alone while I chase my dreams.

What's a girl to do?

"Okay, movie night it is."

The rest of my afternoon shift flies by with thoughts of spending time with my best friends. We've all known one another since kindergarten, and we've been inseparable almost as long. They keep me sane and grounded, while also helping me enjoy my crazy and flighty side. Together, we're the perfect balance of harmony and chaos.

Kristi is a whiz with anything that runs on any type of computer. She got caught hacking in to the county's government website and combing through discrepancies in their accounting, but she used the embezzlement evidence she found in exchange for clemency. She vowed only to use her talents for good—to help people rather than hurt them. Now, several agencies identified by initials, and a few that aren't identified anywhere on paper, have recruited her to join their ranks when she finishes college.

Doug is a great guy and an all-around jock. He plays a different sport every season, always the captain of whatever team he's on, and even manages to fit in a few more outside of school just for fun on the weekends. Skilled in football, wrestling, competitive swimming, and baseball—he has his pick of college teams to play for and scholarships to accept. But he has a good head on his shoulders, and he's taking his time before making a decision. He's weighing his options for the future and not allowing anyone to pressure him.

Phillip is a musical genius. He's in our high school band, of course, but he also has his own band. His parents started him in music lessons early, and no instrument has proven to be out of his league. As if that talent isn't enough, he's also a phenomenal singer. He has the voice of an angel and the range of an opera singer. He's going places with all his talents, without a doubt. I wouldn't be surprised to see him on a world tour, with screaming fans all jockeying for his attention.

I've been blessed with amazing friends, all talented in their own right. All fantastic people, regardless of what their gifts are. While I've never been jealous of them, only thrilled with their accomplishments, I have often wondered how I fit in with this group of overachievers. Aside from my good grades, there's nothing outwardly remarkable or extraordinary about me. Unlike my friends, I don't have any hidden talents that'll make me the next superstar. I can operate a computer, but I have no clue how to break in to a secure system and find anything of value. Somehow, I lack the coordination needed for almost any competitive sport, outside of running. I couldn't catch a baseball if my life depended on it, and I sure couldn't throw one to someone else. Let's not forget that music—both playing and singing—doesn't come naturally to me. In fact, most people cover their ears when I sing, and understandably so.

I haven't figured out where and how I fit in life in general yet.

Our little town is far too small to support a movie theater, so we have to drive more than an hour to the next larger town. On the ride over, Kristi, Doug, and Phillip all talk excitedly about what they're doing after high school graduation.

"I'm not going on a senior trip like the rest of the class. My parents have been saving money my entire life for my graduation present, so I'm returning the favor and we're all three going on a two-week trip to Europe with part of the money."

"That sounds awesome, Kristi! I'm headed to New York City with my parents. We're taking in a couple of Broadway plays and a concert at Carnegie Hall. I'm sure we'll hit all the usual tourist spots while we're there, too." Phillip beams with pride.

"We're all too much alike. My dad and I are doing an MLB game circuit across several states. My mom will join us after a couple weeks for a beach vacation. It's so hard to believe I won't be with you guys every day anymore after graduation. After the baseball game trip and time at the beach, it'll be time to start my own training at college." Doug's revelation startles me. I didn't expect to lose any of them so soon.

While I'm excited for all three of them and so proud of what they've planned for their futures, I can't help but feel left out. What do I have to share?

Oh, I'm staying here, in Aspen Springs, and helping Nana

run her gardening business. Forever. We're not going anywhere on vacation over the summer because that's our busiest retail season.

That doesn't exactly fit with the theme of the evening, and I feel like a complete buzzkill for even thinking it. So, I keep quiet about my lack of plans and nonexistent future and focus on theirs instead. If I can't live it myself, at least I'll live vicariously through them.

"Doug, I can't imagine not seeing you again for months on end after graduation. That just doesn't seem right at all. We've spent our whole lives together. What am I supposed to do without you?" I gently elbow him in the side, knowing there's no other option, but not liking it, nonetheless.

"You'll just have to come to my games and watch me play." He cuts his eyes over at me and grins.

"You picked one and signed?" I grab his arm, waiting for him to spill the details. I'm surprised he hasn't already shared this with us before now.

"Just made a commitment today. I'm moving to Tuscaloosa, my friends. I'm starting as a fullback with the University of Alabama football team. I'll be at football camp the day after our beach vacation ends."

We all congratulate Doug, noting that celebrations are in order. But I already feel the twinge of loss in my chest from knowing that day will be here much faster than I'd like.

After the show, the drive back to Aspen Springs is spent dissecting the plot and comparing it to the book.

We've yet to find a movie that was actually better than the book, but this one was at least very close. There are some things that simply shouldn't be messed with—and taking liberties with changing the script from what actually happened in the original story is one of them.

Kristi had picked Doug and Phillip up at the school since they were both at practice, one at football and the other at band, so I jump out of the car too.

"I can walk to Nana's shop from here, Kristi. Save you a trip out of your way. I had a great time tonight. Thanks for driving us. I'll talk to you cats tomorrow."

"Just be careful, Sara. I don't mind driving you up there. It's not like it's too far or anything."

"Come on. Nothing ever happens in this sleepy little town. I'll be fine. Be careful driving home—watch for deer crossing the road."

So much for famous last words, right?

On the stroll to the shop, my mind was on everything my future didn't include while I watched all my friends as they left me behind. One by one, they'd all be gone by summer's end.

I had no idea that when I reached the front of Nana's store, my entire perspective on life would change, and I'd be focused instead on Nana disappearing...then on my own unusual disappearance.

CHAPTER 3

Present Day

My head is on a swivel as I push up from the ground to my knees, looking all around me to get my bearings and try to figure out what the hell just happened. Nothing seems familiar at all, and the anxiety builds in my chest until a strangled cry escapes my throat. Out of instinct, I cover my mouth with my cupped hand to muffle the sound. Growing up in dangerous animal territory taught me to always know my surroundings. But I don't know anything here. Terror grips me in a way I've never experienced before.

I can't speak. I can't breathe. I can't even move. I'm frozen still, staring in disbelief, contemplating curling up in a fetal position until I wake up back at home. Safe, with Nana looking after my every need.

After I don't even know how long, I manage to pull my

faculties together long enough to force my legs to cooperate. I dust the grass and dirt off my pants as I stand. Nana's consistent admonition to never give up won't allow me to keep feeling sorry for myself. Sticking my head in the sand and pretending won't save me from my circumstances.

This is really happening. Regardless of how much I want someone else to take care of me right now, there's no one else around. My survival is solely on me right now.

The trees surrounding the large clearing I'm in are enormous—much taller and broader than the ones I'm used to seeing. Green grass and soft moss cover the ground under my feet. Wildflowers in a vast array of colors grow in large clumps where the warm sun streams through the canopy high above. I stand still and strain my ears for sounds of life anywhere nearby. The only sound I can make out is flowing water, just down the hill from where I'm standing.

Not knowing where I am or where the closest civilization may be, I decide to make my way to the water. That's one substance I'll need sooner rather than later. I can live without food for a while, but I won't make it long without water. Whatever animals lurk in the dense forest have the same natural instinct, so I'm taking a calculated risk by making this choice. Not knowing what kinds of wildlife I'll encounter makes my gamble significantly more dangerous.

By walking as lightly as possible, I hope to keep my presence unknown for as long as I can. It's taking all my knowledge of living in the wild, rugged countryside to keep my wits about me. Black and brown bears, moose, and mountain lions are territorial and deadly animals at home. With the similar foliage and landscape in this forest, I'm only guessing there are also similar creatures here. Sometimes ignorance is bliss, but sometimes it can also be fatal.

The ground under my feet starts shaking, and I quickly realize what I thought was a low roar in the distance is actually stampeding horses racing toward me. When I whirl around and look up the hill, I can't believe my eyes. An army of men wearing matching metal battle helmets and body armor are charging toward me. The swords they wield have electricity flowing through them. They zap and hum noisily before making a loud crack when the arcs of light slice through the air, jutting out ten feet in front of them to kill anything in their path.

They're riding hard toward me with their swords drawn and pointed right at me. Even as far as I am from them, I can feel the anger flowing from their eyes and the current charging the air, ready to strike me at any time. Their livid rants echo in my mind, flowing from theirs as clearly as if they were standing next to me and screaming in my ear.

I've violated their sacred land somehow. I'm not allowed to be here—they think I've crossed the border to their forest without permission, and they're apparently not a forgiving mob. My reflexes take over, and I break out in a sprint down the hill. Not that I think I can outrun their horses by any means, but I can only hope to somehow get across the unknown border before they reach me. My heart is beating so hard, it's likely to jump right out of my chest. Sheer panic makes my legs run faster than I realized I could. This situation is growing more and more perilous with every passing second.

Since the trees are incredibly close together, there's no way the horses can gallop at full speed toward me, so I dart to the right, straight into the dense forest, and continue my mad dash to reach the river. Behind me, I hear limbs breaking and twigs snapping, but the thunderous stomping has all but ceased since most of the angry crowd tries to follow me through the woods.

If all else fails, I'll dive in and swim downstream underwater to try to elude them. That's the last resort option, though, since I don't know what lives in the water any more than I understand why my presence on their land is so offensive.

When I look over my shoulder to gauge their proximity, I get a good look at one of the men chasing me. He's removed his helmet, giving me a full glimpse of his face. He's strikingly handsome, with sharp, angular features. All perfectly balanced and symmetrical. His hair extends down his back to his waist. It's board-straight and platinum blond, making his sky-blue eyes stand out.

Unless my eyes deceive me, his ears are pointed.

Like an elf.

Only he's tall—very tall—and he's sitting atop an enormous horse while staring at me with murderous intent.

The three seconds of catching my breath and considering an alternative plan are over. I have to make my feet and legs move, regardless of how badly they're burning from the exertion. When I reach the water at the bottom of the hill, I see another group of people riding horses toward me, talking and laughing among themselves. At first glance, they look like ordinary people. They're also not brandishing weapons and screaming at me like crazed banshees. At least, not yet…maybe that's because I'm not on their land.

The commotion behind me gets louder again, and I look for a way to cross the river without just diving in. One of the riders ahead notices me and lifts her hand, pointing in my direction and drawing the others' attention to my predicament. They take off at full gallop toward me, several drawing strange-looking guns from their sides.

I'm caught between two angry hordes, unsure of what move to make.

"Jump! Jump across the river! Hurry!" I barely make out the shouts over the sound of hooves hitting the ground mixed with the water rushing by. One of the women riding with the pack motions for me to come toward her.

I hope this isn't a cruel trap.

But their clothes are similar to mine, so I make the decision to trust them. Plus, they're not actively trying to kill me, unlike the furious horde of battle-dressed men still yelling angrily.

With the elves quickly closing in behind me, I back up a few steps, run toward the bank, and give the best impression of an Olympic long jump I have inside me. My last thought when leaving the bank is, even if I don't clear the entire span to the other side, at least it gets me closer to the other bank—soaking wet or not. The side where seemingly normal humans are waiting and encouraging me to join them.

With my arms and legs flailing in the air in an attempt to increase my momentum, I realize I'm still airborne long after I should've already landed according to the standard rules of physics and gravity. But I'm still in the air until I've cleared the water and safely land on the other side. They form a protective fence around me with their horses. Their weapons are drawn and aimed at the outraged crowd that's still keen on killing me.

The thoughts of the group surrounding me filter through my fears, giving me reassurance of their intentions. They're actively defending me. One of the riders assumes I simply got lost in the woods while walking from the city to their village, making an innocent mistake by crossing onto the forbidden land.

Not knowing what I'm dealing with, where I am, or why I'm here, I decide it's best to go with that excuse for now. When facts about this place become more apparent, maybe I can tell them the truth. For now, I'll wait and get more information about where the village is and why anyone would assume I'd get lost in the woods. Perhaps later, I'll reconsider telling them the truth in the hope they can help me figure out what happened to me.

"Give her back to us, Saban. She was on our land, so she belongs to us now. She will answer for her crimes." The man who removed his helmet earlier pierces me with the angry glare of his coal-black eyes as he speaks. I could've sworn they were blue a few seconds ago.

"That will never happen, Rycan, and you know it. She made a simple mistake. A small group of girls ventured into the woods to enjoy this beautiful day. She simply got separated from the others and lost her way. We've been out searching for her—and we're taking her home now that we've found her."

The two men stare at each other while my heart beats in time with every second that ticks by. My eyes dart back and forth between Saban and Rycan, and my allegiance is currently aligned with the one who's actively trying to save my life.

Saban is as stunningly handsome as Rycan, but in a different way. He exudes a natural sex appeal that draws women to him—like a moth to the flame, getting burned when she gets too close, but willing to take the gamble on the off chance the feeling is mutual. He looks like he's a few years older than me, with close-cropped scruff covering his strong jawline. His jet-black hair is slightly longer on top than on the sides, naturally messy and spiky in a way that suits him perfectly.

The women riding in his group all have similar thoughts in mind—they're salivating over him, hanging on his every word, and waiting for him to take their feelings for him sincerely. So far, he hasn't chosen a life mate, knowing it's forever once he does. Each one is vying for his affections, fighting for his attention, and silently begging him to choose her to fill that role.

With good reason, too. Saban's muscular frame makes the enormous draft horse he's riding seem small. The air around him crackles and sparks with innate authority and charm. His casual demeanor, sitting relaxed on his horse, unaffected by the daggers flowing from Rycan's eyes, belies his underlying strength. His muscles are coiled, ready to react with lightning-fast reflexes should his enemy try to make a move.

I've never seen eyes the shade of gray as his. They change from a light gray to a dark gray with his thoughts and moods. Right now, they're so dark, they're almost charcoal. He hopes Rycan pushes the issue. The bad blood between them is long-standing, going back over several years of increasing animosity, and Saban is more than willing to finish whatever this human-elf feud is by ending Rycan's rule forever.

"Keep her for now, Saban. You should send her to your private school that you reserve for your precious royal bloodline. Next time she gets 'lost' in our woods, I'll send her back to you in pieces." Rycan turns his hateful gaze back to me when he finishes his threat. "I'm sure we'll meet again."

Rycan and his merry band of elves turn their horses around and ride away, leaving me with a new problem to solve. Saban blatantly made up the entire story about my getting lost in the woods while out with a group of friends. Now he'll want the real story, and not knowing the size of the nearby city or their smaller village, I have no idea what the odds are that he knows everyone who lives there.

He waits until Rycan is out of sight before turning his attention directly to me, assessing me from head to toe. For the first time in years, I purposely open my mind and let my intuition take over. The thoughts from the group surrounding me flow through my mind like water cutting a path through rock, knocking against the sides and creating trails with indiscriminate force. The trick is identifying the real ones from the fake, the notions thought in jest versus the ones truly believed.

The shade of his irises lightens to a stainless-steel sheen right before my eyes. I watch with rapt attention, mesmerized by both the hue of his eyes and the thoughts swirling in his mind. Thoughts of me. Wondering who I am, intrigued he hasn't seen me before, and a desire to change that for the foreseeable future.

"Saban, we should get going. You'll be late for your sister's engagement party if we don't leave for the castle now." One of the women who desperately wants to marry Saban tries her best to turn his attention from me to her.

Hoping to head off the questions I don't want to answer, I quickly add my part before an inquisition can begin. "Thank you for coming to my rescue. Please accept my apologies for any trouble I've caused. I'll head straight to the city now."

Every word I've spoken is the truth, even though I don't know which way the city is or what I'll find if I reach it.

"Not to seem rude, but I'm surprised we haven't met before now. Do you live in the orphanage compound? Is that why your parents haven't brought you to court at the palace? As beautiful as you are, surely they would've presented you as a possible mate for me if they were able." His war face was intimidating, but his smile is entirely disarming and much more dangerous.

It's no wonder all the ladies in his company want to baptize me in the river and hold me under the water a few minutes too long.

"My parents died when I was just a baby. I never knew them, so I'm not sure what they would've done, given the chance. I'd like to think they would have introduced us, but I'm afraid we'll never know." I smile in return, hoping my explanation settles his curiosity.

"In that case, maybe you should come to the castle with me right now. We'll get dressed up, then we'll eat, drink, dance, and celebrate my sister's upcoming nuptials."

I look down at my clothes, dirty and torn from my escape from the beautiful but angry elves. "As much as I'd love to join you, I probably shouldn't. My clothes aren't exactly appropriate for a party in the castle, and I literally have nothing to wear to that kind of event. Please give your sister my congratulations and wishes for a long and happy marriage."

"You are nothing like any other girl I've ever met. It's so refreshing. What is your name, beautiful lady?"

Make up a name, the voice warns.

"I'm Sara Meneres." Only slightly different, but close enough to play off the mispronunciation as a case of nerves or misunderstanding if the occasion arises.

"Sara, I like that name." He says my name a few more times, putting a different emphasis on the vowels each time. "It's very original."

Not where I come from, I think to myself.

"Well, Sara, I am Lord Saban Strydor, but you can call me Saban. Since you've never visited court before, you probably don't recognize me. My father was Sagran Strydor. I inherited the responsibility of ruling our kingdom when he died last year. That includes fostering relations with our bordering nations, as you just witnessed."

"That's a lot of responsibility for one man to bear. That's very impressive, Saban."

"I do my best. Now, back to our date tonight. My sister has plenty of clothes you can wear. If there's something you need that she doesn't have, the palace staff will get it for you. Now, is there any other reason why you can't be my date for the party?" He slowly arches one eyebrow, waiting to destroy my next excuse. But I don't have one— not one that won't arouse even more suspicion anyway.

"In that case, how can I turn down such a generous offer? I would be honored to be your date tonight."

"Thank you for not making me beg. My next move was going to be to climb down off this horse, drop to my knees in front of you, and plead shamelessly until you relented. You just saved me from an extremely humiliating display." Mischief dances in his eyes, and his smile turns sultry. His full lips only enhance his handsome face.

"But Saban, we don't have an extra horse for her to ride. It's cruel to make her walk all the way to the palace." The same girl has yet another reason to get rid of me.

I really need to get this girl's name because she'll stop at nothing to keep me away from him.

"Good point, Shania. We can't have that, can we? Here, Sara, take my hand—you can ride with me."

He reaches down, and I slide my hand along his forearm until I reach his elbow. With no effort at all, he lifts me from the ground, and I throw one leg over his horse. With my front to his back, I wrap my arms around his waist and hold on with all my might. I've ridden horses all my life, but these are not like any horses I've ever seen by any means. They're twice the size of a Clydesdale, with broad backs and long legs.

"Hold on tight. These horses were specially bred to fly when they take off running. They're incredible animals."

When he said the horses fly, I assumed he meant it as a metaphor for running fast. He didn't. He means they can literally fly—like Pegasus, but without wings. They run, jump, and soar over great distances, much like I did when I jumped across the river. Everything about this place and people I've met so far is surreal, like a vivid dream I don't want to wake up from because it feels so real. But I must be dreaming because there's no other rational explanation for what's happening.

"This is incredible, Saban. You must ride them every day just to experience this feeling of freedom." My face is close enough to his ear that I don't have to shout over the sound of the rushing wind.

"I'm glad you're enjoying the ride. That gives me the incentive to take them out more often—and ammunition to get you to go with me." The charming smile on his face is more than a little facetious. He knows the effect he has on all the women around him more than he's admitting. Right now, he's merely making sure he brings me under his subjection too.

"You told me to call you Saban, but I have a question. Are you actually the king? I'm sorry I don't know much about how palace life works. You must think I'm a complete idiot."

"I don't think you're an idiot at all. Most people don't know all the details unless they're active in court. I'm not a king. Not yet, anyway. To be given the title of king, you have to be born into the royal bloodline. If there's no royal heir, you have to be voted into the position by the royalty of the neighboring kingdoms. As you can tell, there's at least one kingdom still holding out on that vote. To be honest, there's likely more than one. So, for now, I'm still a lord. But not for much longer—I have big plans."

Their monarchy system is obviously different from what I've studied in school, with kings and queens and lords, all the titles I've never fully committed to memory. But there's definitely a hierarchy system here that he's trying to work to his advantage. From our brief interaction, I already know he wants the title of king so bad he can taste it. He lives in a castle and holds court, waiting for potential mates to be presented to him as if they're dolls on a display shelf.

With his flirty demeanor and quick wit, I can't help but wonder if he's the type that takes them down and shows them off, only to discard them just as quickly, like yesterday's garbage.

CHAPTER 4

When we reach the castle, I'm more confused than ever. I naturally assumed this place was still stuck in the medieval period when I first saw everyone riding horses. Kings. Lords, metal body armor, swords, and crossing the country with horses and carriages. In hindsight, the electric swords and futuristic guns should've been a dead giveaway. But then again, nothing here fits the typical mold at home. I also expected the castle to be ancient—with candles to light the way and outhouses or chamber pots as bathrooms. I'd read the castles of old were drafty and uncomfortable to live in. They were hard to heat and cool, especially since they lacked the modern convenience of central heat and air conditioning units. Naturally, I thought Saban's castle would be much the same.

I couldn't have been more wrong.

"The horses need to be fed and watered before you

turn them back out to pasture. Mix the oats and the alfalfa together." Saban hands his reins off to one of his stable hands after he dismounts, then he turns and helps me down. "Come with me, beautiful. I'll show you to the guest room where you can get dressed for the engagement party."

He must sense my hesitancy as I look down at my clothes. After riding the flying horse, I can only imagine how my hair and face must look. This has got to be the worst idea in the history of this world.

"Don't worry, Sara. You'll have everything you need and people to help you pick out which dress to wear. Now relax, because you and I have a lot of dancing and flirting to do over the next few hours. Plus, as beautiful as you are now, I bet you'll light up the entire room when you finally smile, and I wouldn't miss that for all of Easthaven Crest or the entire world of Covis Realm." He winks at me before placing his hand on the small of my back and steering me toward the palace.

Easthaven Crest? Covis Realm? That's where I am? What the hell?

From the outside, this place is the stuff little girls' dreams are made of—beautiful ivory-colored stone, with high walls, towers, turrets, and the massive keep standing tall at the center point of the wall. But the most beautiful part is the main house.

Actually, "royal palace" is a better term to describe it. The enormous structure is topped off with a navy dome and spires reaching toward the heavens. The light-blue accents and navy-blue dome against the white walls sparkle in the sun, like a supernatural sign confirming the magic held inside the golden gates. And there are many gates, all fortified by heavily armed guards.

Inside the high walls surrounding the castle, the gardens take my breath away. My first thought is of Nana and how she'd love to see all the greenery, flowers, and shrubs that were professionally and strategically placed to make the lush green lawn and immaculate residence even more gorgeous. These plants aren't from my world—they're much more vibrant, more colorful, and much larger—and not a variety I've ever seen before.

I fight the urge to pinch myself to make sure I didn't hit my head when I fell. Maybe I'm passed out in the forest and fantasizing all of this.

Then the warmth of Saban's hand seeps through my shirt. I smell the fragrant flowers mixed with his spicy, masculine scent. Do they have cologne here? I can only assume they do because any man who naturally smells as good as he does would be lethal to the female population. I chance a glance over at him, watching his every movement as he walks through the gardens toward the palace courtyard. His air of confidence precedes him, making people step out of his way rather than him giving way to them. His shoulders are broad, his chest is thick, and his legs are as wide as tree trunks. If not for the warning ringing in my ears, telling me to be careful with him, maybe I'd also fall under his spell without a second thought.

But then again, I've never really been that type of girl. I never went boy-crazy when my hormones kicked in at puberty. Of course, I've had my fair share of dates and boyfriends, but I haven't met anyone yet who truly held my heart—or even my interest—for very long. Saban may not be able to change that in the long run, but I can certainly see the appeal he holds. When he feels the weight of my stare, he cuts his eyes toward me. The playful and flirty glint in them makes my heart skip a beat, then a slow smile covers his handsome face.

"In this light, your eyes are such a pale violet they're almost pure purple. I've never seen such a beautiful shade on anyone else in the entire realm. You're special. I felt it from the moment I first saw you. But now, that feeling is much stronger." He stops walking and turns to fully face me.

When his fingertips brush against my cheek, I inhale a sharp breath and hold it, unable to release it or move away from him. This is more than electricity arcing between two bodies. More than chemistry holds us hostage. An instant and intense connection is alive between us, tethering us together with an invisible chain that seems unbreakable. He feels it too—I can sense it in his thoughts, see it in his expression, and feel it in his touch. He reaches his other hand for mine, gently holding it while we stand rooted in place.

Who is this stranger? How has she so fully enraptured me with nothing more than her spirit? How can I convince her to stay in the palace when I've only just met her?

The thoughts stream from his mind to mine like water from the river flows into the ocean. The feelings attached to the queries slam into me like a speeding train, mixing with my own unsorted thoughts and sensations, making me question which emotions are mine and which are his. I force my body to breathe again, releasing the long-held breath slowly to help calm my racing mind and heart. Each passing second gives me time to soothe my ragged nerves and sort out the jumbled mess in my mind.

Saban wants to get to know me better without scaring me off. Moving in to the castle would solve several immediate problems—the most significant being I'm homeless here and have no idea how to get back to my world. I sift through his thoughts, looking for any inkling he's onto my plight, but there's no suspicion there. The orphanage must be full and turning out young adults frequently. With that story conveniently in place, I won't bother adding to it and potentially complicating matters. I'll just have to be extra careful not to mention my past experiences that would invite more questions.

Saraya, follow your instincts. Don't be afraid of your feelings. Everything will be okay.

The voice that speaks to me sounds closer, almost as if someone is whispering in my ear. It feels like the same voice I've heard all my life. It's uniquely nondescript. I can't tell if it's a male or female voice. I don't know if it's real or if I've made it up. But I've learned to trust it and believe whoever is behind it has the best of intentions for me.

Saban and I are still locked in a staring contest but without the usual accompanying discomfort. Gazing into his eyes makes me feel as if I'm at home…at peace with the world…where I should be. While I was leery of him just a few minutes ago, his thoughts and feelings that are a part of me now are reassuring. I can't help but wonder if mine are a part of him now too.

"You'll think I'm crazy for what I'm about to say." He sounds unsure of himself, something I'm sure is a foreign sensation for him.

"Try me."

"Move in to the castle…permanently. You can work here, and plenty of the staff lives here full time. I can't explain it, but I know you belong in my life. Since you don't have any family to turn to, this is the perfect solution. Then you and I can spend more time together in the evenings, getting acquainted, learning everything there is to know about the other. It's a crazy request, I know, and it sounds like a really smooth line some playboy royal would use to entrap a new mistress. That's not my intention, I promise. I just can't seem to stand the thought of you not being near."

"Let's see how the rest of the day and evening go first, then we can revisit your request. You may decide you can't stand the sight of me after you realize I have two left feet while we're dancing." My smile is genuine, putting him at ease. I can dance with no problem, but this excuse gives us both an out if we come to our senses later.

"Fair enough. But I should warn you—I'm a very

skilled dancer. I can lead you all over the dance floor and never once get my toes stepped on. You won't get rid of me that easy." Without warning, he leans down and places a soft kiss on my cheek. The warmth from his lips makes my cheeks flame, my heart flutter, and butterflies come alive in my stomach. "This is Addilyn. She'll show you to your room and help you get dressed for the evening. I'll be the impatient one at the bottom of the stairs, pacing back and forth until I see you again."

I didn't even see anyone else approach us.

When he releases my hand, the fog clouding my mind clears enough for me to gather my wits again. I watch Saban walk away for a moment before turning my attention to Addilyn. She smiles sweetly at me, prompting me to return the gesture. Given her beauty, I'm surprised Saban isn't head over heels for her. Addilyn is tall and svelte, with her long, curly hair perfectly styled, her fashionable clothes, and her nails all beautifully polished. Her dark skin is smooth and glows with a heavenly sheen. Her full lips and soft brown eyes would make anyone jealous.

"Hello, it's nice to meet you. Saban isn't acting like himself today. He didn't introduce us or give me any instructions on what he wants. I've never seen him so taken with anyone in all the years I've known him. It's good to see he's finally met his match." She taps her finger on her lips while studying me with equal parts amusement and fascination. "He said he'd be impatiently waiting for you, so my guess is you're his date for the engagement party tonight."

"Yes, I am—because he wouldn't accept no for an answer. I'm Sara, by the way. He didn't even give you my name." I laugh, somewhat nervously, and her bright smile returns. "I have absolutely nothing to wear, and he volunteered his sister's wardrobe to clothe me for the evening."

"Now it makes sense. I'm the royal fashion stylist, so I clothe most everyone who lives in the palace. I have the best job in the realm, if I say so myself. Come with me. The only time they'll take their eyes off the bride-to-be tonight is when they're looking at you." She waggles her brows and flashes a devilish grin.

The thoughts and feelings flowing from her are all benevolent—so far. She reaches for my hand, and I take hers, hopeful to have made a friend and ally in this world. A tingle courses through my veins when we touch, and she releases an audible gasp. Her eyes grow wide, and her bottom jaw drops open. She pulls me close to her while nervously glancing around us.

"Let's get out of here before someone starts asking questions."

Yes, someone like me. What the hell is happening?

She pulls me with her, walking at a brisk pace until we reach the fifth floor of the palace. Inside the enormous guest bedroom, she locks the door behind us and closes the curtains.

"Addilyn, what's going on? Why are we in hiding all of a sudden?" The vibes she's putting off still aren't harmful, but she is terrified of something. Or someone.

She stops pacing midstride. "You honestly don't know, do you?"

"I guess not because I have no idea who you're so afraid of, or why, or what caused it." *But I'm all for you filling in the gaps. Right now.*

"We have a lot to talk about, Sara. Unfortunately, we don't have enough time at this moment for me to tell you everything you need to know. There's no way you're from Covis Realm, though. I would've already known about you if you were. Did you come here from the outside world?" She already knows the answer to that question. She's waiting to see if I'll confirm her suspicions.

"You're right. I'm not from here. I have no idea where I am, what the hell is happening, or how to get back home."

"Why do you trust me enough to tell me? I know you didn't tell Saban or his groupies."

I shrug, not sure I'm ready to give away all my secrets just yet. "I get a good feeling from you."

"That's because you're a mage, and you recognize your own kind. But mages are killed here, Sara, so you can never tell anyone what we are."

I'm a mage? What?

"Killed? Did we go back in time to the Salem witch trials or what?"

"I've heard of Salem, but I can assure you it's much different here. We didn't eat a fungus that caused hallucinations and hysteria. We have actual magic in our veins, and it scares those in power who don't have it. Mages were outlawed many years ago. They were hunted and murdered because of their gifts. The bloodlines are hard to break, though, and magic skips generations, only to find its way back to the chosen. Keep your magic secret, Sara."

"Addilyn, hold on just a minute. I'm having a hard time with all of this. You're saying I'm a mage. I have magic in my veins. I can do spells and all that shit. And people here want to kill me because of it. The only thing that makes sense to me is you did eat the fungus and you're hallucinating all of this. I'm not a mage. I don't have magical powers. I don't know spells or ride a broomstick or cook in a big, black cauldron."

She walks to me and grabs both my hands in hers. The zing I felt earlier is amplified ten times. "Do you feel that? That's how we know one of our own. It can't be simulated by anyone. You're one of us, my dear. You said you get good vibes from me, which is a way of saying you can read my mind. So, tell me, am I lying?"

I drop the wall I've constructed around my senses and allow the stream to flow freely again. But this time is different. Instead of thoughts and feelings making themselves known, images fly through my mind like a movie playing on the silver screen. Addilyn's childhood, being taught how to use and control her magical gifts. How to hide them from outsiders. How to cloak them.

"Holy shit. That has never happened before. Did you do that, or did I?" I search her face for an answer.

"You did, Sara." Her smile is slightly sad...for me. "You're a very powerful mage."

"So, we don't have to learn spells or use ingredients and all that jazz to use our powers?" I didn't see any of that in her memories.

"No, that's all superstition and make-believe stories the other world has created about us. Our magic comes as naturally to us as their blood type does to them. I'd be honored to teach you everything you need to know, but we have to be very careful. Whatever you do, don't breathe a word to Saban about it."

"Trust me, I'm not talking to anyone except you about this. Saban asked me to move in to the palace. He mentioned working here too. All he knows about me is I'm homeless. He thinks I'm from the orphanage, and I didn't correct him. If I accept his request, can I work with you? Then no one would question the time we spend together."

"That's a brilliant idea, Sara. Take him up on his offer. Believe me, he's never been that generous with anyone in his life, so you're meant to be here. As far as your training, I'll make sure that happens. There are plenty of reasons why you and I would spend time together once you move in to the palace.

"Now, let's get you dressed and ready for the gala tonight. Saban is already under your spell, figuratively speaking. Wait until he sees you after I'm finished with you. That boy will be madly in love with you by the time the clock strikes midnight."

CHAPTER 5

"Isla is Saban's sister and the bride-to-be. Tonight's party should be all about her and Gerard, but don't be surprised when you steal the spotlight from them. Everyone will wonder who you are, partly because no one has ever seen you at court before, but mostly because you look absolutely stunning." Addilyn steps to the side of the full-length mirror, giving me an unobstructed view of her work.

The reflection in the full-length mirror on the wall renders me speechless.

My only hidden talent is the ability to sense the thoughts and feelings of others. I'm not the star player on the girls' basketball team. I'm not the one who can jump the highest and spike the volleyball onto the other teams' heads. In fact, I've never been more athletic than hiking or climbing trees. But my clothing of choice has always been more like a tomboy than a girlie-girl. Maybe because of all the time I've spent in the woods and helping Nana with her flower and herb gardens.

But now I'm rethinking my entire life's strategy.

The deep purple ball gown has a floor-length skirt that's full and layered with translucent ruffles covering the satin skirt underneath. The strapless bodice has a sweetheart cut, covered in shiny jewels. Addilyn pulled my long blond hair off my shoulders into a stylish updo, with curled wisps strategically placed for emphasis. Soft tendrils of curls hang loose around my face, and delicate jeweled earrings dangle from my ears. The color of the dress accentuates the light shade of my eyes, and the soft smoky eyeshadow she chose makes them pop like never before. The ivory lace fingerless gloves trail up my arms as if I'm adorned by real flowers and complete the princess ensemble.

"Addilyn, I have no words. You are a miracle worker." I turn and look over my shoulder, gazing into the mirror and not believing it's genuinely me I see in it.

"Only because I had a beautiful canvas to start with. Saban won't be able to take his eyes off you tonight." She beams with pride.

"I'm not so sure that's a good thing, Addilyn. The less attention I draw to myself, the better."

"It's too late for that, my friend. I've never seen him look at anyone the way he did you. When he said he'd be waiting at the bottom of the staircase for you, he meant every word of it. He'll make sure none of the other men reach you first. In case you haven't noticed, nearly every woman in Easthaven Crest is after Saban Strydor."

"Yes, I have noticed. It was hard to miss all the daggers being thrown at me from the eyes of the girls surrounding him. They were riding the flying horses. Do you have any idea what they were doing out there?" I hate not having all the information at hand, especially in my current circumstances.

Addilyn narrows her eyes and tilts her head to the side, examining me with all too keen eyes that see far below the surface. "You and I will have a long talk after the party tonight. For now, let me give you the highlights of where you are."

When I don't deny her assumptions about me, she motions for me to follow her into the adjoining room. Between the sitting room, the dressing room, the walk-in closet, and the bedroom, this suite is larger than my entire house back home. The whole back wall of the expansive room is one enormous map with so much beauty and detail, I have to fight back the tears. This is the first time since I landed here that I have any hope of figuring out a way back home.

"This is absolutely beautiful." I stare in awe at the intricate detail drawn on the map.

"Everything you see on this map is called Covis Realm. It's divided into several kingdoms, or nations. This area is Easthaven Crest, where all the humans live. Though they are different from the humans from your world—don't bother denying it—because they live a lot longer and have more unique characteristics."

She didn't even have to take an extra breath to challenge me.

"Starting from the northwest corner, there's Elderwater Basin, with all the natural pools, lakes, and streams. That's where the merpeople live. Next to it is Timbergarde Pointe, the rolling hills and valleys where the shifters make their home. The northeast corner is where the Nightside Mountains are and where you'll find the vamps and dragons."

"Stop right there. Vampires are real?" I'm waiting for the punch line to follow.

Addilyn laughs at my wide-open eyes and slack jaw. "Yes, they are. But the fact that you asked about vampires being real instead of dragons first cracks me up."

"I can believe dragons are real much easier than the walking undead, stalking around at night, drinking blood, and killing people."

"You think they can only move at night? No, my friend. They are just like you and me. You may even see a few here tonight. Saban is doing all he can to win their favor. Okay, below where the merpeople live is where you'll find the elves. I understand you already met a few of them. Rycan, their military leader, doesn't like any humans on his land, and they know when anyone crosses the border. There's a long-standing rivalry between him and Saban. The elvish land is called Elen Sevin. It means 'sacred home' in the elvish language."

"I thought Rycan was going to kill me. Even with Saban defending me, Rycan glared at me with those piercing black eyes, and I felt his hatred in my soul."

"Their eye color changes with their mood. If they were black, he definitely intended to kill you. But what do you mean, you felt it? Is that an expression in your world, or did you actually feel something?"

"Oh, I felt it. The hate, the anger—rolling off all the elves chasing me like a tsunami hitting me with full force. But when they stopped, he was the main one still trying to get to me."

She grabs my face, leans in close, and stares deep into my eyes. I can't sense her thoughts, so I have no idea what she's looking for all of a sudden. How did she shield her thoughts from me?

"Who were your parents? Where are they?"

"I never knew them. They died when I was little. My grandmother raised me."

"She raised you in the other world?" Her eyebrows draw downward, and her eyes narrow to mere slits.

"Yes, she did. My mom was her daughter, and Nana was heartbroken after losing her only child."

While that's the truth, I have no idea what the whole story is since I only learned of the "other world" a few hours ago. Needless to say, Nana's bedtime stories didn't include all the details regarding Covis Realm, Easthaven Crest, or all the magical creatures that live here. Some of her tall tales may hold the clues I need to navigate this unfamiliar world, if only I could remember all she told me.

Just as Addilyn's long stare begins to unnerve me, her gaze softens then she slowly nods to herself. "I think there's more to you than even you know, Sara. Whatever it is, hopefully you'll tell me the full story eventually. For now, let's finish the map. This entire area below the shifters and vampires and above the humans is affectionately known as the Veil."

She sweeps her hand along part of the map, but there's nothing labeled in that area. It's merely the border between Easthaven Crest and Timbergarde Pointe. "I don't understand. Why isn't the Veil on the map between the humans and the shifters?"

"Because that's where the mages live, and our kind has been outlawed for many years now. We had to create a cloaked community to hide who we are. We go there to practice our magic, learn new spells, and recharge from the oppression we feel from the humans."

"What would happen if they found out?" Ice runs through my veins because, in my heart of hearts, I already know the answer.

"They would have a mock trial then sentence us to death us for being mages. People like you and I are actually mages. There's a subtle difference from witches as you know them. Mages don't practice the dark arts, but the witches do."

"Then witches are bad, and mages are good?"

"Not exactly. Just like every other creature, there's good and bad in all of us. But we can choose to feed one more than the other. Witches use their powers to hurt others more than they help. They focus on revenge and retaliation against anyone they don't like, so we use that term to define them. Mages never set out to use their powers to hurt anyone. They will only do that if they're defending a life—their own or someone else's. For the most part. But we can make mistakes or act out in anger and frustration sometimes."

When she pulls out the shoes that match my ball gown, I can't contain my laughter. "Ballet flats? With this gown?"

"I don't want your feet to hurt after dancing all night with Saban. You can thank me tomorrow morning."

"I'll thank you right now—I appreciate how you're looking out for me. These shoes are so cute. The color matches my dress impeccably, and the jewels match the ones on my bodice. They're perfect."

Now that Addilyn is finished decorating me with more jewelry than I could ever imagine, the hummingbird-sized butterflies in my stomach take flight, and my nerves kick into overdrive. I've never left Montana before, much less attended a royal event. As the date of the brother of the bride.

Too much has happened too soon. I'm not entirely convinced I'm not dreaming all of this after falling out of a tree and hitting my head. But no matter what's actually happening to me, the more information I gain, the faster I can help Nana. Keeping my thoughts focused on her and my end goal is the only way I can make it through tonight.

"When you're rubbing elbows with everyone who's anyone in this kingdom, just remember you wouldn't be there if Saban didn't think you belonged. You may run into other mages. They probably won't admit it, but they're every bit as interested in being his mate as those women who were riding with him today are. Shield your mind from them so they can't read your thoughts."

"How do I do that?"

"Rub your index and middle finger across your forehead and say *'mentis celare'* to yourself. That will hide your thoughts from anyone trying to read them."

I do as she instructs then immediately feel the walls inside my mind rise in place. "Wow. That was different. I've never felt anything like that before. I mean, I had to learn to control the flow of other people's thoughts so listening to them wouldn't make me crazy, but this is not the same at all."

"We have a lot of work to do." Addilyn shakes her head at me with a smile on her face. "For now, go have fun with your hot date."

I'm so nervous as I walk down the corridor toward the ballroom, I can't even feel my feet. It's as if I'm floating on air. When I reach the end of the hall, I step onto the open landing overlooking the entryway below.

There, at the bottom of the palatial staircase, is Saban.

Our eyes meet, and his thoughts flow freely to me... and all the background noise fades to silence.

CHAPTER 6

The blush creeps up my chest to my neck, finally filling my face as I make my way down the stairs. The long purple train of my dress follows behind me, making me feel like a princess descending the keep toward her prince. Saban's thoughts filter through mine, forcefully taking front and center in my mind. The feelings attached are equally as strong, hitting me like waves crashing onto the shore.

"I can't believe how beautiful you are...and you'll be on my arm all night."

"Every unattached man, along with a few already taken, will try their best to take you away from me. I'll do whatever it takes to stop that from happening."

"Where have you been all my life? Why haven't we met before now? Now I know exactly why no one else could hold my attention."

The initial possessive thoughts morph into more carnal ideas.

His hand wrapped around mine.

Our lips pressed together.

His tongue tracing the lines of my neck and along my exposed collarbone.

I reach the bottom of the steps before his mind has time to wander any further, though I know where he was headed next. I can feel my temperature rising inside me the same as the heat inside Saban. His desire to claim me as his mate is palpable—literally, in my case. Though I'm not familiar with all the details of claiming a mate in this world, I can tell it's a significant milestone and a decision that's not made lightly.

Despite how warm and fuzzy his intense emotions make me feel, I'm not ready to be claimed or mated to anyone. Especially someone I don't know and in a world that's not my own.

He extends his elbow toward me, and I wrap my hand around it. I'm infinitely grateful for the flats I'm wearing since I can't walk in heels to save my life, but the height difference between Saban and me is significant. I feel small and dainty next to him, something I've never experienced before now.

"You look absolutely stunning, Sara. Every man here will be jealous of me tonight. I'll have to be on my toes to stop anyone who tries to steal you from me." He softly kisses the back of my hand.

"Thank you, Saban. You look very handsome yourself."

He's wearing a black tuxedo with tails, a white shirt, and a black bow tie. The entire ensemble obviously was tailor-made to fit his immense frame. We both already know every female within a fifty-mile radius is clamoring for his attention, so there's no need to state the obvious.

Most of the people we pass by watch us walk into the ballroom together with an amused expression on their faces. Their thoughts are all along similar lines. *Saban has finally met his match.* In this instance, I don't think their definition of "meeting his match" is quite the same as mine. They're referring to his mate as his match, the life-long commitment philosophy I'm actively avoiding getting caught up in.

On the one hand, it's flattering to be thought of that way. On the other hand, I must respectfully decline. Thanks, but no thanks.

A few single ladies throw the intentional eye daggers in my direction, but I'm not concerned with their opinions of me. Envy is a strange sensation to experience from someone else's view. They're jealous because they think I've taken him away from them, but they don't even stop to consider I just met the guy a few hours ago. They're envious because they want to be the one on his arm right now.

Not a single one of the jealous crowd has attempted even to say hello to me, much less get to know me before deciding they hate me. They could at least dislike me based on something with merit rather than their own insecurities.

Saban stops walking to chat with someone. Though his attention is elsewhere, he still manages to pull me closer to his side. I can't help but smile as his own insecurities are bleeding through. He's getting his fair share of eye daggers from the young men around us. One bold young man seizes the opportunity while Saban is engaged in a conversation he can't easily excuse himself from.

"Hello, there. I know I haven't had the pleasure of meeting you before. What's your name?" He lifts my free hand and presses his lips to my knuckles, letting them linger there a second or two longer than usual decorum would dictate.

"Hello, I'm Sara. And you are?" I extract my hand from his grasp without being too apparent of my intent. He gives me a sleazy used car salesman vibe, and his head is strangely devoid of feelings or images. Not like when Addilyn shielded hers from me, though. It's as if he doesn't have an internal monologue before his thoughts are voiced.

Some people only joke that they have no brain-mouth filter. Apparently, it's not just a joke, though.

"My name is Valerian, but most people call me Vale. I'm one of Saban's friends. Our mothers are lifelong friends. How did you and he meet?"

"Sara accidentally crossed the line and was in Elen Sevin. I happened to ride up at just the right time to assist her." Saban's interjection into the conversation is notice-able but also welcome. The fewer times I have to explain how I crossed some invisible barrier, the better.

"Oh, I bet Rycan appreciated that. We all know how much he loves humans, especially ones who dare to step foot in his kingdom. Don't worry about it, Sara. We've all done the same at one time or another. Once when I was in the woods hunting, I tracked the deer across the border without realizing it. I had to give up my prize stag because Rycan demanded its head or mine for my mistake." Vale chuckles at the mishap, but I see a glimpse of the scene in his mind. It was much more severe than he's saying. He was much closer to losing his head than the deer was—until Saban interfered and negotiated on Vale's behalf.

Maybe Saban is a decent guy after all.

"Saban helped me out of a challenging situation. He kept Rycan from killing me on the spot. I'm very thankful we met when we did. Otherwise, my encounter with the elves would've turned out very differently."

The pride emanating from Saban is evident on his face and in his stature. He stands a little taller. His chest sticks out a little farther. The sexy smirk on his face is more pronounced. He really is a stunningly handsome man, so his reaction to my praise of him surprises me. If I were a betting person, I would've said he was accustomed to others extolling his deeds when I first met him. Now, I'm not so sure.

I've watched the jocks at high school receive applause and compliments from their teammates and everyone else trying to be accepted into their inner circle. Those guys hold their heads high, keep their expressions schooled, and barely nod to acknowledge anyone has spoken to them.

Instead of letting it roll off his back like most guys do, Saban is soaking it in and enjoying it openly.

"Saban, didn't I tell you to throw those ragged shoes away and have new ones made? And that tuxedo—it's so old, moths have probably started eating it. When's the last time you've had a haircut? I swear, you'd do anything to embarrass me beyond repair."

Saban cringes then stiffens beside me. Vale's smile drops, and his eyes turn to mere slits as he tries to hold his intense anger inside him. My eyes swing between the two men before turning to locate the source of the angry female voice directed at Saban.

When I find her, I'm instantly revolted. By her dress and demeanor, she was once a beautiful woman with a world of class and high stature in the community. But the years have not been kind, and the abundance of alcohol has not been a friend. She moves toward us, the drink in her hand sloshing over the sides from her unsteady gait. Even without reading her mind, I'd recognize the resentment in her eyes...and it's aimed directly at Saban.

For some reason, I need to know why that is. What did he do to her that was so terrible, she'd humiliate him in a room full of everyone he knows? I focus solely on her thoughts, and her mind becomes an open book to me, as if I'm flipping through the pages from picture to picture until I find the memory I need. This has never happened before, maybe because I've spent a lifetime trying to filter out the thoughts rather than letting them come to me. But this time, I'm seeking them.

Those are more questions I'll have to ask Addilyn later. For now, I have a limited amount of time to venture into her thoughts before she reaches us and I'm expected to interact with her. Almost like a fuzzy movie on a silver screen, her thoughts play in sequence in my mind's eye.

Saban and his father leave the castle together early one morning. They're as close as brothers, this father and son pair. They're laughing and playfully gouging at each other on their way to the stables. Their laughter echoes off the surrounding mountains, carrying down the glen from the castle and filling the morning air with love.

Sagran approaches his usual horse and begins to walk it toward the tack room area when he notices a loose shoe. He lifts the horse's foot and pulls off the shoe, pitching it to the side with a look of disappointment.

"Ah, I'm sorry, son. Doesn't look like I'll get to ride with you today after all. Zeb threw a shoe, so I can't ride him today. I'll have to get our farrier to fix it later." Sagran stands and wipes the dirt from his hands.

"But we've planned this all week. We never get to spend time together anymore, just the two of us." Saban drops his shoulders and turns to put the tack back in its place.

"You're right, son. I'll ride one of the other horses. They need attention too. What about Zora? She needs more time under the saddle."

"You can try her. You may spend more time correcting her than actually riding her, though." Saban chuckles, but he's not

overly concerned. He and his father are both skilled horsemen, so there's not much they haven't encountered before.

"Today is as good a day as any to start her training. We'll have fun, no matter what."

Saban's smile brightens his face as he rushes to gather the tack once more and prepare his horse for the ride.

"You two just be careful. I expect you both back in time for dinner tonight." She steps up to Sagran, lifts up on her toes, and places a kiss on his lips. He returns the kiss and slides his arm around her waist.

"Don't you worry your pretty little head, Giselli. We'll be back before you know it. You and Isla should go off for some girl time while we're gone. Then the four of us can eat together tonight."

"I may take you up on that suggestion. Maybe a little shopping is in order. I have a feeling Isla and Gerard will be engaged sooner rather than later."

Sagran growls, but he has a content grin on his face. "Don't talk about my little girl getting married anytime soon. I'm not ready for that day yet."

Giselli laughs and swats him away. "Ready or not, that day is coming, my love. Hurry back to me. I love you."

"I love you too. See you this evening."

"I love you too, Saban." Giselli grins devilishly at Saban, who blushes noticeably. "No matter how old you are, you can still tell your mom you love her."

"Love you too, Mom," he mumbles in reply. Giselli and Sagran have a good laugh at Saban's embarrassment then he joins in, laughing at himself. "Happy now?"

"Yes, as a matter of fact, I am."

Sagran and Saban ride away on their steeds, smiles intact and waving to Giselli until they're out of sight.

The scene cuts to later in the evening, when Giselli stands outside the castle, awaiting her husband and son's return. The sun begins to set, and a figure gallops at full speed up the hill toward the palace. Terror strikes her heart, fear gripping her throat with its cold, unfeeling fingers to prevent her from making a sound.

Saban swings his leg over the back of the horse, jumps down, and runs toward the door, yelling for their servants to follow him. He tells one to get the doctor and where to meet them. Giselli grabs him on his way back, and he finally realizes she's standing there. The dread and distress in his eyes reach out and grab her, making her knees buckle where she stands.

"Zora spooked on the trail with Dad on her back. She reared up and fell over backward. They went over the side of a steep embankment. Mom, I don't know if Dad will live. He's hurt very badly. I had no choice but to leave him to get help."

"Mom"? This hateful woman is Saban's mother?

Sagran died before Saban had a chance to reach him. Giselli has blamed her son for her husband's death since the day they went riding at Saban's insistence. She can't see past her own grief to realize her son has carried this unnecessary guilt for more than a year. She has criticized his every move, his every decision, his very being to the point he actively avoids being around her.

But he's trapped tonight. He's here to celebrate his sister's engagement. He looked forward to spending time with me. Then Giselli emerged from her wing already inebriated, incredibly cross, and prepared to pick a public fight, knowing Saban wouldn't fight back and hurt her further.

But she doesn't know me.

CHAPTER 7

"Mother." Saban keeps his face neutral to prevent agitating her further. "I'd like you to meet Sara. Sara, this is my mother, Giselli Strydor."

"It's a pleasure to meet you." I lie like I've never lied before. It's not a pleasure, but I'll give her the benefit of the doubt.

"You should get away from him while you still can. Before you end up dead, too." She points at me with her index finger; the others remain wrapped around her glass.

"Funny you should mention that. Saban saved my life today. I would've been dead had he not interfered on a stranger's behalf when he was under no obligation to help. As I was just saying to Vale, I'm very thankful for Saban." I smile sweetly, not giving away the underlying reason why I feel the need to defend her son when she won't.

Saban and Vale both look at me with astonished expressions. A quick glance into Saban's thoughts tells me no one talks back to Giselli. She's apparently become hateful and bitter since her husband's death, feeling she's had someone taken away from her far too soon. I can sympathize with her loss. I've lost my entire family, but her son still wants to be an active part of her life. She should be grateful to still have family members who love her.

Giselli glances up at Saban, and I feel the ice around her heart melt ever so slightly.

"You have every right to be proud of your son. He's fearless, and he refused to stand aside even when an army of elves demanded it. You've done a wonderful job of teaching him to be an honorable man. Not that he won't make mistakes. We all do, right? But in the short time I've known him, I've learned a lot about his character from his actions."

She quickly wipes away a tear before it drops on her cheek.

"I noticed they just replenished the finger foods. Would you like to have a bite to eat with me? I don't know about you, but I'm famished. We can leave the boys to finish trading their hunting stories while we get to know each other better." I'm trying—for Saban's sake, I'm really trying.

"That sounds lovely. I would like that, Sara. Thank you."

Not that I think I can solve their family problems over a cucumber and cream cheese finger sandwich and hot tea, but even a little bit of improvement counts. Simply a starter conversation would be better than what I witnessed between mother and son just now. I will use everything I have at my disposal to gain the upper hand and keep it.

As we walk toward the tables full of food, she loses her footing and stumbles. On instinct, I reach out to help steady her, and I'm pleasantly surprised when she lets me. I hook my arm around hers, so it appears we're just walking and talking instead of her leaning on me to make it the short distance to the table. She pats my arm in appreciation and understanding of my actions, despite her inebriated state. We reach an empty table near the food display, and I deposit her in a chair.

"What can I get you to eat?"

She names off a few food items she likes, and I assure her it's no trouble for me. Before I turn to leave, I pick up her glass and hand it to a passing server. Another tear is quickly dabbed away, but she doesn't argue. When I return with our plates, the servers have left glasses of water on the table for us. Giselli stares at her drink, watching the beads of sweat drip down the sides of the clear glass.

"Here you are. I grabbed a couple fresh scones when they came out, along with clotted cream and jam, of course." I slide into the chair beside her and place my linen napkin on my lap.

"Did Saban really save you today?"

"Yes, he did." I recount the version of the story I know is safe to tell, emphasizing how scared I was and how I didn't know what to do. But Saban stepped in and saved me in so many ways, and for that, I'll be eternally grateful to him.

"You must think I'm a terrible person. He couldn't have had anything nice to say about me." She can't find the strength to lift her eyes to meet mine. "Not that I'd blame him. I don't like myself most of the time."

"He hasn't said one bad word about you."

That gets her attention, and her gaze flies up to mine. When she finds no deceit in my eyes, the tears well up in hers. "I'm surprised. Now that I've opened the door, I suppose it's only right that I tell you the entire story."

"You can tell me whatever you feel comfortable sharing. We just met, so I have no expectations of anything."

"You're young and beautiful. But you have a gentle spirit that draws others to you. That asset probably also means you carry others' burdens on your shoulders. It makes you easy to talk to and to share personal details with, and with your big heart, you won't turn someone away when they need help."

I would swear she was a mage if I didn't already know she wasn't. There was no surge of electricity when we touched. That means she can't be one. Right?

"I'm more than willing to listen and help you if I can. I don't want you to feel obligated, though, because you don't owe me anything."

"I want to share, and I appreciate any insight you can give me."

She recounts the details of the memory I already

know, adding bits and pieces from other times in their lives as color commentary and additional information to help the pieces fit together. But the gist of the problem remains the same—her grief has blinded her to the truth, the blessings she has, and what she should hold on to with both hands.

"What if it wasn't Saban's fault?" I ask the blunt question because I want to stun her. I want the first answer that comes to her mind.

"Then it would be mine." Her voice is almost a whisper. She doesn't want to say it out loud, hear the words, or admit the possibility.

"No, Giselli. It wasn't your fault. It wasn't Saban's fault. It wasn't even the horse's fault. It was simply an accident. My parents were killed when I was a baby, but it wasn't anyone's fault. No one caused it. No one created the circumstances that took them away from me. Accidents happen, regardless of how many precautions we take to avoid them. I've lived my entire life wishing I had siblings, wishing I could spend just one day with my family, and knowing that can never happen. If I were in your shoes, I would spend every spare minute I had with Saban and Isla, making memories and having fun. Because we never know when our time will be up."

She's so overcome with emotion, she can't speak. I decide to give her a minute to regain her composure, so I stand and put my hand on her shoulder. "I'm going to get us a few more scones. We're celebrating tonight, right? We can afford to splurge a little."

She smiles and nods. Her eyes are watery, and her face is splotchy red, but the smile is genuine. When I return to the table, Saban and Vale have joined us, and the three of them are having a polite conversation. Color me surprised...and pleased. I put one plate in front of Giselli and retake my seat with the other. Servers make their rounds, handing out cups of what smells like the fresh aroma of coffee. The mixture of food and coffee seems to help Giselli sober up more with each minute that ticks by.

"Are those for me?" Saban asks with a wink.

"No, they certainly are not. I picked these out especially for me. But I will tell you where you can find more." I grin and start slathering the cream and jam on my sweet goodies while Saban and Vale laugh good-naturedly with me.

"Keep your seat, Saban. I'll grab some for us, and we won't share with the ladies." Vale chuckles as he makes his way to the food line.

Saban leans over to whisper in my ear. "I'll share everything I have with you after what you've done tonight. You have my undying loyalty. All I know to say is thank you, but that is horribly insufficient under the circumstances. On my honor, I pledge to stand by your side, come what may."

"You don't owe me anything, Saban. You saved my life today—I'm the one who owes you. Talking to your mom wasn't a hardship or an inconvenience. It was my pleasure."

"My pledge stands, Sara. You've more than saved my

life. You've saved my family." He places a chaste kiss on my cheek. There's nothing sensual behind it, only pure gratitude.

"Saban?" Giselli waits for him to look at her before continuing. "You look so handsome tonight. You're so much like your father—in both your personality and how you carry yourself. I'm extremely proud of you...and I love you."

Saban stands and is at her side in an instant. He helps her up from her chair and holds her in his arms. A vision of a little raven-haired boy clinging to his mother's leg and giggling so hard he can barely remain upright pops into my head, and I know it's in Giselli's too.

"That is such a beautiful song playing. Maybe the two of you should take advantage of it and enjoy a slow dance." My suggestion is well received, and they walk off to the dance floor hand in hand.

When Vale rejoins me, he glances around the room, looking for them for a moment. "You must be a miracle worker."

"No, nothing like that. I just told her about losing my parents and how I wish I had one more day to spend with them. Accidents happen, and they're no one's fault."

"She must really like you to listen to you like that. People have tried to talk to her about it for the past year, but she wouldn't hear it."

"Sometimes it takes a kindred spirit. Someone else who has lost everything, who can point out what's left to live for."

"This pretty much guarantees Saban will never leave your side." Vale doesn't sound too pleased about that, for whatever reason. To be honest, I'm not sure how I feel about it either.

Before I can formulate a response, a young lady with thick black hair, bright blue eyes, and a headband of large red roses rushes up to our table. She's dressed in an elegant floor-length white gown that molds to her perfect form. Her white gloves reach her elbows, giving even more of a sophisticated air. The bewildered expression on her face only makes her more beautiful.

"Vale, what are Mom and Saban doing dancing? How did this happen?" Her forced whisper isn't nearly quiet enough to be a secret.

"Isla, this is Sara. She's Saban's date tonight. She had a talk with your mom, and the next thing we knew, Giselli and Saban were mother and son again." Vale nods toward me as he speaks, keeping a sly grin on his face.

Isla jerks her gaze to me, her eyes roaming over my face until she's memorized my every feature. "It's so nice to meet you, Sara. I heard the rumor as soon as I walked out of my bedroom, but I didn't buy it. I couldn't believe my brother had finally taken an interest in someone, but I've never been happier to be so wrong. Whatever you said to Mom to soften her heart, don't stop now. Our little family has been to hell and back over the past year."

She wraps her arms around my shoulders and squeezes. "Thank you, Sara. Thank you so much. You've just made my engagement party the best day of my life."

"I'm happy to help, really. But all I did was share my story with her. Your mom did the rest."

She pulls back, her eyes level with mine, and gently shakes her head. "Somehow, you softened her heart. You're a good influence—on Saban and Mom. I'm an excellent judge of character."

"Well, I appreciate your kind words. Congratulations on your engagement. This is such a beautiful party, and you look exquisite in that dress." The gentleness in her eyes reveals a level of humanity I haven't witnessed in anyone else I've encountered here so far.

Saban and Giselli rejoin us at the table when the song finishes. Everyone tries a little too hard not to stare at them, but we're all waiting for one of them to share even a morsel of information. Saban takes the empty seat next to me with gratitude swimming in his eyes. He takes my hand in his and lifts it to his lips for a sweet kiss. While the others engage in a conversation about the party, I lean closer to Saban.

"How was your dance?"

"It was exactly what we needed. We had a good chat under cover of the music. Obviously, one dance won't cure all our problems, but it's a solid chance at a new beginning."

"I'm happy to hear that. A chance is all you need."

"Couldn't agree more. Would you care to dance with me? All I need now is a chance to get to know you better." The sexy smirk on his face is exactly why no female between eight and eighty can refuse his charms.

"I'd love to dance. Take me away from this table before I eat all the finger sandwiches and embarrass us both tonight."

I'm graced with a full smile as he stands and offers his hand to help me up. "You could never embarrass me. All you have to do is say the word and whatever you want is yours."

He pulls our entwined hands to his heart and simply stares into my eyes for a moment before walking to the dance floor. With my arms around his neck, his around my waist, and our chests pressed together, I'm keenly aware of both the instant attraction between us and the sense that fate has somehow thrust us together.

Even with the strange circumstances of my arrival in this world.

Fate did bring the two of you together. He is your destiny, Saraya.

That voice in my head again. But...*Saraya?*

CHAPTER 8

"You and Saban definitely seemed cozy tonight." Addilyn can barely wait to grill me about my evening as she helps me out of the ball gown. She hands me a pair of silky pajamas, and I pull them on before plopping down on the bed.

"Addi, have you ever felt something for someone that hit you so hard and so fast, it made your head spin? Feelings you can't rationally explain and can barely even acknowledge because it's way too soon?" Not only do I need Kristi here with me right now to help me navigate these unfamiliar feelings, but I need her brutal honesty to tell me if I'm absolutely crazy. I don't have any experience in the falling-hard-for-a-guy arena, so I have no idea if what I'm feeling is real or just a fleeting fantasy.

"Wow. This is more serious than I thought. Tell me everything. Leave nothing out. Not one single detail." She takes a seat next to me on the bed after putting away the dress.

For my story to make sense, I have to start from the very beginning—when Nana disappeared, and I fell into this strange new world. Then when I ran into the angry elves and my savior, Saban. All the assumptions and allowing them to believe the details they supplied for my story. I explained how all my life, I'd filtered out the voices until I couldn't hear them anymore, but when I arrived here, I knew I had to let them flow again. The dangers of not using my gifts were too steep.

Addi sat in stunned silence as I rattled off all the details leading up to how I got here.

"We know all about the other world, of course, since our society was built as a mirror image of yours, with a few distinct differences. I've just never met anyone who was able to pass from there to here the way you did. Your power levels must be off the charts.

"The mages and wizards who created this realm sealed the original spells they used, so no one who came after them could reverse it. Doors occasionally open between our worlds, but only when powerful magic is involved. Our realm is hidden by ancient magic that's older than anyone here and wholly unbreakable, even by the most powerful of our kind."

"This is fascinating. What's the same and what's different here? I have no idea what to expect." Maybe I should've stayed here with her and learned more about this world instead of going to the engagement party.

"We've evolved and adapted to modern times the same way you have, only at a slightly more advanced rate. Our flora and fauna have evolved faster as well. The original mages and wizards left the old world because of the constant wars, diseases, and hatred mankind harbored in their hearts. Over the years, we've made a few advances they didn't consider.

"For one, the orphanage where he assumed you lived is used as a last resort. We don't have children here by mistake. No underage pregnancies can happen. When a human couple decides to have children, there are intentional steps they have to take, or it won't happen. The magic inside our realm is incredibly powerful, even if some are afraid of it. We've all but eradicated diseases and illnesses, which is why we live so long. We've also adopted stricter antipollution measures.

"But we'll finish this part of the conversation later. Tell me about Saban and these strong feelings you've developed for him over a few hours. Let's dissect what's going on there."

I find it much easier to talk about falling through a door from another world than admitting to my feelings for Saban.

"From the moment we laid eyes on each other, we just clicked. Our personalities mesh. We have the same sense of humor, and we get along so well. After we danced and ate and talked and laughed and enjoyed a couple glasses of that delicious champagne, Saban and I walked out onto the balcony to spend some time alone.

"It was already dark, so all the bioluminescent insects and plants in the forest surrounding the castle were entirely stunning. Saban thought I was awed by the view from the castle, so I didn't correct him. That was gorgeous too, but I've never seen a forest so alive before. My amazement at the world around us is what prompted the deep conversation Saban and I had next.

"The whole time we talked, I fought the feelings stirring inside me. I've had a small, still voice inside my head, guiding my steps and helping me along. The voice feels friendly—it feels like my nana speaking to me. It told me Saban is my destiny. But, Addi... I'm too young to think about anyone being my forever. Only, that's all I can think about now. Saban. What I hesitate to label as affection for him. My desire to be near him all the time is borderline psychotic. None of this makes sense."

"Actually, it makes perfect sense...for this realm. Just not for yours and what you're used to. Here, the more time you spend with your mate, the stronger your bond grows. We don't spend years dating, getting to know each other, going through all the drama-filled ups and downs we've heard your world does. A few people from the Covis Realm kingdoms have traveled back and forth between the portals. They always come back here, though."

"Well, that actually makes sense. I guess that's where we got all the tales of vampires, werewolves, and witches, huh?"

"Absolutely. Although, I have to tell you, the tales we've

heard from your world regarding our races are *so* far off the mark. It's amazing how facts are misconstrued and spread as the truth. Now, back to Saban. You're not finished with that part of the story."

"When he kissed me, I thought I'd died and gone to heaven. His lips were so soft. His touch melted me from the inside out. With that single kiss, I was ready to pledge my heart to him for all time. I'd become one of those girls in high school I used to make fun of—the ones who found a different 'perfect guy' every week. Even though my life goals felt a million years away, I had goals—*have* goals—I want to accomplish before even thinking about marriage or kids or anything like that. Not to mention finding my grandmother and getting her to safety. But it's taking every ounce of strength inside me not to run to his room right now and spend all night next to him. Who is this person I've become? I don't even recognize her."

The corners of Addi's lips curve upward, but the smile doesn't quite reach her eyes. "You've had a long day. I don't expect you to understand everything that's been thrown at you in the last several hours. If you have that strong of a reaction to him, and he feels the same, the two of you will be linked. It's how the natural law of our world works. When you meet your soul mate, your soul knows."

"Are you saying there's someone for everyone here? You just keep looking and waiting until you meet the one person you'll spend your life with?"

"It's not quite as simple as that. I'm sure you date in

your world, right? If you're romantically interested in someone, you spend time together and see if you're compatible?"

"Yes, of course."

"We do that here too. It's not as if everyone wanders around aimlessly until they bump into their soul mate. The difference is when you actually find that person, no one else matters. No one else can fill that empty place in your heart and soul anymore. You can date, you can spend your days and nights with someone else, but it'll never feel quite right. Does that make sense?"

"I'm afraid so. No one will ever hold a candle to Saban, and if I try to move on from him, I'll never be fully happy."

"Not as long as he's alive. Same for him when it comes to you. Love sucks, huh?"

"Yes, it does." We giggle like little girls. "By the way, how old are you?"

"By your world's standards, I'm about twenty. Instead of magic, humans here live for several hundred years. We age much slower than the people in your world." She shrugs at my shocked, slack-jawed expression.

A light rap on the door snaps me out of my surprise. "Who could that be at this hour?"

"Who, indeed?" She sniggers and shakes her head. "I think we both know who it is. I'll step into the other room and give you two some privacy."

The giddiness nearly escapes my throat as I rush to the door. *Damn, Sara, desperate much?* I force myself to walk the rest of the way and slowly crack the door open. His handsome face comes into view, my heart skips a beat, and whatever plan I had to remain cool and collected flies right out the window.

"I'm sorry to show up like this. It's already so late and I'm sure you're ready to go to sleep, but I had to see you one last time." He leans against the doorframe as he speaks.

His tired eyes skim over my silky pajamas and instantly morph into a heated mixture of longing and need. I grip the doorknob to remain rooted in my current spot and keep myself from flying into his arms. The intense attraction is mutual. The powerful yearning and craving for the other are shared. Saban and I are in this thing together—whatever it is.

I only hope we're not burned to ashes by the white-hot desire.

"I'm glad you did. Do you want to come in for a minute?" I hesitate to ask him that question because I don't want to seem too forward, but I'm also not ready for him to leave either.

"I'd love to, if it's not too much trouble."

"Not at all." I open the door farther and let him pass by me. He walks to the small sitting area and sits on the couch, so I leave the door ajar and join him. "What's on your mind?"

"You." He links our fingers together and pulls me closer to him. I happily oblige.

"What a coincidence. You were on my mind too. Anything else?"

"Tomorrow, I have to go with Gerard for our standing meetings with the surrounding kingdoms. There's nothing special happening, but we can't miss it. We're expected to be there to represent Easthaven Crest. My mind will be on you all day even though I can't be with you."

"I'll be here when you're finished with your meetings. Addilyn will keep me busy tomorrow, teaching me everything I need to know about the palace and the work. The time will fly by, and you'll be back before you know it." I gently stroke along his jawline, my eyes automatically drifting to his full lips.

"Any time away from you will be long, drawn-out, and pure hell. But I'm all for making up for lost time when I see you again tomorrow night." He leans down and presses his lips to mine. I have no choice but to respond in kind—my mind and my body are under a spell. His spell. He ends our kiss but keeps his lips close enough to brush against mine as he speaks. "If I don't leave now, I'll never go. As much as I hate to say it, I have to say good night now."

"Good night, Saban. Sweet dreams…until tomorrow." With one last, lingering kiss, he stands and walks out the door.

"There's absolutely no doubt about it. You both have it bad for each other." Addi stands in the doorway to the adjoining room, smirking at the lost puppy expression on my face.

I shrug and purse my lips to the left. "I have to admit you're right. So now what happens?"

"You live happily ever after, of course."

"Why do I get the feeling that's the furthest thing from the truth?"

"Because, my dear, Saban is a human and you're a mage. The laws are crystal clear—when a mage is discovered, she's killed. Humans and mages are not allowed to be together, Sara. It's one of the most absolute laws and why our kind has to hide in the Veil. I think we should go there tomorrow while he's away at the council meeting. You can meet the others and start learning how to use your powers in a safe environment."

"Yes, okay, let's do that. I have to get my mind back on finding my grandmother and not letting some man distract me from my goal."

"Easier said than done in this case, my dear. But I'll help you any way I can."

Addi leaves, and I climb into the extra-large and ornate bed. The mattress is soft and cushiony, enveloping me in a warm embrace while I attempt to sleep. But my dreams haunt and confuse me, causing me to toss and turn all night. One minute, it's pure ecstasy and what real dreams are made of. The next minute, all hell's breaking loose and I'm running for my life again. Only this time, everyone descends on me with pitchforks and lit torches, ready to burn me at the stake.

"Are these dreams or premonitions?" I rub the sleep out of my eyes and force myself to sit up on the side of the bed.

Whoever said dreams and premonitions are mutually exclusive, Saraya?

First things first—I need to identify the source of the voice in my head before it drives me crazy.

CHAPTER 9

After I spent a few early morning hours learning the ropes around the house, Addi and I left the sprawling palace on foot. My mind keeps taking me back to medieval times, so I'm always looking for horses and carriages, knights in shining armor riding their trusty steeds, and people who live way behind the modern times.

But this place is magical, pun intended, and has the coolest, most futuristic vehicles I've ever seen. Addi simply rolls her eyes at my amazement every time one passes by on our way to the Veil. She insists we can't use transportation to get there because we have to maintain a low profile when we disappear behind the invisible curtain.

Good thing I enjoy getting my exercise outdoors.

When Saban mentioned the village and the orphanage, my mind pictured dirt streets, wooden buildings with straw roofs, and old-timey clothes. Nothing could be further from the reality of it, though. As we walk through the city, the sleek, modern, multistory buildings tower over the clean streets. The people on the sidewalks hurry by in their avant-garde attire, pushing the boundaries of what I usually see in fashion, but killing it, nonetheless.

"You're cute." Addi glances at me with a clear side-eye expression. "You come to us through a magical door and automatically assume you stepped back in time a few hundred years."

"First, get out of my head. Second, I can't help it. Castles and kings and fights for the throne became all but extinct a long time ago in my world."

"Maybe in that sense, but I'm sure the constant fight for political gain is well underway. Every kingdom is the same. My world, your world, other worlds. Someone is always power-hungry, and the innocent people trapped under their rule always pay the price."

"You're right. That does happen everywhere."

A vehicle approaches from behind then slows down to idle along beside us. When we lean over to glance inside, I'm surprised to see Gerard's smiling face behind the wheel. "You ladies need a ride somewhere? I have a business meeting with some of the local merchants, but I'm early so I have plenty of time to give you a lift."

"Thank you for the offer, Gerard, but we're enjoying the beautiful weather today. Plus, we're still in the middle of our girl talk." Addi giggles and shrugs innocently.

"All right. I'll see you two later, then." He smiles then drives away.

Gerard is an extremely handsome man with his neatly styled mixture of light and dark blond hair, alluring blue eyes, and deceptively devilish smile. He has an innate charisma about him that makes people want to talk to him and captivates their full attention. Isla is a lucky woman. He dotes on her every need and want, putting her front and center of his world. They were adorable to watch at their engagement party. So much in love, so full of life, and so thankful for all their friends and family celebrating with them.

When Gerard is out of sight, we make a sharp left turn down a side street and walk at a brisk pace until we're out of the city limits and approaching the thick forest that's home to the Veil. The trees are taller and bigger around than any I've ever seen. Their full branches and broad trunks make walking in a straight line impossible. Moving through the tangled underbrush is difficult at best. We wind through the dense brush until the sunshine from the outside world dims and the glow from the flying insects lights our way. I release a sigh of relief when we finally find the trail and can move faster.

The first clearing we reach takes my breath away. In the tops of the trees, high above the forest floor, are magnificent houses connected by wooden walkways and bridges. The canopy is alive with magic and people and music and singing. Birds of every color flutter through the air, their chirps only adding to the harmony.

"Are we in the Veil now?"

"We are." The pride she feels for her secret home is palpable—and with good reason.

"This place is amazing. It's beautiful, but it even feels different from the rest of this realm. There's a peace here that settles over me, making me calm and relaxed. Happy, even."

"You can feel that after one visit?" Addi turns to me, trying to read my thoughts.

"Yes, and I can also feel you trying to get into my head. Why couldn't I feel that before now?"

"Beautiful girl, what is your name?" An older woman steps out of one of the enormous trees, silhouetted by the light from inside. Her silver hair and dark brown eyes give her wrinkled brown skin an ethereal glow. She walks up to me and takes my hands in hers, looking deep into my eyes and seeing me with more than our normal vision.

"Sara."

She cups my face in her hands, and tears well up in her eyes.

I'm not sure what's happening, but I don't get a negative vibe from her. Her intense scrutiny makes me slightly uncomfortable, but not because I think she poses any threat. The longer she stares at me, the more her expression changes from interest to disbelief. She's shocked for some reason, and that can only mean what she's about to say will change my life. Again.

"Is it really you, sweet girl? Saraya, have you returned to us?" The tears spill over onto her cheeks, flowing unchecked as they drop to the forest floor below. Her face is alive with a mixture of love, relief, and fear in equal measures. My mind is spinning, and I don't know what I should focus on first.

Saraya. I've only heard that name whispered from the voice that invades my mind. And only here, in Covis Realm. What does all this mean? My thoughts swirl and steal my ability to speak, leaving only confusion in their wake.

"Come with me. I'll explain everything to you. Don't you worry. It'll be all right." She gently pats my face before taking my hand in hers and leading me inside the enormous tree. "I'm Ginevra Crowe, the leader of this order."

The staircase curves around the inside of the trunk, all the way up to the top where another door leads out to the walkways connecting the trees. Curtains of tiny colorful lights stream down the walls, twinkling in a mesmerizing pattern, making it nearly impossible to look away. Shades of white, gold, pink, green, blue, orange, red, purple—and every color on the spectrum in between—brighten the steps and light our way. That's when I realize they aren't simply lights at all.

"Are those…fairies?" I literally can't trust my own eyes.

"Yes, they are. The fae are friends of the mages and help keep us safe. Their magic is a little different from ours, but no less powerful. They're better hidden from the humans because they can remain as small as a firefly or take on their full adult size whenever needed. They've been extremely loyal allies." Ginevra walks through the door at the top of the stairs and turns to me with a sly grin plastered on her face. "Yes, we do have a better way to reach the top than taking the stairs every time, but I thought you'd enjoy seeing all the details on your first visit."

"Busted. Get out of my mind." I chuckle to myself, knowing I could've shielded my thoughts if I'd wanted to hide them.

"I don't have to read your mind to know what you were thinking after climbing that tall tree. We're all thinking the same thing." She laughs good-naturedly as she steps onto the sky bridge connecting the trees. "No one can accuse us of not getting our exercise in today, right?"

"Exactly. Honestly, taking that route didn't bother me. I love to climb trees anyway. You simply showed me a new way to do that today."

We move inside an actual tree house and take a seat in the comfortable living room. The limbs above act as ceiling beams. The floors are rough-cut wood planks that have been coated to make them smooth. The walls are floor-to-ceiling glass panes, giving a complete 360-degree view of the surrounding forest. All the furniture is made from the wood of the trees, colored in earth tones. The couch is extra wide, overstuffed, and strewn with coordinating throw pillows.

"Ginevra, I think I could live in this place and never leave the Veil. You have a gorgeous view. It's quiet, peaceful, and surrounded by nature." I lean back, and the soft sofa envelops me.

"See what I mean? I told you Sara was different from the other mages, Ginevra." Addi laughs out loud as she plops down on the couch beside me and playfully nudges me in the side with her elbow. "It's pretty refreshing, actually."

"Do you know why she's different, Addilyn?" Ginevra's tone catches my attention, and I turn my gaze to her.

"No, but I'm all ears."

"So am I." With my elbows on my knees, I wait impatiently for an explanation.

She makes quick movements with her hands in the air, and a white cloud forms from her actions. Then the cloud shapes into specific forms before morphing into something like a projection screen, complete with moving images just like a movie.

"Many years ago, all the kingdoms of Covis Realm lived together in peace. Each nation had its own borders, but we were also neighbors who looked out for one another. Mages were a vital part of every community— humans, elves, merpeople, shifters, and vampires. We helped bridge the gap between the different types of beings in our world. Mages created a commonality among the vastly different backgrounds.

"There are bad elements in every culture. You'll always have criminals, regardless of how advanced you think your race is. Someone comes along and wants to tip the scales of power in his or her direction. That's why no one looked too hard into the murders and disappearances when they first started. The crimes were sporadic, and the victims didn't seem to have a connection. There was no obvious rhyme or reason. Until it was too late, and by then, we'd been blind for too long."

"I don't understand. How were you blind for too long?"

"The victims were all killed with magic. No apparent wounds—no lightning swords, no guns, no marks on the body that would suggest anything else could've caused the deaths. The realm was outraged, calling for the head of the mage who was responsible. It was the first time our world had experienced a serial killer, and it was more than jarring. It turned nation against nation. Ethnic group against ethnic group. Suspicion clouded the minds of people who had been friends all their lives.

"Then the humans started 'testing' others to see if they were a mage or not." She uses air quotes and rolls her eyes.

"What kind of test?"

"Complete nonsense. The humans held women down, twirled a crystal pendulum over their hearts, and if the stone turned a certain color, they were deemed to be a mage. Out of sheer panic, they sentenced those accused of being a mage to death and carried out their sentence immediately. Of course, those who tried to dispute the test were declared mages and also killed. It was a very dark time in our world." Ginevra squeezes her eyes shut, bows her head, and breathes deeply until her chin stops quivering.

"That is terrible. I can't imagine witnessing such a complete disregard for life." My heart is pounding inside my chest so hard I'm surprised they can't hear it knocking. There's more to this story, I know, because *Saraya* hasn't made an appearance yet.

She takes a deep breath and meets my gaze head on. "You were barely a newborn when the troubles began. When the executions started, the search for mages carried on for months, growing in intensity and ferocity. Your mother, Wren, was the queen of Easthaven Crest. By the time the angry mob went after her, the mania had hit an all-time high. Her mother, Zula, took you and left this world before they could hurt you."

"My grandmother's name is Sue." I don't want to believe this reality.

"In the other world, yes. We called her Zu for short, so Sue was a natural conversion for her to fit in."

"The mob killed my mother?" My question comes out barely louder than a whisper.

"I'm afraid so, sweetheart. I'm so sorry to be the one to tell you this, but you have to understand who you are. You're the—"

"What about my father? What happened to him?" I jump up from the couch, barely containing the chaos inside me that's threatening to boil over at any second.

"He died trying to protect your mother. They loved each other so much, and he wouldn't abandon her when the angry citizens came for her. You understand what this means, don't you?" Ginevra moves to my side and wraps her hand around my forearm. "You know what I'm about to say."

"Don't say it. I don't want to hear it. Where is my

grandmother now? She disappeared in my world, I fell through a hole in the forest and wound up here. If she's here, I only want to find her and get us both back home as soon as possible." I rub my hand across my forehead and drop my chin to my chest.

This cannot be happening. I feel as if I'm Alice in freaking Magicland.

"Zu was my best friend, Saraya. I loved her like a sister, and it broke my heart when she left here. She and I cast a powerful spell over you that day to cloak your true identity from the inhabitants of this world until your eighteenth birthday. We knew the person behind the atrocities would keep searching for you. If you were killed, nothing would stand in their way from taking over.

"On your next birthday, the spell will be broken, and your true identity will be known. If Zu disappeared from your world, then she was found because they were looking for you. There's no way to free her without giving away your identity."

"I know I'll regret asking this, but there seems to be no way around it. Are you saying the magic murders were all a setup to take over the throne from my parents?"

She nods.

"And by killing me, the path to the throne is wide open for the taking?"

"Yes. As long as an heir lives, no one else can claim the throne, even if they have the votes from the other kingdoms. We've managed to persuade most of the others not to give it away...to wait for the rightful heir to return."

Ginevra's hesitant but hopeful expression causes me physical pain.

I don't want this role.

"Who was behind the mass extermination of the mages? Who started the panic?"

"We were never able to trace it back to the original source. All we know is it was a powerful and dark warlock. One highly seasoned in his magic and deeply entrenched in his hatred. Your mother was a powerful mage who was well-known throughout the kingdom and celebrated until the murders started. He used those events to turn the people against her and make them afraid of what she could do. But, as with most who gain power, he wanted more. He wanted the power of the Easthaven Crest throne."

"That means he's still out there, waiting for me."

"I'm afraid so, my dear."

"Good. He won't catch me off guard like he did my parents. I'll be ready for him to make his move. When can I start my training?"

CHAPTER 10

"Don't worry, Sara. I've been sworn to secrecy for anything regarding mages my whole life. I couldn't tell anyone your secret even if I wanted to—the spell prevents it. But I'm glad you didn't ask me to stay behind when Ginevra took you to her home. At least you don't have to bear the weight of the world alone. That takes a heavy toll on your shoulders." Addi has been nothing but supportive and reassuring since we left the Veil.

"Thank you for everything you've done, Addi. I'd be completely lost without you. Not that I want to burden you with my problems, but I'm glad you're on my side."

I think she knows I'm teetering on the verge of freaking out, and she's trying to keep me talked off the ledge. Whether that involves hunting down every warlock in Covis Realm or running back to my plain and ordinary world, neither of us can say.

I spent the better part of the day in training—reading illegal books, watching how others use their magic, and learning how to listen to the elements and use them to my advantage. When I brought up the voice in my head, guiding me and talking to me as if someone were right beside me, whispering in my ear, Ginevra's interest was piqued. She cautioned me about allowing that voice in. It could be as benevolent as my grandmother reaching out to me, but it could also be a trap designed by the warlock to lure me into the open before it's time.

The trick is distinguishing friend from foe when it's only a murmur in my head.

I don't see the problem here.

As a side note, sarcasm is mainly lost on the people of this world, and yet it seems to be my first language. We're still working through the language barrier.

After we finished in the Veil, we went into Easthaven Crest so Addi could show me around and train me on how to do her job. Since we're working together in the castle, I need to learn what's expected of the royal fashion stylist. Although, as she pointed out, Saban and Isla are not royalty, regardless of how hard they've tried to get their titles changed. We won't split hairs over that, though. I'm planning to fly under the radar for as long as I can. I'd still rather find my grandmother before my coming out party, though.

Speaking of flying, I did learn I don't need a broom, despite what all the myths say and Halloween costumes show. Most mages aren't capable of actually taking flight.

Only a handful of documented instances have occurred in their entire history, and it wasn't with a broom of any shape, form, or fashion. They levitated from sheer power, mostly under need or duress, but of their own volition.

Learning my way around the city was a good distraction from the seriousness of the rest of the day…and the heaviness in my chest when we walk into the castle. Now that I know my parents weren't killed in a fluke accident, I'm having a hard time hiding my true feelings. My only saving grace right now is knowing Saban couldn't have been the one to do it since he's barely older than me, in my world's age. He would've been way too young to have been involved.

But was his mother or father? Did they want the throne and power? Did they want to set up Isla or Saban as the ruler of the kingdom? As if I didn't already have trust issues, now they're multiplied by a thousand. With the added complication of the intense attraction between him and me, and the whole "you're my mate for life" thing, I'm a walking contradiction of feelings and convictions.

Addi and I take the numerous packages we bought on our shopping trip to the room known as the castle's master closet. It's one large walk-in closet that's bigger than the house I grew up in. All the clothes, shoes, and accessories anyone could ever want or need are neatly arranged by event type and size. This will be my official job in the palace.

OVER THE NEXT SEVERAL WEEKS, ADDI SHOWS ME THE ROPES in working the master closet and the inner workings of the castle—as far as anyone else is concerned, that is. We take a detour on our daily trip to the city and continue my training in the hidden forest of the Veil. My abilities and skills with casting spells and using magic without saying a word grow by leaps and bounds every day. Watching the others and learning from an entire tribe of supportive women has done wonders for my own abilities.

Every evening when I finish my shift at work, Saban waits to escort me to dinner, admire the numerous stars in the night sky, or just spend time together walking in the scenic gardens and forests. Every moment helps me learn more about Easthaven Crest, about Saban, and about what I have to do in the coming weeks. He's been attentive and affectionate…and patient. He's expressed multiple times how he's ready to take our relationship to the next level, to announce to the kingdom he's found his soul mate and is prepared to live with me for all eternity.

I've been hesitant to fully commit to him, and I know he senses it. In this world, mates can't resist each other, so I know my reluctance to advance our relationship is confusing to him. But I'm no ordinary mate, and these are not ordinary circumstances. I'm torn, and I don't know which way to turn.

The stolen kisses in the hall aren't enough anymore. The unmistakable yearning between us is growing harder and harder to resist. I feel it every bit as strongly as he does. One of our recent escapades had us lying on a blanket under the stars. It was a beautiful evening, not a cloud in the sky. The glowing creatures of the night were out in full force.

He'd been baring his soul to me, telling me all of his dreams of being king of Easthaven Crest one day. He wasn't facetious in the least—he'd shared intimate details with me he'd never told anyone before.

"My parents put this grand idea of being king in my head when I was little. I used to wear a tablecloth tied around my neck, pretending it was the king's robe, as I strutted around the house. A stick served as my sword— but not just any sword. One that had been blessed by a dragon and worthy of knighting my loyal protectors. I'd pretend all my subjects loved me, I took good care of them, and that was all there was to being king.

"Of course, now I know better. Being in charge mostly means finding a diplomatic compromise that pisses off the fewest number of people. Even that's usually a stretch. But I still want the chance to prove my worth. I have this sense deep inside me that I'm meant for greatness...not the mundane world of being a servant."

He was earnest and open with his feelings. Showing his vulnerable side others didn't get to see. But there was so much he didn't know that I did. Facts I knew and couldn't share. Information that would completely change the dynamics of our relationship if I revealed them. Keeping those secrets made me feel as if I had betrayed his trust in an unforgivable way.

I knew I was the heir to the throne...and as long as I lived, he couldn't have it.

A great sadness settled over my heart and my mind. When he turned to me with his eyes so trusting and full of love, his soul laid open, and his lifelong pursuit shared in such an honest manner, the dam inside my mind broke. He leaned down to kiss me, pouring every emotion, sentiment, and desire into it, and a tear trickled down my cheek.

Torrential rain poured from above though no clouds were blocking the twinkling stars. We were both soaking wet by the time we ran back to the palace. He attributed the downpour to a freak of nature.

He was very close to the bull's-eye on that call.

This is part of why I'm so wishy-washy and indecisive about my feelings for him. When I'm with him, I only want to be with him. When we're apart, the conflict inside me nearly tears me apart.

Should I stay here in this world, on this path, and claim my right to the throne?

Should I find Nana and escape back to our ordinary and comfortable life, forever hiding from shadows and dark warlocks?

Despite Saban's declarations of love, I'm not convinced he would accept my claim to the title—or my status as a mage. Especially not as a queen mage...mage queen... whichever. If I came forward now, after we've spent so much time together, he'd think I'd been undermining him all along.

I have to wait until the cloaking spell is lifted and my true identity is indisputable. Then I'll know exactly how he responds when I tell him the full truth.

Addi is the only person in this palace I can fully trust.

One of the special magic tricks I learned from the others was how to communicate by reading minds and allowing mine to be read in return. Now Addi and I can send messages to each other telepathically and keep our conversations far away from eavesdropping ears.

While we work inside the palace, we have a full conversation about Saban and his family's possible role in my parents' demise without saying a word.

"I've never seen or heard anything that would make me question them, Sara. From what I understand, Sagran was your father's steward and stood in his place when needed. If the warlock is still looking for you, it can't be because of Saban's father. He died in a horseback riding accident."

"You think I should trust Saban?"

"To a degree. I wouldn't tell him anything about your magic or who you are. Just remember, if you two are truly meant to be mates, the link between you will eventually become too strong to break. Just take it one day at a time, but keep your secrets close to the vest for as long as you can."

"Do you believe in this lifelong mate theory?"

"Yes, I do, and I believe he's yours. There's no such thing as coincidence, Sara. Especially not one of this magnitude. He's enraptured by you. You're smitten with him. He's ignoring all the other women who have tried to capture his heart over the years. You're the only one who exists in his mind now. And speak of the devil…"

"Sara?" I turn to find Saban filling the doorway, his sights set solely on me. "I'm sorry to interrupt you when you two are so busy. Can I borrow you for a minute?"

"Of course." I can't deny the pitter-patter of my heart or how the wings flutter in my stomach when he's near. "I'll be right back, Addi."

"Take your time. I can finish this." She smiles knowingly, but I can't help but feel guilty for leaving her to do all the work alone.

Saban turns to step into the hallway, away from Addi's line of sight. I swipe my fingers across my forehead and shield my thoughts while no one is looking. It's not that I don't trust her, but there are some things I want to keep to myself, especially at the moment. While I'm sorting through my feelings for Saban, I don't need her sorting through my thoughts and deciphering them for me.

Plus, I don't know who else may be lurking in the shadows, waiting to pounce on my mind.

"Our council meetings ended earlier than I expected. I'd like to get away from here and spend some time alone with you. What do you say?"

Gone is the cocky, confident Saban. In his place is a vulnerable, sincere man. I wonder if he realizes how much more appealing this version of him is—the genuine person behind the masked façade.

"I'd love to go with you. What do you have in mind?" Any thought of playing hard to get just evaporated into thin air. I blurted out my consent without even thinking about it. Maybe there is something to this mate ideology they have.

"Are you up for going out on the water? We can take the boat, swim for a while, and have dinner on deck."

"That sounds perfect. Let me change my clothes, and I'll meet you at the main entrance."

"Awesome. I'll be waiting for you." He presses his lips against my knuckles, but his eyes remain glued to mine, making my insides heat from the intensity.

I step back into the master closet and approach Addi with my eyes wide open. "We're going out on the boat, swimming, and having dinner on the water. Can you help me pick out what I should wear?"

"That's what I live for, Sara."

She grabs my hand and pulls me along to another corner of the room. After rifling through the drawers and finding the perfect bathing suit, we move to the hanging racks to find clothes appropriate for a formal dinner. With everything neatly stored in a designer beach bag, she sends me on my way to meet Saban.

As promised, he's waiting by the front door, already changed into his casual clothes. When I approach, he senses my presence and turns to face me. A smile splits his face in two, making him even more handsome than usual. I can't deny my reaction to him every time he's near. The attraction is undeniable, and the powerful draw he has on me is unmistakable.

"Ready to go?"

"I'm ready. I've never been out on a boat before. This is exciting." I take his outstretched hand, and we walk out to the car.

We climb into the sleek vehicle. There are no wheels or tires; it merely hovers above the ground. With a little acceleration, we're essentially flying to our destination. The inside is as impressive as the exterior. Buttons and lights cover the control panel, but Saban manages them with practiced precision and ease.

"The marina is private. It was named after our last king, Taeral Nemertes. He was well before our time. My father said the people of the kingdom loved him so much, they didn't care that he was actually an elf. He was adopted and raised by human parents, our king and queen at the time, when his parents were killed in a tragic accident out at sea." Saban is making casual conversation, but I'm hanging on every word, soaking up every bit of information I can.

My dad was an elf? What?

"What happened to him?" It takes every bit of the strength I have to keep emotion out of my voice.

"You know all about the edict against mages, right? They were deemed too dangerous to our society overall. I mean, we all know they still exist, so we turn a blind eye for the most part, as long as they're not causing trouble. But even in Taeral's time, there was a law against a mage being queen. It simply wasn't allowed, the same as today. Imagine the kind of influence a queen mage would have over a king's decisions. Who knows how many times she'd use her magic to convince him to do what she wanted, you know?

"Anyway, when the kingdom learned our queen, Wren, was a mage, they revolted and attacked the castle. King Taerel died trying to protect his queen. He refused to leave her even though the people wanted him to remain their king. It's a tragic love story, isn't it?"

"Yes, it is. Do you think that law against mages still has a place in today's society?" I want to scream, curse, and punch him in his perfect face all at the same time. His story is vastly different from the one Ginevra told me. Now I fully understand why people at home say history books change the story based on what they want future generations to believe.

"I think there's always room for improvement. I'd like to think we've changed and evolved since that happened. Some may have been unfairly judged and condemned to die when they were actually valuable members of society. Some of the pieces of that past are sketchy for me, honestly. I've asked questions about what happened and why, but no one wants to answer them. It's as if they're ashamed of their contributions to the widespread panic and want to put it as far behind them as possible."

"If you were king, what would you do differently?"

"That's a tough question, but one I need to put a lot of thought into if it's ever to happen. I would be much more tolerant of other people and promote how our differences make us stronger. One or two bad apples shouldn't be allowed to spoil the whole bushel, and I think that's exactly what the last generation allowed to occur. We may have to start with laws that govern when and how magic can be performed to make everyone feel safe and level the playing field."

I know I put him on the spot with that question, but I still get the sense his idea would result in significant violations of civil rights. Come to think of it, do they even have civil rights in this world? There's so much I don't know or understand.

"Here we are. Ready for a little playing on the water and leaving all our burdens behind?"

"I'm so beyond ready to have a little fun." That is the honest to God truth. It was only a few weeks ago when I complained about having a dull, ordinary life. Now, I wish I could return to it, blissfully unaware of civil wars, mass genocide, and grand political schemes.

CHAPTER 11

I'm utterly speechless as we walk down the pier toward where the boat is docked. The water is a gorgeous shade of crystal-clear emerald green. The waves lap gently at the hulls of the ships as we walk by, vibrant fish dart back and forth, and sea gull chirps carry on the light breeze. There's so much here that's the same, and so much that's the complete opposite, as home. Keeping everything straight and separate is proving more and more difficult.

When Saban stops and extends his arm toward the gangway, my mouth drops open. His boat is actually a luxury power yacht, complete with a captain to navigate and a crew to attend to our every need, leaving us free to roam the multiple decks without a care. As I cross the bridge to the boat, something in the distance catches my eye. At first, I thought it was a dolphin breaching the water in a full jump and flip, but dolphins don't have human heads and long, flowing hair.

This detour from real life is exactly what I need right now. There are actual mermaids in this water. I can only hope one will approach me when Saban and I eventually enjoy a dip in this beautiful lake. I have so many questions, I wouldn't even know where to start. It's times like this when everything that's happened over the last forty-eight hours feels like a vivid dream. Nothing is real, everything is made up in my mind from a collection of books, movies, and tall tales. If I could wake up in my own bed with Nana rushing me to get dressed for school, I would never take it for granted again.

"She's a beauty, isn't she?" The heat from Saban's body seeps through my shirt from behind me. "We can go anywhere you want on this boat, princess. Just say the word, and I'll make it happen."

"She is gorgeous. It even rivals the palace with this view of the water. Maybe you should consider becoming a pirate and living at sea instead."

Saban laughs. "If only pirates weren't merely fairy tales."

Huh?

"Who says you don't deserve a fairy-tale life?" I laugh it off, pretending I already knew that. Even though we're enjoying downtime, I have to remember to keep my guard up. Invading his thoughts and reading the signs are the keys to keeping myself alive.

"*We* deserve one," he clarifies. "What do you say we

change into our swimsuits and enjoy the sun before it starts to set?"

"I'll race you—except I don't know where the finish line is, so you'll win."

"Come on, I'll show you around the ship while the captain takes us out into the open water. Once we anchor, we'll jump in and explore the coral reefs and shallow caverns."

As I expected, the interior of the ship is ultra-modern and every bit as decadent as the palace. However, I wasn't kidding when I suggested living on the boat and just sailing from port to port for a while. I think getting away from the charged political atmosphere would turn Saban into a different man entirely. My stateroom has every amenity known to man and then some.

Changed and ready for a little sun and surf, I rejoin him on the outside deck. He's shirtless, lying back on a cushy lounge chair, with mirrored shades covering his eyes. I've been swimming with Doug and Phillip plenty of times back home, but seeing Saban like this takes my breath away. His muscular chest is broad and solid. His six-pack abs appear to come naturally to him, and they stretch and flex with his every breath. His long legs are thick and muscular. He's not aware yet that I'm standing here, gawking over his finely tuned body.

I manage to make my feet move and take the chair next to him. He lifts his head, and even though I can't see his eyes, I can feel them roaming over my body from my head to my toes. I know precisely when he lingers on certain areas longer than others. The desire building inside him feels like a physical being, an invisible bond reaching out to me with the sole purpose of joining us as one.

"Princess, you are gorgeous. Every perfect inch of you."

"Princess" is a new nickname he recently started calling me. It makes me wonder if he subconsciously recognizes me somehow. But that's impossible, so I push the notion out of my head.

"Thank you. You don't look so bad yourself. I'm not drooling, am I?"

He chuckles and hands me a chilled glass of freshly poured champagne. Then he lifts his glass for a toast. "To my beautiful princess, who has breathed a new spirit of life into me and given me a reason to become the best man I can."

"To both of us." I clink my glass against his and drink to the sentiment.

The ship comes to a halt and the captain weighs anchor, so we grab the snorkel gear, put on our fins, and jump into the clear emerald water below. I'm pleasantly surprised by how warm it is. With my mask and snorkel in place, I dive down and savor the brilliant colors of the schools of fish and the expansive reef.

When I surface for air, Saban suggests we swim to the shallow waters where the boat can't go and take a leisurely lap there. I heartily agree, so we set off toward the shore of a small island. As the sandy bottom comes into clearer view, more vibrant fish surround us, along with plants and animals darting in and out of hiding places in the coral. We swim along the bend in the shore until the ship is just out of sight, giving us more privacy.

I've always been a mountains and forest kind of girl, but I'm in heaven right now and I never want to leave this water. Mermaid life is right up my alley today. We move to the shore, resting on the sand as the waves wash over our feet. Saban sits behind me, his legs on either side of me, and gently tugs me backward. My back meets his chest, his natural warmth seeps into my skin, and his arms encircle me. With the bright sun above, the clear water ahead, and a sexy man at my back, I couldn't ask for a better setting.

"You know, sometimes I wish I could read your mind." The soft murmur of his voice flows past the shell of my ear on his warm breath.

If only he knew how hard I tried to stay out of his mind. To give him the common courtesy everyone should be afforded. But when we're close like this, and his thoughts are so loud and contain such emotion, it's impossible not to hear them.

"What do you think you'll find in there?"

"That's just it. I'm not sure. I'd love to root around in there and flush out your true feelings for me." His tone is both hopeful and apprehensive. He hopes for the best and fears the worst.

This constant pushing away and pulling closer is hurting him as much as it pains me. The last thing I want is to hurt him, especially when he's been nothing short of my savior. He's been patient and kind, loving and affectionate, giving and thoughtful. And my heart does nearly leap out of my chest every time I think of him. Every day, my feelings for him grow stronger. I've given him nothing of myself compared to the bounty he has presented me.

I want to give him my heart.

All these secrets I'm keeping are shredding my soul to pieces. But they're not mine to share, and too many lives are at stake. So, I'll bear the burden as long as I have to. I imagine this is only a fraction of the stress the crown actually contains. Selfishly, I'll take his love and give him mine in return…until the reckoning day arrives.

I shift in the sand and turn to face him. When I say the words, I want him to see my eyes and feel the spoken truth.

"You really don't know how I feel about you?"

He shakes his head, but the hopefulness in his expression belies his answer.

"I'm crazy about you, Saban. I've never felt this way about anyone before, in my entire life. And I know without a doubt that no one could ever take your place in my heart."

He cups my face with his hands and presses his lips to mine, his kiss full of gratitude and relief. "I was beginning to think something was wrong with me. How could I be so sure about my soul mate if she didn't love me in return?"

"I'm sorry I made you doubt yourself and me. I've never told anyone this before, but losing my parents has affected me in so many ways. I've been afraid to give my love to anyone else. The pain of that kind of loss is unbearable and not something I've been eager to relive. But I've realized something important in the last few weeks we've been together."

"What's that?"

"The pain of not giving you my love hurts just as much. If the time comes when I have to face losing you, I'd rather know I gave you all my love while we were together."

"You'll never lose me. I'll always come back to you, no matter what happens. Even death itself couldn't keep me from you."

Please remember your vow when the time comes.

I'm not sure which of us moves first. He lifts me as I turn to fully face him. I straddle his lap as he lowers me down. I slip my fingers through his hair as his hands sear the exposed skin of my back with his unique brand. He slides his tongue against mine the moment I open my mouth for his taking. The thin material of my bikini bottoms is hardly a barrier to the growing hardness I feel under me. My hips rock of their own accord, seeking more from the only man who has ever, or will ever, stirred this kind of desire in my soul.

He breaks our frenzied kiss only to resume his ministrations on the sensitive skin covering my neck. With nips, licks, and bites, he works his way down to my collarbone. I slide my hand over his perfectly chiseled chest and across the muscled indentations of his stomach. The feral growl from deep in his throat only gives me more confidence to continue my exploration.

As my hand moves lower, his mouth follows suit. His warm tongue glides between my breasts, languidly lavishing attention there until my fingers trace the tip of his erection. His hips surge upward, pushing against my core and making me whimper with need. He grips my sides with such force, I'm sure I'll find bruises there. But I don't feel an ounce of pain—only sheer pleasure.

The rustling in the trees and brush and the heavy fall of footsteps behind force us to separate abruptly. Realizing we aren't alone on this island makes my chest tingle with anxiety, wondering who's there and how much of our public display of affection was just witnessed. Saban and I both watch with rapt attention as the visitor draws nearer.

Then a beautiful young woman with thick purple hair steps out from behind the trees. Her steps falter for a moment, and her expression is one of complete shock. She didn't know she was stepping directly into a love scene right there on the beach. Her eyes dart between Saban and me for a moment before recognition sets in.

"Saban. How are you?" Her tone is cordial but detached. "I didn't expect to see you here."

"Hello, Talia. This is Sara…my mate. Sara, this is Talia. She's from Elderwater Basin."

"You're a mermaid?" I ask a little too excitedly. I have no idea if everyone else has seen or met a mermaid before.

I should've probed Saban's mind a little to find out, but I'm too far beyond excited to stop myself now.

"Yes, I am." Her demeanor toward me is much warmer. "It's nice to meet you, Sara."

"It's very nice to meet you, Talia. I don't mean to sound rude, but I have so many questions for you. About your kingdom, about your culture in general. Maybe I'm the last person in the realm who hasn't met a mermaid before." I shrug off my ignorance.

"Not at all. We're normally reclusive, so I'm not surprised. But I'd be happy to sit and talk with you for a while." She smiles warmly, and the kindness reaches her eyes. It only falters when she glances at Saban.

"In that case, I will take my leave and give you two ladies some privacy. If it's okay with you, I'll swim back to the ship and have our meal brought to the beach." He raises his eyebrows when he looks at me, waiting for my approval.

"That sounds perfect. Thank you, Saban." In a flash, he's cutting quickly through the water toward the ship, leaving me alone with a real mermaid. "Talia, do you prefer to sit here on the beach or relax in the shallow water?"

"In the water, if you'd like. That'll answer one of your questions anyway. Yes, I have legs on land and a fin, complete with scales, in the water."

"Let me see." I can barely form a whisper in response. Getting to see this transformation is unbelievable.

She chuckles as she steps into the lake then gracefully

submerges the lower half of her body in the clear, shallow water. My brain can barely believe what my eyes see. Her legs and feet meld into one appendage. Then a tail fin pops out, and shiny scales in an array of green, blue, pink, and purple emerge, covering her legs like colorful sequins glimmering in the late afternoon sun.

"I know this sounds incredibly rude, but I mean no disrespect. Can I touch your scales? Please?"

"Sure." She flicks her tail fin up out of the water, and I run my fingertips along the smooth arrangement of scales covering her legs.

"You're absolutely amazing. Is there any way I can become a mermaid and swim off into the sunset?"

"I'm not sure it's quite that easy." Her laugh is contagious but not mocking. She can tell I'm sincerely in awe of her transformation.

The conversation flows effortlessly as she and I float in the warm water. She describes the underwater kingdom of Elderwater Basin in such vivid detail, I can see it as clearly as the beach in front of me. I ask all kinds of stupid questions—about the men, their babies, their way of life. She answers every inquiry without the least bit of judgment in her tone.

Her attitude changes when the sound of the dingy being started catches our attention. I turn to watch Saban skipping across the water toward us, but her warning leaves me skeptical and hesitant once again.

"You're sweet, Sara, and I've thoroughly enjoyed getting to know you. So, I feel as if I have to say this to you or I won't be able to live with myself." She purposely glances over my shoulder at Saban. "Be careful with that one. All is not as it seems with him, and you'll need all your wits and cleverness when the time comes. Do everything you can to keep your powers at their full strength."

Talia touches my hand and the familiar zing of mage energy courses through my skin.

CHAPTER 12

"How was your outing with Saban yesterday?" Addi casts a sideways smirk at me on our daily trek to the Veil.

"It was great at first. Then we stopped on this little island to chill, and a mermaid showed up. That was cool, but when Saban left us alone, she warned me about him. She and I had a great chat about her kingdom and the merpeople, but when he was on his way back, her attitude completely changed. I'm not sure what to make of it."

"Did Saban notice anything was different?"

"No, he didn't have a chance. I thought he was bringing food back from the ship for a beach picnic, but he was coming to tell me we had to hurry back to the palace. Some kind of emergency meeting with the officials from all the kingdoms. Saban said he'll be away for several days, along with his court officers. Do you know what that's about?"

"Not a clue. But if it's with the leaders of all the king-doms, it's something major. That usually only happens when we've had a breach with the outside world, when we're at some kind of risk of being exposed. Or..." She turns her gaze to me, concern etched in her drawn brows and expressive eyes.

"Or what? Don't leave me hanging here."

"Or if they've learned the heir to the throne has returned." She grabs my hand, and we take off in an all-out run toward the woods.

"Don't you think you're overreacting? I mean, there's a strong protective spell over me for a while longer yet."

"And yet, you still somehow fell through an opening into our world before the cloak was lifted. How do you think that happened? Maybe you did it yourself, but maybe you didn't, and it's that chance we can't take."

Well, when she puts it that way.

When we're safely behind the Veil's borders, Ginevra sits with us while I recount everything that happened from the moment Talia stepped out of the trees until now. Ginevra pats my hand with her cold, wrinkled one to help calm my nerves and reassure me I'm not alone.

"One of the first things you need to know is mermaids can see the future, as it stands at that moment. It's always changing based on the decisions we make every day. Nothing is written in stone. The future is very fluid, like a fast-flowing river. The emergency meeting is concerning, no doubt. Her warning about Saban should be taken seri-ously, though. You should stay as far away from him as possible. We can't be too careful about any of this until we distinguish friend from foe." Ginevra leans back in her chair and narrows her eyes in deep concentration.

"But Saban is Sara's mate, Ginevra." Addi's eyes dart between the two of us, waiting for direction on how we're supposed to handle this part of the problem. "How is she supposed to stay away from him?"

"He's what?" Ginevra jumps to her feet and stares down at me. "Is this true?"

"From what I understand of how mates work in this world, yes. He and I both feel the connection. It grows stronger every day, and it becomes harder and makes it harder to stay away from each other. He even introduced me as his mate to Talia yesterday."

"Oh, child." She quickly masks the deep vein of torment that flashes across her face, but the effects hit me square in the chest just the same. Everything she feels flows directly into me. Fear, alarm, sympathy, and sadness. "That does complicate things."

"You think? What am I supposed to do?" The need to do something propels me out of my seat. I pace back and forth across the room, wringing my hands and racking my brain for a solution. "What am I talking about? I don't even believe in this soul mate business. Can't I just stay here, hidden behind the enchantments covering the Veil?"

"For a while, yes. But if he's your mate, the forces pulling you together will be too strong. You won't be able to remain here without him, and he will be tormented without you. These next few days away from you will be hard enough." Ginevra turns and stares out the window, looking at the trees, but her thoughts are far away.

"Are you saying this time apart will provide a definitive answer to the question that's been on my mind the last few weeks? If I'm not going crazy from thinking about him night and day by the time he gets back, then he's not actually my mate?"

"You have a strong stubborn streak, and you're fiercely independent. That combination makes it more difficult to sway you. It may take a little longer for the separation to bother you. We'll see how this time apart goes." Ginevra doesn't turn around. "We'll use this reprieve to advance your training. You can stay in the Veil in one of our guesthouses. If he is your mate, these next few days and nights will be especially long and difficult."

The door opens, and another mage steps into the room. I recognize her from my previous sessions. Her name is Aris, and she's very talented in her magical abilities. I've learned a lot from simply watching her work and letting her thoughts invade my mind.

"Hi, Sara. Are you ready to take your powers to the next level?" Aris grins, a bit of mischief twinkling in her eyes.

"I'm absolutely ready. Lead the way."

She and I walk out, heading to the forest floor to practice. "No more stairs for you. You've earned the right to a little fairy dust. Kobi, if you don't mind."

I follow her line of sight to a tiny fairy hovering just over my shoulder and smile. "Hello, Kobi."

"Hi, Sara. Are you ready to fly?" Kobi grins back at me and rubs her hands together. Sprinkles of fairy dust rain over me, and my feet lift off the floor. "Now, just think about where you want to go."

The tingling in my stomach makes me laugh but I do as she says, and I'm gently lowered to the base of the tree. Aris claps encouragingly then motions for me to follow her. I look up at Kobi with the biggest smile on my face. "Thank you, Kobi. That was awesome."

"My pleasure, Saraya." She winks before flittering away, disappearing into the distance by blending in with the natural flora and fauna of the forest.

"Up until now, we've worked on the basic tutorials of what you'd need to control your magic. You've learned a few tricks and tips—reading minds, having conversations, minor spells, and conjures. Now we'll start the real work. Offensive and defensive spells, special maneuvers, and creating safe zones."

"Let's do it. I have a couple questions I'm hoping you can help me with first. I asked when I first came here, but it was so hectic, I didn't get an answer."

"Of course. What's on your mind?"

"Why do I have a calmness that settles over me when I'm here? And why can I feel others trying to get into my head here but not out there?"

She looks at me as if she's waiting for the punch line. Then she realizes I'm serious. "That's amazing. The calmness is because you're in your element—you're at home with the other mages, and deep down, you sense it. The power flowing through the Veil is full of white energy, and your spirit feeds on it, in a good way. You can feel the others trying to get into your mind here because you're more in tune with the magic inside you while you're here. We need to find ways you can take that same focus back into Easthaven Crest with you. If you can channel the level of white light contained in the borders of the Veil, you'd be unstoppable."

"Is that not the same as stealing power from my sister mages?" I don't want to be accused of pilfering magic from my allies.

"Not at all. The magic here increases because of how much we use it. If we were able to do the same out there, the air would be full of excess white energy. But we have it contained inside our enchanted area, so it has nowhere else to go. But a mage vessel would be a tremendous sight."

"That also sounds kind of scary."

"There's nothing scary about the white light. It's the darkness you have to be wary about overtaking your mind. Don't let your thoughts go down that path, no matter what happens or who hurts you. Anger and fear will take much more away from you than they'll ever give you."

"Have you had a lot of interactions with witches and warlocks?"

"I've had a few run-ins with them. The witches are

always trying to recruit mages to their covens. There's strength in numbers, and the more people they have in their clutches, the stronger their collective magic becomes. Warlocks are more elusive than witches. Their main goal is always gaining all the power for themselves. They don't want to share it with anyone."

It's only a matter of time before the warlock behind this coup makes himself known. I'm not looking forward to facing off with him, but I do want to get on with finding Nana and living the rest of my life in peace. Whether that life will be here, I can't say right now. Every day I'm here strengthens my magic and makes it harder to imagine returning home and forfeiting everything I've gained...and everything I still have to achieve.

Aris leads me to a trail that takes us deep into the forest, away from all the mage homes and shared spaces. The trail ends in a large opening where the carpet is so thick and vibrant green, it almost doesn't look real. The sun is bright and warm, the birds chirp in the distance, and a light breeze blows around us. The scent of honeysuckle, cedar, and pine fill the air, another reminder of the forest behind the only home I've ever known.

And my friends. I haven't seen them in weeks. They must be worried sick about me.

"Clear your mind, Saraya. Your thoughts are getting the better of you, feeding on your fears and worries. Focus on the here and now, what you need to accomplish to reach your end goals. If you bring your friends into this now, you'll only put them in danger. The warlock knows you're here. He can sense you, and he will use anything and everything you care about against you." Aris closes her eyes, inhales deeply, and leans her head back to soak in the sun.

Following her cue, I do the same, letting the worrisome thoughts fade away and the calm serenity of the forest take over. When I focus on what's around me, glimpses of forest creatures flash behind my eyes. Squirrels scurry from one tree to another, romping and playing with one another. A doe and her fawn walk silently, picking out choice morsels to graze on while remaining vigilant against any threats. Birds nab insects off the ground and out of the air. A black bear rolls a fallen tree over and claws the ground underneath in search of grubs.

"Excellent." Aris's soft voice pulls me out of my trance.

"What's excellent?"

"You're a natural. We all have animal spirits. You may know them as familiars. When we match with one, they allow us in without hesitation, letting us see the world through their eyes. You just did that on instinct."

At first, I'm not sure what she means. Then I realize I wasn't merely watching the animals of the forest from afar. I was one of them. "I didn't know…"

"It's okay. That was your first time, so it's normal not to recognize the difference. Close your eyes, clear your mind, and go back to that place. Then tell me which animal represented your spirit."

I do as she says and seek my animal spirit again. When my vision becomes clear, I look down at the big paws and backward at the long, lean body. And its flicking tail.

"It's a mountain lion."

"Powerful, lethal, fiercely protective of its own, and unmatched in stealth. Certainly not a creature to be underestimated." Aris sounds impressed. I'm just thrilled my animal spirit is a mountain lion.

"Will this mountain lion recognize me on sight? Will I ever see it?"

"Yes, and yes. That animal felt your spirit reach out, and it answered. That bond will never be severed, and she will fight to the death to protect you. She considers herself as yours now." Aris nods toward the edge of the forest. I follow her line of sight until my gaze lands on the most beautiful creature stepping out of the shadows.

My heart knows her on sight.

She strolls up to me then turns and rubs her side against my leg like an overgrown house cat. I kneel beside her, run my hands over her thick coat, and rub my face against hers.

"Laurelai," I murmur against her nuzzle. She puts her paw on my shoulder, hugging me to her, and I hear her whisper my name inside my mind.

"With white magic, you can enter other animals' minds to see through their eyes, but your bond will only be with this animal." When Aris scratches Laurelai behind her ear, she makes a soft purring sound.

"She knows she's loved. I can feel what she feels, and I can hear her thoughts."

"It's the same for her too. You don't have to speak out loud for her to hear you. I've never seen a mage and her familiar bond so quickly. Fate has spoken."

"I've waited for you all my life, Saraya."

CHAPTER 13

With Laurelai watching and guarding from the sidelines, Aris and I begin tapping into my untested magic. My mind is wide open to allow her full access to read it and guide me when I need more help. She directs me to clear all outside thoughts and focus on the white light emanating from everything around us—the trees, the grass, the fairies hiding under the leaves and behind the bushes, and my familiar. It's even flowing from both of us. I can see it in Aris's thoughts.

"Yes, I can see the light in others, whether it's light or dark. You can as well, and that'll help you quickly determine who's a friend and who isn't, unless they've cloaked their energy."

"Wouldn't that mean they're not friendly?"

"No, not necessarily. There are many reasons why you'd want to keep your energy hidden. Ginevra has always taught us to be very careful about who we allow to see ours. Our enemies are cunning and will stop at nothing to erase us from memory, so it's best not to give them ammunition against us when we can prevent it. Yours is hidden because of the cloaking spell, so stop worrying about who has seen it before now."

"That makes sense, and thanks for putting my mind at ease. Now show me how I can see others' energy."

"Let's use Laurelai as an example. You can tell when an animal is a threat by the color of their energy. Focus your thoughts on her heart—not the actual heart beating in her chest, but her nature and temperament. What do you see?"

When I do as Aris says, I feel the energy pulsing inside me, buzzing like bees around an enormous hive. The separate vibrations fuse into a single source, and faster than a snap of my fingers, Laurelai's golden coat glows in a white sheen. I laugh nervously, amazed at the smallest act.

"You're so beautiful, Laurelai. Inside and out."

"Now, let's do a test so you can see the difference," Aris says to me. "Laurelai, I want you to imagine someone hurting Saraya."

In a flash, my familiar's energy turns from bright white to a deep red, the color of murderous intent. Her lip snarls, she bares her teeth, and she springs to her feet, ready to pounce in my defense. Her demeanor leaves no doubt she'd kill for me.

The feeling is mutual.

"Perfect. Thank you, Laurelai. Your mage is safe. You

can rest again." Aris chuckles lightly. "You would pair with a mountain lion. I sense the same resolve in you that's in her. You're stronger than you realize, Saraya."

"This is amazing. What's next?"

"Next, you learn to pull that energy into you and send it back out as a directive. Our relationship with the light is symbiotic. It wields its power through us, and we channel it to create magic. One doesn't exist without the other, so what we send out is always with the utmost respect for the light. Always both a request and an expectation, but never taken for granted."

"So, I can draw it into me and ask it to do anything I want?"

"Pretty much, yes. Just remember, if you ask the light to do something out of malice, you'll automatically invite the dark energy inside you. Even if you don't mean to or want to turn to that side of magic. For example, if you're upset with someone and throw a spell at them to hurt them in some way out of anger, you invite the dark magic in. You can apologize all you want later, but that mark is still inside you. There's a fine line between using magic to protect yourself or someone else and using it as a means for revenge."

"I understand, and I'll be cautious with controlling my emotions. What I had in mind is much cooler than that anyway."

"Let's see what you've got, then." Aris walks to the edge of the clearing and stands beside Laurelai. "Take it away."

My first solo attempt at using such powerful magic

may be overly ambitious, but this is a test of what's genuinely inside me as much as it's to demonstrate my skill level for Aris. I draw in as much of the white energy as my body can take before it feels as though it'll crack apart from the intense buzzing in my every cell. Then I focus it on one objective and wordlessly direct it to do as I ask.

Fly.

With my face tilted to the sky, I imagine the white energy pushing me off the ground. My feet leave the earth beneath me, and I hear Laurelai in my head, cheering me on from the sidelines. I can see it, feel it, and taste it— soaring through the treetops is almost within my reach. When I open my eyes and look down, I'm hovering a couple feet off the ground, but I can't seem to gain more traction than that. A bird takes flight from a branch nearby, soaring into the wild blue yonder, while I'm stuck in this meadow, unable to join it.

Then I crash to the ground with an ungraceful thud. My knees buckle under me, and I tumble the rest of the way down on my side. Aris eyes me from beside my familiar, and I wonder what she's thinking, but I purposely block it. I'm disappointed enough in myself, so I don't need to hear anyone else's interpretation of my failure.

"It's not a failure." Aris crosses her arms and locks her gaze on me. "You didn't fail. You lifted off the ground. With the sheer determination in your mind, I thought I'd see you soar like a phoenix right before my eyes. But you took your eyes off your goal. You looked around at the circumstances and what your mind believed to be true, and you lost sight of what you wanted to accomplish. This level of magic takes time, patience, and practice."

I stalk off into the forest to be alone for a few minutes. My own ambition drives me to places I don't always want to go. My adamant belief I had to go off to college to be successful wasn't correct. My strong-willed conviction that life in Aspen Springs would never be enough failed the test. And now, the complete and total letdown of not achieving what I believed I could is almost crushing. Almost. As I calm my mind, her words filter through the noise in my head until my attention is on what I can achieve instead of what I can't.

She's right, of course. I tasted a morsel of success and pouted when I couldn't finish the whole cake by myself. I'd built up the expectation in my own mind, thinking I should be able to do something very few in history have managed. Holding my focus on the goal at hand will keep me alive when this cloak over me lifts. My every step must be in the right direction of building my skills so I can stand on my own two feet when the time comes.

I emerge from behind the tall trees and darkened forest, ready to face the light again. "Okay, I'm shaking it off. What's next?"

"It's time for you to meet A.M." Aris grins devilishly, letting me know she's about to reveal yet another level of magic.

"Who is A.M.?" I glance around but don't see anyone. With a swish of her hand, Aris conjures a being out of thin air. She looks real in every way, but her mannerisms are a little too stiff. Her movements aren't fluid enough to pass as an actual living person. But the attention to detail in creating her is impressive.

"A.M. is our Artificial Mage. She has state-of-the-art artificial intelligence, learning from every interaction and applying it to the next scenario. We've used her to train young mages how to counteract dark spells. Because we can't create the spells without taking the darkness into ourselves, we use her to do it for us since she's completely fake, only running off the programming built into her quantum computer. She's far superior to the binary computers in your world. Her responses are infinite and diverse, able to change based on how she reads the signs around her."

Aris and I practice for hours, with Laurelai watching and helping, pointing out when the artificial intelligence training robot was about to hurl an offensive magic spell my way. Aris helps me decipher the energy levels, the deviations in energy flow, and the almost imperceptible changes in A.M.'s demeanor.

We move through the paces of learning to harness the energy surrounding others to anticipate their next move. Even slight tremors in the flow of light around a dark witch or warlock can help me identify when they're about to throw what I've affectionately dubbed a magic bomb in my direction. Reading their aura, for lack of a better word, can give me the split-second advantage to incapacitate them before they're able to cast a dark spell on me.

When we finish at the end of the day, I've almost mastered the art of intercepting and obstructing dark spells. My mind is mush and my body is tired, but I feel as if I've accomplished more today than on all the others combined. One of the harder skills to master was connecting with animals other than Laurelai and using my powers to see through their eyes. After my disappointment in my attempt at flying, I wasn't about to let the ability to telepathically communicate with other animals elude me. When I finally became proficient at it, I knew exactly how I'd use my newfound talent.

But that'll have to wait until I'm alone and confident my thoughts are shielded.

Aris, Laurelai, and I stroll through the woods on our way back to the Veil. After a long day of exhausting mental work, we don't have a lot left to say. The silence of the forest is calming, taking me back to the time I spent in the woods behind my home in Aspen Springs. Every little thing reminds me of Nana, but one of the magical tricks Aris showed me today was how to sense Nana's presence.

She's here in Covis Realm, and she's alive. I can't pinpoint exactly where she is, and Aris said the cloaking spell is so potent, I won't be able to break it. But I'm stubborn and refuse to accept that as the definitive answer. My bond with Nana is resilient. I know if I can feel her, then she can feel me. Maybe with both of us reaching out, we'll be able to communicate.

My thoughts drift back to Talia's warning—keeping

my powers at full strength, needing all my wits and cleverness, and about Saban.

You think about him a lot. Laurelai cuts her big gold eyes up at me. I swear she arches one eyebrow at me. *He must be very important to you.*

I'm not sure what he is to me, to be honest. The term soul mate has been thrown around a lot lately about us, but that's not a label I'm comfortable with just yet. I reach over and scratch her head behind her ear. Her muscular body brushes against my leg, and her purring engine cranks up to high. I'm still amazed by her. *The only mate I'm sure about is you, Laurelai. You understand me.*

I do understand you, Saraya, more than you know. When I meet Saban, I'll know if he's your soul mate or not. If he's not, his jugular will be extra tasty. She releases a playful growl, making me jump and laugh at the same time. *Oh, there's something else you should know. No one else can hear our conversations, even if they're actively reading your other thoughts.*

And you feel everything I feel? Know everything I know?

Yes, and I can find you anywhere and at any time. Our bond can only be broken in death.

I wonder if Nana had a familiar before she escaped Covis Realm with me. She never mentioned anything that I can remember. But then, the bedtime stories she told me about this place were so long ago, I can hardly remember them.

Laurelai, do you talk to other familiars?

Not so much. Cougars are solitary animals by nature. We're extremely territorial and protective of our families. There aren't many other animals that will cross paths with us.

Fierce. Loyal. Protective. Solitary. You and I do belong together. I smile down at her, and she responds in kind by baring her teeth, fangs and all.

If your grandmother did have one, I'm sorry to say it's probably dead by now. Once we've bonded with a human, we need the connection to thrive. Seventeen years is a long time to be apart and survive. But I'll keep my ears open; maybe I'll even become a social butterfly to gain information.

Don't hurt yourself.

Her laughter echoes through my mind as her chirps ricochet through the forest. She drops to the ground, rolls onto her back, and lets me rub her belly. *Good one, Saraya. Your sense of humor is different—good different. You bring a new zest for life to this world.*

"Do I even want to know what this is about?" Aris asks. She's smiling, but the sentiment doesn't reach her eyes. There's a deep sadness there. Without asking, without reading her mind, and without knowing...*I know.*

Her familiar died.

The pain must be unbearable at times like this, watching Laurelai and me together.

"She likes my sarcastic sense of humor. She's the only one in this realm who seems to understand it." I chuckle lightly while scratching my cougar's belly. "Now I don't want to go back to the palace and leave her. Would they look at me funny if I strolled in with a cougar as my house cat?"

"They would definitely look at you funny. Besides, her place is here in the forest. You know, she's still a wild animal. But just because she's not beside you doesn't mean the two of you can't talk. You can have entire conversations with her the same way you do with Addi."

"My brain is about to become very crowded. I'm going to start charging rent."

Even Aris laughs at that wisecrack.

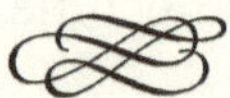

CHAPTER 14

When I'm alone in my bedroom, my thoughts drift over the events of the past couple of days. I spent another day training with Aris, Addi, and Laurelai. Ginevra watched from the edge of the forest, chiming in with tips and tricks as the day progressed, but generally only observing the advancement of my powers.

The new skills I've acquired in such a short time make the energy hum and whir inside me like a jet engine preparing for takeoff. The intensity is incredible and only makes me crave stronger powers. I want to practice every minute of the day so everything will come naturally to me when I need it most.

You need to rest, Saraya. We'll practice more tomorrow. Good night, my lovely human.

Good night, my beautiful cougar. Stay safe out there. I'll see you in the morning.

I feel Laurelai relax before she finally succumbs to sleep, nestled in the darkness of the forest. When the day comes and we're finally free to be ourselves, she'll have a home with me to come and go as she pleases. For now, my sights are set on distinguishing my foes from allies. Assured I'm alone and my shields are up, I sit cross-legged on the floor and focus my thoughts on Saban. The cloudiness around his face clears, and I can see him plainly through the sharp eyes of a tawny owl perched on a windowsill behind him.

Part of me feels this is an unforgivable invasion of privacy, but the voice in my head encourages me to continue my quest. I sense a benevolence behind the message, though I have nothing else to compare it to yet. For the sake of my sanity and peace of mind, I stick to my decision to check in on Saban and find out what's happening wherever he is.

His sister, Isla, and her soon-to-be husband, Gerard, are with Saban, having dinner and drinks at a table alone. Representatives from every kingdom in the realm are in the grand dining hall of an immensely elaborate castle. Through the owl's eyes, I take in every feature of the room and realize Saban and his family are guests of the elf king —Rycan's father, Ruvaen Zyldan.

The tables are separated by ethnic groups, emphasizing the division among the diverse types of beings. If this world hasn't conquered stereotypes and dislike of differences, I wonder if my world will ever achieve commonality. The table of humans keeps their voices low, their arguments no louder than a harsh whisper, but the tension in the air is thick. I can feel the stress rolling off Saban like stormy seas crashing on rocky shores.

"Saban, you have to be very careful. The other kingdoms are starting to talk about restoring the mages' rights. You know we can't allow that to happen. Can you imagine the complete chaos and anarchy of allowing them to roam freely among our people?" Isla shudders at the very thought, and I feel my pulse hitch upward. I never would've believed she was like this when I first met her.

"Why do you think that's so wrong, Isla? That law was put into place during a different time, and frankly, I'm not even sure I agree with how they handled it then, much less now." Saban lifts his wineglass to his lips, but it's simply a diversion. He's not even drinking it.

"Lower your voice," she hisses, an angry expression covering her features. "How can you say that with a straight face? You know how livid Mother would be if she heard you. We can't trust them, Saban. They use their powers against us, to control us, to get their way above everyone else."

"Do you even know any mages, Isla? Can you say you've met one and she took advantage of you?" Saban pins her with a pointed glare, daring her to lie to his face.

"Of course not. I'm too strong-minded for that to happen. But many people in our kingdom can't say the same, and we have a sacred duty to protect them. Don't you want to be king, Saban? Do you want to be known as a weak warden or a strong king?"

Saban leans back in his chair, scrapes his hand over his face, and releases a long sigh. Reaching out to his thoughts, I probe his mind to learn his true feelings and intentions. My heart aches for him. His mind is full of memories of trying to please his family, doing what they wanted him to so he could earn their approval, and denying himself with every step of the way.

He doesn't want to pursue this course of action against the mages. He also knows if he's the lone opposition to restoring their place in society, the other kings will never include him. If he doesn't sway them to his side, his family will never accept him because they'll see him as a failure. He carries the weight of the world on his shoulders and the fate of the mages in his heart.

Do what's right, Saban. Not what's easy.

If Isla knew I was pushing my thoughts to Saban, she would accuse me of using my magic to control him. Nothing could be further from the truth. I want him to make the best choice, do the right thing, and steer the kingdom on a noble path—all on his own. This decision must be his and his alone. He has to show he's the honorable man that I believe him to be...that I hope he is.

"Of course I want to be a strong king. But I also want to be known as a just king and rule true to my conscience. Part of that strength is knowing what's right and wrong, and acting on it. Consequences be damned. I don't believe genocide is the answer, Isla. It wasn't the answer all those years ago, and it's not the answer now. How would you feel if all these other races decided humans were no longer a valuable part of the realm? What if they passed a law that allowed them to kill us on sight? Would you change your mind then?"

Isla glares at Saban, unwilling to respond and validate his argument. She also doesn't trust herself not to become loud and draw unnecessary attention to their conversation. Gerard reaches over and takes her hand in his before lifting it to his lips.

"Sweetheart, I admire your resolve, but I think Saban is right in this argument. We need to take the high road, welcome them back into the fold, and show we can make this a better world than our older generations did. This is the only way we can move forward from the atrocities of the past. An entire race shouldn't be judged and punished for the cowardly, delinquent acts of a few." Gerard speaks gently, purposely keeping his eyes soft and a small smile on his lips. He knows how to disarm her anger and hatred with a few well-spoken words and strategically placed kisses.

"Very well. If the two of you can be the bigger person and accept that rabble, I suppose I can too. But I'm not going to be the one who breaks the news to Mother. That's all on you, big brother."

"This won't be the first time she's been disappointed in me, and I doubt it'll be the last. You worry about your upcoming wedding, and I'll deal with your mother."

"She's your mother too."

"Stop reminding me."

They both laugh it off, but Saban's unease about how

his decision will be received is still as strong as ever. However, I feel a swell of pride in my heart for his bravery and display of character. Next time we're together, I'll have to find a way to bring it up and commend him for his actions so he'll know he has my support.

King Ruvaen stands, and a hush falls over the room. His keen eyes move over the crowd, assessing each person as he comes to them. His gaze stops when he reaches Saban's table, his eyes narrowing in the corners when he notices the owl through the window. The edge of his mouth twitches, his lips lifting ever so slightly before he masks the smile trying to overtake his face.

"Before we say goodnight, I wanted to take this opportunity to thank each and every one of you for coming. I believe we've had a productive few days, even if we don't always agree on the pertinent issues. The mistakes of our past must be rectified for our realm to move forward as one cohesive world.

"Many of you don't remember those dark days, when every single being was suspected and accused with no just cause. As long as we permit the status quo, we will never realize our full potential. On that note, I'd like to raise a toast to everyone here. For listening to the proposal, for voicing your opinions, and for representing your kingdom in the best way possible. Here's to a brighter future for all of us."

Rounds of "hear, hear" ring out through the great banquet hall. People lift their flutes of champagne in celebration and agreement. One group begins to clap, and soon the echoes of applause bounce off the walls. Smiles light up the room. My gaze stops when I see Rycan seated beside his mother. His handsome face beams with pride and happiness, a stark difference from the murderous anger I experienced from him firsthand.

Isla moves, catching my attention, and all joy flees when I look at her. She's utterly annoyed and fuming just below the surface. She plays nice in the face of the vast opposition in the room, but her deep animosity toward mages is there, nonetheless. I was completely wrong about her.

Rycan stands and takes his dad's place with a message and a toast about the collaboration and cooperation he has experienced during this emergency summit. I'm listening to him intently, trying to glean a crumb of information about what made the meeting an emergency. Is it because they know I'm here? Are they considering putting Saban on the throne? Has something else happened that hasn't been announced to the masses yet?

"You know, you should really be more careful about eavesdropping on a group of sovereign leaders in a closed-door meeting. Parking an owl directly outside the window to spy on us isn't exactly clandestine behavior. You could've chosen a branch to hide him on at the very least."

Ruvaen stands tall and confident, staring down the owl I'm currently inhabiting.

"Though I don't know *who* you are yet, I know *what* you are. I haven't raised the alarms on your subterfuge...

because our world needs you. Be careful and trust no one. Your life is in grave danger. Perhaps more than you realize at this point. When you find yourself in dire need of help, come here to Elen Sevin. Remember these words *'Dryadalis qui sanctuarii.'* I will give you sanctuary within my borders. The elvish army will defend you with their lives."

He turns and walks back inside the palace as if nothing happened…and I'm left with cold chills running up my spine.

I look back at Rycan and find him staring in my direction. The only problem is I can't tell if he's looking at Saban or the owl. With the long-standing feud between the two men, Rycan's icy glare could very well be a direct challenge for Saban. But after the way he chased me down with his army of elves for no reason other than stepping foot on his land, his scowl could be aimed at me instead— or, more accurately, my owl. If his father recognized I'm using an owl to spy, maybe Rycan can sense it as well.

When the owl moves to the other side of the window ledge on my prompt, Rycan's eyes follow.

Well, shit. I'm totally busted. Or my owl is. Whatever. Same difference. They know I'm here. They know I'm listening. What else do they know?

Before I can stop myself, I probe Rycan's mind. I have so many questions that can't be asked aloud but need immediate answers. Once inside, I open my mind and let the thoughts flow, running backward until I latch on to a memory regarding the emergency meeting.

Whatever could you be looking for inside here? Whoever you are, you're young, inexperienced, and clumsy. Like a baby. Run along now, baby girl, before you hurt yourself.

His shields around his thoughts clamp shut as fast and abruptly as a door slamming in my face. Seeing his cocky smirk from across the room only adds insult to injury. But that single memory I found in his mind is firmly implanted in my own now.

One of the elves is secretly a wizard with ties to the Veil. He told Ruvaen the heir to the Easthaven Crest throne has returned to Covis Realm…and she's a mage.

Known or not, I'm walking around with a huge target painted on my back now.

CHAPTER 15

*A*fter taking advantage of the time for extra training and practice on my last day without Saban in the palace, I'm surprised how much I'm looking forward to seeing him again. Just as his car drives up the long driveway, I walk outside to enjoy the sunset after finishing work for the day. He jumps out of the slick, futuristic vehicle and rushes toward me. Inside my chest, the deep-seated urge to be close to him explodes, making my feet break out in a jog to meet him halfway. I leap into his waiting arms, and our lips lock in a heated kiss in front of everyone.

"You have no idea how much I've missed you. I should've smuggled you into the meetings with me despite their strict rules." He kisses me again before finally putting my feet back on the ground. "Let me change clothes, and I'll join you on your walk. I could use some fresh air."

"Sounds good to me. I'll wait right here."

I watch him walk away, ignoring the twinge in my chest that's at odds with the warning in my head. I'm not part of his family, and it's only been a few weeks since he reconciled with his mother. When he's forced to choose sides and face the consequences, I'm well aware I can't compete with that bond. Potential soul mate status won't earn me any extra points when that time comes.

That time being the day I announce my intentions of taking over the throne.

This is not something I've agreed to lightly. In fact, I only made the final decision today, after an intense conversation with Ginevra. She made me understand how imperative it is to the entire kingdom to have the best ruling family in place to take care of the people. She also stressed how seriously my parents took their roles in the community. I feel a deep sense of obligation to follow in their footsteps, but I also see a profound need to change the current mindset in Easthaven Crest.

What I don't feel is a sense of entitlement. The thought of being responsible for an entire kingdom scares the shit out of me. But announcing that I'm a mage, in this political climate, downright terrifies me.

"You know he's crazy about you, right?"

My head jerks in the direction of the deep male voice beside me, and I find Gerard with one side of his mouth lifted, watching me as Saban rushes into the palace.

"This all feels surreal, to be honest." I'm not sure how else to respond, but my answer is still the truth.

"What feels surreal?" He tilts his head to the side and draws his brows down. He studies me too intensely in our brief encounters. Reading his thoughts doesn't reveal anything incriminating, but the strange feeling vibrating from his spiritual energy won't stop.

"The whole finding my soul mate thing. Even though I've heard of it happening to others my entire life, I never really believed it would happen to me. And I never dreamed it would be with someone like Saban. It's just still all so new." I shrug and smile, lowering my eyes to the ground.

"I know what you mean. Sometimes I wonder how I got so lucky to have found Isla. She is the love of my life."

Yes, she is quite the treat, isn't she? My shields are up, just in case, but my sarcasm would be lost on Gerard anyway.

"You two seem very happy together. She couldn't take her eyes off you at the engagement party. The big day is coming up soon, isn't it?"

"Two weeks from tomorrow—but that's two weeks too long for me. I'm ready to exchange vows right now and make it official. Isla won't hear of it, though. She's put a lot of time and thought into our wedding, so I'll wait, however impatiently. When she's finally mine forever, the wait will be worth it." Gerard's left eyebrow disappears under the hair swept across his forehead, and a smile brightens his face. But the way he leers at me makes me uncomfortable, and I want to get away from him as quickly as possible. "It's hard to believe you've been here with us for two months already. Isla and I haven't had a chance to get to know you well enough. The four of us should plan a double date soon."

"Absolutely. That sounds like fun. I'm sure you're busy until after the wedding, but Saban and I will be ready when you are."

"I'm sure we can find some time to relax and unwind before the wedding. The time away from the planning will do us all some good."

He's persistent, I'll give him that.

Saban trots out of the palace just in time to save me from continuing this small talk. I've never been skilled at idle chitchat, even with my friends back home. I prefer comfortable silence over painful conversations that go nowhere.

Saban snakes his arms around my waist, pulling me tightly against his chest. "I'm so ready for a quiet walk in the woods with you. Are you ready to go now?"

"That sounds perfect. Let's get lost for a while." Any reason to get away from the prying eyes around here is a good excuse.

We say our goodbyes to Gerard and begin walking toward the trail leading into the forest. Saban wraps his big hand around mine, and the connection between us fires on all cylinders, lighting up all my senses at once. He feels it too, and our gazes quickly shift to find the other.

"Why do all the solutions to all the problems I'm dealing with seem so much clearer when I'm with you? We have these meetings, yet so many still seem angry and ready to go to war. And for what? Because they won't accept reason."

His pensive expression catches me off guard. These arguments over mages are taking a toll on him, pulling him in opposite directions and making it impossible for him to find a solution. The sudden vise around my chest makes it hard to breathe. How can I tell him the truth of what's to come? How can I admit to the facts I've purposely kept from him?

"What solution seems clearer now?" I feel like an undercover spy, asking questions and gathering secret intelligence to use against him later.

His sincere smile only makes me feel worse.

"Love. Love is the answer. If we simply accept others as they are, allow our strengths and weaknesses to balance us as a kingdom, and give everyone the benefit of the doubt, we'd be a much stronger nation."

The trail into the forest is wide enough for us to walk side by side, but he puts his arm around my shoulders and pulls me against his side anyway. I wrap my arms around his waist, and we meander along the path, in no hurry to get anywhere specific. The creatures of this world still fascinate me, even after the weeks I've spent here. Colorful and different, the trees, birds, insects, and animals still hold my attention.

I stop along the way and bend over to admire a gorgeous flower in full bloom. Saban watches me with an amused expression. "What? Why are you looking at me like that?"

"You find beauty in the most ordinary objects, the things everyone else passes by without a second glance. Like this bloom everyone else only sees as a weed. But not you, Sara. You inspect it, touch it, smell it, *ooh* and *aah* over it. Your enthusiasm for the simple things in life makes me rethink everything I've ever believed. You amaze me, and I don't know how I've lived this long without you in my life."

His words strike a chord deep inside me. I stand up straight and stare at him wordlessly. Without any experience in this arena, I don't know how to respond to him. So, I do what I always do—I deflect the sweet compliment he just gave me. "I'm sure you've managed just fine without me around, Saban. When we first met, you had an entire horde of girls surrounding you, all desperate for your attention and affection. Any one of them would still kill me if it meant you'd choose her. Granted, I'm not like any of them, so I'm sure that makes anything I do seem odd by comparison."

He steps toward me with a predatory swagger in his step and a sexy smirk on his face. "There's no comparison to you. Those girls aren't worth a minute of my time— none of them. From the moment I saw you, I knew you were the one for me. I'm simply waiting for you to realize the same about me so we can tell the rest of the kingdom. I'm ready whenever you are, my love. However long that takes."

I've tried not to use my powers for ill-gotten gain, I really have. But I find myself crossing the line between need and want when it comes to prying in his thoughts. I've heard my fair share of smooth lines from guys with a forked tongue. What he just said is either the best pickup line in history, or he's the most understanding man in the world. He knows I'm hesitant and he feels my doubts, but he's willing to give me time to work it out on my own.

When I open myself to his thoughts, a wave of affection hits me with the full force of a tsunami. His thoughts filter through, hoping I feel the same eagerness to take our relationship to the next level and a desire to express his love for me. Simply knowing my feelings don't match his nearly brings tears to my eyes. The last thing I want to do is hurt him, but I can't force myself into something that doesn't exist on its own.

"Saban, I hope you know I'm not playing any games with you or stringing you along. My life hasn't been easy, and I have a hard time trusting others. This feeling between us is so new, so out of character for me, I don't know what to do with it. These are my issues, my flaws, I know, and you shouldn't be the one to pay for them. I'm not capable of just opening up and throwing my heart out there so soon."

"You don't have to explain it to me. After my dad died, I shut everyone out for a long time, even though I still had the rest of my family. You didn't have that luxury, so it makes sense that you're more guarded. But I'm not going anywhere. I'm right here, waiting for you regardless of how long it takes for you to feel comfortable committing yourself to me. One day you'll realize I'm willing to stand by your side, no matter the cost."

He leans in and presses his lips against mine. This kiss doesn't have the heat and urgency in it that the others have. It's much more chaste, but it also holds so much more depth and meaning. He's declaring his love for me without expecting me to say he's my soul mate too.

My heart shatters into a million pieces in my chest, stabbing me with the jagged edges for extra measure.

I could take the easy road and give in to the incredible fondness I already feel toward him. What I feel for him is as close to love as can be, I know that deep down. If I never reveal who I am, I could live happily ever after with my soul mate in the same palace I'm in now. If I deny my true self—the mage and the heir to the throne—at this moment, I'll make him the happiest man in Covis Realm. In return, he'd do everything in his power to make me the happiest woman.

But I can't do any of those things.

If he's my soul mate, why aren't my feelings as strong as his? Why can't I bring myself to say I love him? Isn't that what normal couples do? Those three little words feel as though they'll choke me to death.

If we're meant to be together forever, why am I caught in this deceit about who and what I am?

And that's the crux of the matter. I can't give him all my love without sharing all of myself.

"I don't deserve you, Saban." *No truer words...*

"You deserve so much more. Let me spoil you while

you're making up your mind. I know you love me, you've already told me in so many words. Maybe it'll help speed along our soul mate status." He winks, letting me know he's at least partially kidding. He picks the flower I was admiring and slides it into my hair behind my ear. "That flower doesn't hold a candle to your beauty, princess."

We continue our trek through the trees, with me pointing out every animal, tree, and flower that's in our path. Saban's amusement with my antics continues, and the ease between us grows. We laugh and poke fun at each other, growing emotionally closer with every physical step we take.

When I reach for his hand, he falters for a moment before falling back into step with me. I look up at him with my brows lifted. "What's wrong?"

"Nothing's wrong. That's just the first time you've initiated contact with me since we've been out here. It feels good to know you want me too, at least a little."

I squeeze his hand in reply, because any words I'd respond with would only kill the moment. My hesitancy is amped up only because of my secrets, I'm sure of it. Under normal circumstances, I'd already be head over heels in love with this handsome, romantic man.

He is very handsome, and he's definitely in love with you. That's obvious without reading his mind. Laurelai is close to us, watching from the shadows.

Laurelai, I'm so glad you're here. I've missed you. Besides being handsome, what else do you think about Saban? I search the forest around us for a glimpse of her golden fur, but she's well hidden.

Unfortunately, I won't ever know how his jugular tastes. He's not a threat to you. But something about him is odd... Her thoughts trail off.

Don't leave me hanging here. What's odd about him?

I can't read his spirit energy. It's not there. She growls under her breath, aggravated with the lack of information.

His aura is missing? How can that be? What does that even mean?

It means it's hidden from us on purpose. But I can't tell if he did it or someone else did it to him, though.

Nothing is easy in this world. Just once, I'd like a cut-and-dried answer. Black-or-white. Yes or no. Friend or foe. There are way too many shades of maybe here, and I don't deal well with ambiguity.

CHAPTER 16

*N*ow that Laurelai mentioned it, I can't help but notice the missing energy that should be surrounding Saban. Why haven't I noticed that before now? Apparently, I've been too wrapped up in training, working, hiding my own secrets, and in Saban himself. Is this why I've resisted giving in to my growing affection for him? Or is this simply another riddle to be solved?

It's not as if I don't have enough on my plate already.

Stop feeling sorry for yourself, Saraya.

That voice again. I have to know if it's her. With all the energy I can muster without being obvious, I gather the light into me and channel it to speak to my grandmother.

Nana, is that you?

Yes, sweetheart. It's me, and I'm fine. Now, quit worrying about me and do what you know you should. The sooner you're queen, the faster we can put all this behind us.

But you never told me any of this. Why would you keep all this from me?

Remember the stories I used to tell you. Everything you need to know is in them.

Those damn tales will be the death of me. I didn't know there would be a literal life-or-death test over them, or I would've listened more closely.

"Do you remember anything about your parents?" Saban's question pulls me from the pit I fell into with my thoughts.

"No, I don't. I never knew them. They were killed during the mage attacks." Technically, that is a factual statement and I did not lie.

"I'm so sorry, princess. I had no idea. This latest round of debates whether to allow mages to live freely among us must upset you. Especially the people who are in favor of removing the restrictions."

Removing the restrictions? That's an interesting way of sugarcoating the truth. But I can't say that, so I find a more diplomatic answer.

"No, actually, that doesn't bother me at all. What upsets me is how they're not treated as equals and given a chance to live their lives. The cowardly actions of a select few shouldn't define an entire race. Can you name one perfect person from any kingdom? I mean, technically, I'm a criminal, and Rycan should've been allowed to kill me for being on his land. Does that mean I'm a threat to you and the elves for the rest of time?"

"Persuasive argument. Maybe you should've been in politics."

He sits on a fallen tree and pulls me between his legs. Standing so close to him sets my entire body on fire. His natural masculine scent mixes with the aromatic cedar and pine trees for a heady cologne. He wraps his muscular arms around my back and pulls me to him until we're only a breath's width apart. My heart races and my chest heaves with harsh breaths as if I've just finished running a marathon. I can't deny my innate and carnal reaction to him.

"I'm not sure I have the temperament for politics. The first time someone made me mad, I'd tell them exactly what I thought of them. It wouldn't end well."

"You know, I don't doubt that for one minute." He smiles—a real one that melts me where I stand. That loud pitter-patter noise is my heart pounding against my rib cage. He's gentlemanly enough to pretend he doesn't hear it or see my shirt moving like I'm smuggling a jumping bean in it. "How about you use that beautiful mouth for something more fun right now?"

Before I can answer, our lips are fused. His tongue swipes across the part in my mouth. I release a whimper, giving him an open invitation. The warmth of his tongue invades my mouth, twirling and twisting around mine. My blood is rushing so fast through my veins, all I can hear is the sound of my pulse thrumming in my ears.

He slides his hands across my cheeks, threading his fingers in my hair. He closes his grip and uses it as leverage to tilt my head, gaining better access to deepen our kiss. My nails dig into his shoulders, holding on for dear life so I don't float away on a cloud of ecstasy. Emotion floods my chest, butterflies invade my stomach, and all reason escapes from my consciousness.

An innocuous thought swirls in the recesses of my mind until it's finally front and center, unyielding and resolute. All that's standing in my way of giving my heart to him completely...is me. I'm holding myself back, looking for a way to run before he has a chance to abandon me down the road. No matter how many times he's declared his intentions and stressed our connection is for the rest of our lives, I've been waiting for the trap door of death to open under my feet.

"Is this real, Saban? Or is this a fleeting infatuation that will disappear right before my eyes?" I whisper to him to keep the universe from hearing my question and taking it as truth.

"This is as real as it gets, princess. You and I are destined to be right here, right now, sealing our love for all time. Don't worry your pretty head over anything, though. I'm not rushing you. We have the rest of forever, and I'm willing to wait for you. There's no time limit on my devotion."

"Aww, aren't they sweet? Two humans in love, enjoying the last hour of daylight in the forest. Don't they know nighttime in the forest belongs to us?"

We swivel our heads in the direction of the angry female voice taunting us. I've heard all about witches and warlocks, but I haven't encountered any before now. Addi and Aris both warned me about their nasty demeanor and penchant for causing trouble when we practiced protective enchantments, counterspells, and defensive magic. Their auras are all glowing red, confirming they're more than ready to throw dark magic our way and watch us squirm.

While Saban's attention is focused solely on the five witches, I pull all the white light into me that my body can hold. Then I silently chant until the protective magic surrounds us. The group advances on us, separating and moving with offensive posturing. I release a lash of energy in their direction—a warning shot over their heads—and they stop in their tracks. Then I cut my eyes to Saban to gauge if he realizes anything just happened. When I'm sure he's completely unaware, I send out another strong warning.

"You're in my kingdom, witches. Attack me and see what happens to your entire coven. I dare you." Saban stands tall, ready to fight to the death. But I'm not prepared to see that happen. His honor won't let him back down, and their magic won't allow them to lose. He can't win this fight alone.

With my gaze locked on the leader, I channel my thoughts directly to her. *Leave while you still can walk away. I won't give you a second warning.*

The energy around us hums, buzzes, and crackles like dry lightning. It's visible to them now, but Saban doesn't appear to see it. When one takes another step toward us, the protective lightning strikes her, and she leaps backward.

A low, ominous growl from the dark shadows brings another warning and an extra layer of danger. Laurelai is poised to attack from her vantage point in the tree. She has the high ground, and the witches know they don't stand a chance when they can't even see her until it's too late.

"Let's go, ladies. We have work to do. These two aren't worth the effort." The leader glares at me as she backs away, afraid to turn her back to me until she's out of my line of sight.

"Maybe I should take you back to the palace now. I'm not afraid of them, but I don't want you to get hurt." Saban turns, pulls me into his arms, and places a long kiss on my forehead. "Are you okay, princess?"

"I'm fine. Don't worry about me. But if you're ready to go back, that's okay with me. It's starting to get dark anyway. Maybe tomorrow, we can head out early to spend the day exploring and enjoying our time in the woods." I lift up on my toes and press my lips against his.

I don't want to appear too eager to leave his side, but inside, I'm dying to get back to the palace and talk to Addi. Those witches outnumbered me five to one, yet they were quick to back down. There's more to this story, and I've had a sneaking suspicion they've all been holding out on me during my training. It's time for someone to come clean with exactly what's happening with me and all the energy vibrating through my entire body.

"I'd feel better knowing you're safe and sound inside the palace." He leans his forehead against mine. "I'm sorry a bunch of witches ruined our plan to lose our way tonight. People like them are exactly why the magic debate is still so contentious."

"It's not your fault. We'll just plan to get lost later."

We walk back toward the castle at a brisker pace than when we wandered into the forest, but I understand his apprehension of running into them again. They could bring more backup next time, and my magic may not be enough to fend them off. For both our safety, this is the best decision.

"Oh, and about getting lost tomorrow—I'm afraid we'll have to get lost in the morning and make it home by late afternoon. Before I left the palace, Isla said she and Gerard want to go out on a double date with us. They want to get to know you better."

"Sounds great."

Not really, but I can't very well say the way Gerard looks at me makes me uncomfortable. He hasn't done anything out of the ordinary. He hasn't said anything inappropriate. Maybe it's all in my head, but something about him makes me leery. I get the sense he's constantly sizing me up, saying things just to gauge my reaction, then filing the information away to use against me at a later time.

He's like the quintessential politician—sleazy, underhanded, and untrustworthy.

Saban and I say goodnight on the platform where the

palace steps split between the two wings. I'm still in the servants' quarters, which is fine with me, but parting from him is harder each time. After a lengthy goodnight kiss and promises to resume in the morning, I head off toward my room. When I reach our hall, I stop at Addi's door and knock.

"Come inside. I heard you coming from a mile away. You were so focused on talking to me, you started the conversation well before you reached me." She laughs and closes the door behind me. "Have a seat. I'll tell you all I know. Anything else you want to know will have to come directly from Ginevra."

"Then there is more you know but haven't bothered to share with me?" I'm trying to keep my temper in check with my friend because I don't know the reasons behind withholding information from me.

But she had better have a damn good reason.

"Have a seat." She sighs then paces while she collects her thoughts. "Your magic is different from most of ours, Saraya. Your father was an elf wizard, and your mother was a human mage. You have a mixture of powers from both races. The elves are very powerful, even without being a wizard. They're inherently skilled fighters and all have limited magical abilities, such as healing, short periods of invisibility, seeing in the dark, and talking to animals. The elven wizards are even more powerful in every way.

"Combine that with your mother's magical abilities, and you have a potentially volatile mixture of magic. One that is more than capable of pushing you into dark magic. While you were learning to use and control your powers, Ginevra thought it was best not to tell you this. She wanted to wait until you were mentally prepared to explore the elven magic."

"If my father was so powerful, why couldn't he stop them from killing my mother and him? That doesn't make sense." She knows the answer to my question, but she doesn't want to tell me. "Addi…tell me. I have a right to know."

"Because the angry mob used you as leverage. They got to you first and forced your parents to do what they wanted. When Taeral realized they planned to kill you anyway, he used his magic to send you and Zu to the Veil so Ginevra could cloak you. He died protecting Wren and you, but he got you out of here first."

I feel as if all the wind has been knocked out of my sails. It's a hard pill to swallow, knowing the people of Easthaven Crest turned on my parents so viciously and without cause, to the point they were eager to murder a baby. "And no one knows who the warlock is who started all this? No one?"

"No, we don't. That hasn't been kept from you. If we knew, we could've made this a safe haven a lot sooner. But whoever he is, he's very powerful. He's remained completely hidden from us all this time, despite all our collective attempts to trace him. I think Ginevra hopes your mixture of elven and human magic will be more powerful than his so we can put an end to his terror campaign once and for all. Like I said, your power is different—and much stronger than the rest of ours. When you're at full power, you'll be a force to be reckoned with, for sure."

"Good. I'm ready for whatever I need to do to open the elf magic door in my mind. The leaders are debating allowing mages back out in the open without repercussions—and most of the leaders are all for it. If that happens while he's still loose, they'll be sitting ducks for him to pick off one by one."

"I'll contact Ginevra and let her know what's going on. She needs to remove the magical block she put on you."

"You forgot to mention that part."

"Sorry."

CHAPTER 17

There's a place between awake and asleep where a mage can visit another mage as she's drifting off. I know this fact now because Ginevra surprised me by hopping into my dreams and using that time to explain my mixed lineage.

"Saraya, I need you to pay attention, sweetheart. We have a lot to talk about. Your powers are about to change significantly. You need to understand what will happen after I remove the block. After your encounter with the witches today, it's not safe to wait any longer."

"I'm listening, Ginevra. Addi filled me in on some of the details earlier."

"She told me. Every elf is born with inherent magic, though not all the same. They each have their gifts. Some can hone and perfect their abilities to become formidable adversaries. A select few are born as wizards and mages.

Those elves are especially powerful in all areas of magic, including many skills no other race has.

"With your heritage, you'll have access to unimaginable powers. That much energy constantly coursing through your veins can be dangerous if you don't keep firm control of your emotions and thoughts. Your first instinct will be to lash out at anyone who hurts you or makes you mad, but you can't give in to that impulse. Even one time could end in disaster, Saraya."

"I'll be careful. I promise. I'm feisty, but I think I've handled everything with a fairly level head so far."

"Memories will return to you after the block is removed. We said you were a baby when this happened, but you were actually a little older. You were almost three. We had to hide those early memories for your own safety. Seeing your mother's face, hearing your father's voice— everything will come flooding in at once. You may even remember the people who threatened to kill you the night the palace was breached. I'm putting my trust and belief in you, Saraya. Trust that you can handle this now and won't turn bitter and angry over events we can't change."

"I understand what you're saying, Ginevra. To be honest, I wish you'd just told me that from the beginning, rather than lying to me about it. I'm having a hard enough time trusting anyone in this realm as it is."

"We all make mistakes, Saraya. We can only do the best we can with the information we have at the time. There's no way I could've known how you'd react had I told you the truth from the start."

"You're right. It's okay. I understand you have to protect more than just me. If I need to vent about anything I remember, I'll come to you and let it all out. I won't go off on my own and blow up the kingdom or anything like that."

"Lie still. I'm removing the spell now." She rubs her fingers across my forehead, whispers an incantation, and pulls the energy of the spell from my head.

A sensation like chains falling away and allowing my mind to open fully envelops me. The extra measure of power surges through my body, electrifying all my cells at once. The memories flood my consciousness—love, loss, hope, agony, fear, and elation grip me all at once. I squeeze my eyes shut, grasp the sheets in both fists, and ride out the storm raging inside me. The conflicting emotions are at war, each trying to take control at the same time.

Then the visions of my early childhood begin to play like a movie on an enormous silver screen. Indistinct flickers of my mom's smiling face looking down at me, my dad's muscular arms carrying me to bed, and Nana holding me close to her while she wept over her tremendous loss.

"Let them flow like the river, Saraya. Don't latch on to one just yet. Let them all out so it'll be easier for you to go back and visit each one later." Ginevra coaches me from the sidelines while I fight to maintain control and composure.

Concentrating on the good and releasing the bad

seems to quench my sudden thirst for vengeance over the events of the past. The love I felt from them when I was little is still alive, wrapping around me like a warm, snuggly blanket. I miss my nana more than I can express, but I'm content knowing she's okay wherever she is. What hurts the most is not knowing my parents and not remembering them outside of the memories I've just recovered.

With a little deep breathing and meditation, I'm able to slow my speeding heart and stop myself just short of hyperventilating. When I'm calm again, I begin to realize the immediate changes in my body. The buzzing I thought would break my entire body into a million pieces is gone, replaced by a mighty humming coursing through my veins. The intensity of the force infiltrating my every cell is beyond incredible—it's intoxicating.

I spring out of bed to my feet, walking around the room to expend some of the sudden, pent-up energy. Though it doesn't make sense, I feel so much stronger—in my bones and my muscles. *"Ginevra, is this possible? Can I be stronger because of this?"*

"Yes, dear. That's the elvish magic flowing through you, doing its job."

This is amazing. I suddenly want to go outside to test my new abilities under the veil of darkness. After throwing on some clothes, I slink through the long hallways of the palace until I reach the side service entrance. From here, I can sprint to the edge of the forest with minimal risk of being seen by anyone. My eyesight in the darkness has changed. Now, I can see everything. Not black blobs. Not indistinguishable outlines. I can make out every tiny detail, even from a long way off.

Satisfied the coast is clear, I take off in a dead run away from the castle. My speed increases with every step until I'm certain the trail behind me is nothing but a blur. When I stop deep in the forest, I'm not winded in the least. I feel amazing and could've kept going for miles and miles.

"Ginevra, I wish you could feel what I feel. I can't even be upset with you for keeping this from me now because I'm too elated."

"That's one of the perks of being part elf, sweetheart. The downside to that is your anger will take you to equally dark places. Remember Rycan's reaction to you when you first encountered him—the intensity of his hatred? Elves thrive on passion, whether it's love or hatred or anything in between."

On my way back to the castle, I decide to slow my speed to no more than a leisurely stroll so I can take in every detail of the forest with my new elvish vision. The vibrant colors of the flora and fauna are even more vivacious, making me want to stop and touch everything I see. The crescent moon hangs high in the sky tonight, casting its soft white glow over the openings in the treetop canopy.

"Look who's back and all by herself. No human bodyguard with you tonight, huh?" The angry witch from earlier is back with her friends in darkness.

"I don't need a bodyguard." I cross my arms over my

chest and issue a silent challenge with a quirk of my eyebrow. "Who are you?"

"Starla Keeling, the leader of the Sisters of Shadowmoon. Who are you?"

"No one you'd know."

"Is that right? If you're no one special, why is your spirit energy cloaked? What are you trying to hide?" She places her hands on her hips and issues her own challenge.

"I didn't know my aura was cloaked. I'm not hiding anything."

"Maybe we should take her back to the coven with us, girls. We can make her tell us all her secrets before we sacrifice her to Dredor and take her powers for ourselves."

"There's no need for all that, Starla. I'll be glad to tell you exactly what I'm thinking and feeling right now." The slow simmer of anger builds in my chest, but I quickly extinguish it. Her challenge is hollow, and we both know it. She's trying to scare me and save face with her coven at the same time.

But I've never been a pushover.

Pulling the white light into me is infinitely more natural now that Ginevra removed the block. Like a magnet attracted to steel, the light is drawn to me, filling every nook and crevice inside. Pulsating and pounding through me, the power behind the magic builds and pushes against me inside like water pushing against a dam, ready to break free.

Starla's jaw goes slack first, gaping open while she

gawks at me in disbelief as my magical strength increases. Her sisters of the night follow suit and begin backing away from me. *"What are you?"*

"Tired of your shit, that's what I am. Don't return to this part of the forest. You're not welcome here. I thought we made that clear earlier." Lightning flies from my fingertips, striking each witch separately and sending them flying through the air. They hit the ground with a thud and mumbled curses before they scurry away.

"Nice job containing your anger, Saraya. You had me worried there for a moment." I can feel Ginevra's smile in her voice.

"It's all under control, G. Don't worry about me. Who is Dredor?"

"I don't know, Saraya. That isn't a name I've heard before, but I'm on a mission to find out now."

FALLING ASLEEP LAST NIGHT WAS NEXT TO IMPOSSIBLE, BUT I managed to get a few hours of rest before meeting Saban for our all-day adventure. He's already waiting in the kitchen when I walk in to have breakfast.

"Good morning, princess. Sleep well?"

"I was too excited to sleep." That's not a lie. It's just not the entire truth. "But don't worry. I'm more than ready to go exploring with you today."

"Your eyes—they're glowing purple even more than

usual. They're mesmerizing." He stands and walks toward me as if he's entranced, not moving his gaze from mine.

I shrug nonchalantly, eager to change the subject. "I'm happy. I can't wait to see what the day has in store for us."

We eat breakfast together, then he ushers me out of the house, pulling me toward the barn. He glances over his shoulder and rewards me with his perfect smile. Those steel-gray eyes darken with mischief and secrets.

"Are you ready?"

"More than ready. Are we flying today?" I'm giddy with excitement.

"Yes, we sure are. I remember how much you loved it, so I thought we'd head out alone. We had too many people with us last time."

"I couldn't agree more."

Saban's horse is saddled and ready to go when we walk inside the elaborate barn. "Do you want to ride with me, or do you want your own?"

"I'll ride with you this time. Next time, I'll take off on my own."

"Perfect. I was secretly hoping you'd say that. I like having you close to me."

He climbs up on the horse then helps me up to ride behind him. With my arms around his waist and my chest pressed against his back, we take off for our secret destination. When we're high above the earth, I tighten my legs around the horse and stretch my arms out to the sides and let the wind flow through my fingers. I can so clearly envision myself flying without the help of the horse, I'd swear it was real.

He takes the long route so we can enjoy the scenic view from above. His trusty steed carries us with no effort at all. We circle a large open field at the edge of the East-haven Crest northern border with Elderwater Basin before coming in for a landing. The edge of the forest is the backyard of a beautiful English cottage. The front yard is a vast, multiacre lake with crystal-clear water.

"Saban…wow. I'm speechless." I turn in a slow circle, trying to absorb all the beauty surrounding me."

"I'm glad you like it. This is my secret home away from home. I come here to relax and recharge after the crowds at court suck the life out of me. No one knows about this place, except you." He tucks his finger under my chin and gently lifts my face to meet his gaze. When his lips touch mine, a surge of heat floods my body. Stronger than before. More urgency and need are embedded in our sensual embrace. Every nerve ending inside me is exposed and overloaded with desire.

When did I become such a sucker for a gorgeous smile and a smooth line?

CHAPTER 18

"We don't have time to do everything I'd originally planned, thanks to my sister. I did try to get out of the couple's date tonight. I told her you and I were still a new couple and we needed time alone. She said we've spent the last several weeks avoiding everyone else, so we have to give her tonight. With her wedding coming up so quickly, she doesn't have much time to spare. Her guilt trip on me worked wonders." He sounds so apologetic, I can't be upset with him because of his sister. If Krista were here, she'd want to give Saban her stamp of approval too.

"We have plenty of time to avoid the rest of the world before we have to get back. What did you have in mind?"

His steel-gray eyes darken for a moment, stealing my breath with the hidden meaning behind them. "There's a canoe behind the cottage. How about a tour around the lake? I can show you the stream that connects it to the river from Elderwater Basin. We may see a few merpeople out today. You seemed especially fascinated with Talia."

"A romantic paddle around the lake? That sounds perfect. I hope we do see merpeople today. They're intriguing to me—how they can change so quickly in and out of the water." I shrug one shoulder and give him a lopsided smile.

"You're cute when you're embarrassed. But you never have to feel that way with me. I want all of you. Wait here—I'll go get the canoe." He winks while flashing that megawatt smile at me, and I feel the blush creep up my face in response to the naughty thoughts about him that flash through my mind.

When he disappears around the corner of the rock house, I tilt my head back and soak in the bright, warm sun. It really is a perfect day to enjoy the lake up close and personal on a canoe. His thoughts drift into my mind, and I open my eyes to find him walking toward me.

The muscles in his arms and chest bulge with the canoe perched on his shoulder, but he carries the full weight of it with ease. No heavy breathing. Seemingly no exertion at all. My lips part and my eyes fly open wide, roaming over his broad chest before dropping to his muscular legs. When my perusal brings me back to meet his gaze, the smirk on his face says it all. He doesn't have to read my mind to know exactly what I'm thinking.

Every moment near him only intensifies the feelings. Without the filter on my elfish powers in place, those feelings seem to have multiplied exponentially. If we make it through this excursion without me shamelessly throwing myself at him, it'll be a miracle.

"Do you need any help with that?" I finally find my voice—and my manners—though it's clear he has it under control.

"I'm good, princess." He waggles his eyebrows at me, wordlessly conveying the double entendre.

Believe me, Saban, when I say I've already guessed that.

He puts the boat down at the water's edge and turns to me with his outstretched hand. "Let me help you in."

Although I don't need help stepping into a canoe that's halfway on dry land, I don't want to deny him a chance to display chivalry either. When I take his hand, a devilish grin covers his face, and I'm whisked into the air before I can shriek in surprise. Cradled in his arms, snug against his chest, face-to-face with this handsome man, I feel my self-restraint nearly break. Our eyes are locked in an intense conversation all their own. If he instigates anything, we will not make it off the shore today.

He releases a long, pained sigh. "You're killing me, princess."

I'm more than a little disappointed when he puts me down inside the canoe on the front seat, but I hide it behind a happy smile. The next move is mine—when I fully commit myself to him. Until then, we'll both suffer through cold showers and unmet needs.

He pushes off from the shore as he steps in then takes the seat behind me. With the oars in hand, we slowly paddle until we reach the middle where the water is the deepest. The lakes here are teeming with all kinds of flashy fish and multicolored coral—the kind I've only seen on TV in an exotic Caribbean island location.

"What are those statues on the bottom?" I lean over the side of the boat to get a better look.

"They're statues of King Taerel and Queen Wren."

My heart stops beating. My lungs stop drawing breaths. I'm not sure how I'm still conscious. I turn in my seat to gauge his response.

"Why did you put them down there?"

"There was a discussion among the leaders about destroying them because of what happened after the mage attacks. The leaders didn't think we should still have their likenesses in the realm, much less in the palace. But I didn't agree with them. I took the statues away before anyone had a chance to take matters into their own hands. When I come here to be alone, I swim a lot. They keep me company when I'm in the water, and they're safe from anyone who would want to destroy them."

"That's incredible of you to do that, Saban. To save important artifacts from Easthaven Crest's history without regarding them as contraband, as most people would. Not many have the extraordinary insight you do. You're able to see past the extraneous information and find the most important points."

He shrugs and averts his eyes, uncomfortable with the praise I'm heaping on him. For all the attention he gets for his dashing good looks, muscular physique, and status in the community, he's not accustomed to being admired for his intelligence. But I find that attribute every bit as sexy as his physical characteristics.

"For what it's worth, I believe you would've made a great king."

His eyes snap to meet mine, searching for confirmation I'm sincere. I am, without a doubt. Gratitude floods his features before he swallows hard, pushing the ball of emotion back down where it belongs. With a slow, purposeful nod, he expresses his appreciation. Then he resumes paddling the canoe, but I sense a shift in his disposition. That little bit of encouragement filled him with confidence, something he could fake with the others but not with me.

"If you were so stoked to see the mermaids, I assume you haven't seen a dragon up close and personal, then?"

"No, I haven't. Are you saying there are dragons in this water too?"

"I've seen two or three here over the years. Not very often, but maybe we'll get lucky today."

"Are they dangerous? I mean, will they attack us on sight?"

"They can be dangerous, of course. But for the most part, if you leave them alone, they'll leave you alone. They have a bad reputation because they've had to defend themselves from cruel people. If someone tried to kill or imprison me, I'd fight to the death too, so I can't blame them for how they've retaliated."

The sun is directly overhead, the hottest part of the day, and I'm beginning to glisten with beads of sweat.

Unable to resist any longer, I lean to the right and let my hand glide through the cool water. I close my eyes, pulling the light into me and focusing on my new powers from my elf father, while Saban steers the boat by switching his oar from side to side. Then the unmistakable sensation of scales underneath my fingers snatches me from my thoughts.

When I open my eyes, we're in the shallow water near an outcrop of rocks, on the other side of the lake from the cottage. A beautiful creature with the most vibrant purple and gold features watches me cautiously, unsure of my intentions. I gasp loudly, causing it to retreat from my touch.

"Don't be scared. I would never hurt you." I extend my hand with my palm up, letting it decide to return to me on its own.

"Wouldn't it be awesome if they could talk to us? I've always wanted to be able to communicate with animals, especially dragons." Saban moved closer behind me without me even realizing it. My focus is solely on the incredible dragon who still doesn't trust me.

With a single touch, her thoughts flow to mine, immediately bringing tears of pure joy to my eyes. "You are absolutely the most beautiful thing I've ever seen. What's your name, huh?"

My name is Fadryth. Are you Saraya?

"Let's call her Fadryth. It means 'the gentle.' It suits her." I gently stroke the side of her face and let the answer to her question flow back to her.

"That's a lovely name. It fits her perfectly."

I heard you were here. That's why I came to meet you for myself. Will you really heal the realm, like the prophecy says?

Prophecy? No one has mentioned a prophecy to me yet. Another little talk with Ginevra seems to be in order.

I don't know anything about a prophecy, but I'll do my best to help the realm.

The dragons and vampires support you, Saraya. Call my name when you need my help. I'll protect you with my life.

She lowers her head and leans forward. Our foreheads touch, and we remain in that position for several heartbeats. I can feel the tension and anxiety leave her body. Her muscles relax, and her tail slices languidly through the water. My hands are on either side of her head, affectionately rubbing her with long strokes. Similar to my bond with Laurelai, I feel a connection to this dragon. She's not my spirit animal, but she is a kindred soul.

Without warning, an evil laugh that sounds like as a shrill scream fills my thoughts. It's so loud, I snatch my hands away from her and cover my ears in pain. Through the noise, I try to focus on the source to pinpoint it. I know without a shadow of a doubt it's the dark warlock trying to force me out into the open with any trick he can muster.

Fadryth hears it too and instantly recoils. Her enormous wings unfurl, and she lifts herself out of the water to perch on top of the rocky ledge. The sudden movement sends large waves rocking our small boat like a pendulum out of control. I'm thrown out of the opposite side of the canoe.

Saban moves to grab me, but the boat is still rocking violently from side to side. Even with Saban's naturally athletic build, he can't maintain his balance. His foot catches on the boat just before he's thrown out, leaving a gaping hole in the hull. The sound of his head striking the rock is so loud, I can hear it from where I'm treading water behind the sinking canoe. His body goes limp just before rolling into the water, facedown.

"Saban!" I scream his name, but he doesn't move.

Knowing I have no time to waste, I kick my feet as hard as I can. When I reach him, I quickly turn him right-side up. I check his breathing. His chest isn't moving. Then I try to find a pulse, but there isn't one. There's no physical way to perform chest compressions while in the water. I have to get him to solid ground.

With my arm wrapped around him, I kick hard, drawing on my elf strength, and power my way to the shore.

"Saban, come on. You can't do this to me now. You have to wake up." Tears sting the backs of my eyes, but I refuse to give in to the terror welling up inside me. That won't save him. We're out here alone. I'm all he has right now. "Think rationally, Sara."

I send the light from me into him, coursing through his veins to keep the blood circulating to his organs. Then I focus on his lungs and draw out the water. When he inhales and begins coughing, I roll him onto his side. The gash on his head looks terrible, but I remember head wounds swell and bleed worse than other locations. I take the outward swelling as a good sign that he doesn't have a significant head injury.

When he stops coughing and seems to be regaining consciousness, I roll him onto his back and use my wet shirt as a bandage to stem the blood flow.

"What the hell happened?" His hand goes to the giant goose egg already formed on his forehead.

"Shh. Just lie still for a minute. You hit your head on the rocks when you fell out of the boat. You nearly drowned, Saban. You scared me to death. We have to make sure you don't have any other injuries I don't know about."

"I'm okay, princess. My head is throbbing, but nothing else hurts." He looks around and realizes we're on the shore on the opposite side of the lake. "How did we get all the way over here?"

How do I explain this? There's no way human me could physically haul him out of the water.

"Umm, Fadryth helped us. She grabbed you, and I pointed to this shore. I wanted to be closer to the horse in case I had to get you somewhere fast for help."

He stares up at me for a moment, both shocked and pleased with my concern for him. "You really do care about me, don't you? You're nothing like the others who have tried to catch my eye over the years, only thinking about what they can get."

"Of course I care about you. This is not an act. I would

never use someone like that, make them believe I cared when I didn't. I can't believe you'd even question that."

A shadow of regret settles over his face, but it doesn't belong solely to him. Isla put that notion about me in his head. She insinuated I only wanted Saban because I have nothing of my own. With him, my life would be easy, and everything would be given to me on a silver platter.

"I'm sorry—"

"Forget about it. Let's see if you can sit up now." I cut him off before he can finish his apology. It's not that I'm not willing to hear him out, but I can tell most of this is coming from his sister. He shouldn't have to apologize for her, too.

I help steady him when he lifts his back off the ground. After a few moments of sitting without feeling dizzy or sick, he's on his feet and gingerly touching his head. That's when he realizes the wet bandage is actually my shirt and his eyes fly to my exposed chest. Not that my bra covers less than a bikini top would, but the moment feels uniquely intimate.

"You covered my wound with your shirt?" His fingers link with mine.

"You needed a bandage, and I didn't have anything else to use."

He shakes his head, then immediately regrets it. "You never cease to amaze me. Come on, let's find one of my shirts in the cottage for you to wear. There may be some first aid supplies in there too."

CHAPTER 19

Saban and I walk to the cottage with our arms wrapped around each other. With each step, the full realization of what just happened strikes me like a hammer hitting a nail. If I hadn't been able to restart his heart...if I hadn't had the ability to withdraw the water from his lungs...if he hadn't started breathing again. There are so many ways today could've had a much different outcome—one that didn't end with Saban walking beside me.

By the time we reach the door, my entire body is shaking after coming down from the sudden dump of adrenaline. Now that the rush of excitement from being in the moment is over, reality is biting me in the ass. I'm supposed to be taking care of the man who almost drowned, not falling apart from the stress of everything.

Apologies filter into my thoughts from Fadryth, but I assure her she has nothing to be sorry about. I would've backed away from that evil laugh if I'd been capable of getting away from it. Everything that happened afterward was simply an accident, one she shouldn't feel guilty over.

I'll be out here, guarding the cottage, in case his location spell worked.

Thank you, Fadryth. I feel safer already.

"You're shaking. Are you cold?" His eyebrows knit in confusion.

"No, I'm not cold."

"Are you hurt?" He grabs me and starts checking for wounds, turning me around and looking over my head.

"No, I'm okay. Where's that first aid kit?" I'm trying to get my mind focused on something else. The task of patching up his head should work.

He narrows his eyes at me for a moment but finally relents. "In the bathroom. This way."

With the supplies arranged on the vanity, I instruct him to sit so I can get a good look at his wound. I carefully unwrap my shirt from around his head. I'm relieved to find the blood has clotted and it hasn't swollen more since I last looked at it. After cleaning it and putting antibiotic ointment on it, I find the largest adhesive bandage in the bag to cover it.

"You'll be as good as new in no time." I try to smile, but the fear attempts to rear its ugly head again.

"Thank you, princess." He strokes my cheek with his fingertips, and I step closer to him, between his legs, and wrap my arms around his neck.

My practically bare chest presses against his,

absorbing the warmth from his skin. Funny, he should be the cold one—not the other way around. I didn't even notice until this moment. Now all I can seem to think about is how close I came to losing him forever.

"You *are* cold. Why didn't you tell me? We need to get out of these wet clothes. Come in here with me."

We walk into the bedroom, and he rifles through the closets and the drawers until he finds something that will work. For me, he picked a long tee and a pair of lounging pants with a drawstring. His shy smile as he hands them to me makes him look so sweet.

"I know these will be way too big on you, but they'll have to do for now. I'll go to the other room to change and give you some privacy."

Before I can object, he's out the door and closes it behind him. The silence is usually my friend—I've always found solace in it before, when I was at home with Nana, wandering through our forest. But now it taunts me, reminding me I have nothing else to focus on except everything that's gone wrong in the last couple of months since I've been in Covis Realm.

He's been one of the consistent bright spots in my life.

I work the wet pants off my legs and take off my bra too. His T-shirt swallows me whole, but it feels comfortable and cozy. The lounge pants are way too big around my waist and too long on my legs, but I figure out a way to make them work, regardless.

When I step out of the bedroom, he's waiting for me in

the hallway. At first, I look up into those gray eyes and feel a swell of peace come over me. He's alive. He's relatively unharmed, just a bump on the head that will heal in no time. He'll have one hell of a story to tell his friends—he nearly drowned in the lake and was saved by a dragon.

Then my eyes drift downward to what he's holding.

My blood-stained shirt is in his hand, and suddenly, I can't breathe.

Literally. Not metaphorically. Not an exaggeration.

My lungs have seized, and all the oxygen has left my body. My chest burns, my eyes lose focus, and my entire body shakes uncontrollably.

"Sara, talk to me!"

I hear the urgency in his voice. I feel his arms encircle my waist before lifting my feet off the floor. Then I'm enveloped in the heat radiating from his body and the softness of the mattress beneath me. This is the serenity I've needed—to feel safe, sheltered, and loved.

"Come on, princess. I need you to tell me what's going on in that pretty head of yours."

"I'm sorry, Saban." I manage to get the words out through my chattering teeth. "You shouldn't be taking care of me. It should be the other way around. I just keep seeing you lying on the ground, lifeless, and it's hitting me all at once. You had quit breathing. I didn't think I'd be able to save you by myself. But there was no one else around to help, so I didn't have a choice. The 'what-ifs' are killing me."

He tightens his arms around me, squeezing me closer.

"Are you sure I quit breathing?"

I nod. "You didn't have a pulse either."

"But you brought me back—without any medical equipment? How?"

I want to tell him the truth—all of it. I want to tell him who I am, what I am, and how I was able to save his life. Maybe knowing the truth about the light and the dark magic will help settle his mind about mages and wizards. But I can't...too many lives are at stake, and revealing myself now could put us both in more danger than we're already in.

"It was nothing short of a miracle, I can assure you of that much. I couldn't stop until I knew you were breathing normally again."

He's silent for several heartbeats. I know, because my head is lying on his chest, and the lub-dub rhythm of his heart thumps against my ear.

"I owe you my life, Sara. I wouldn't be here right now if it weren't for you."

"No, you don't owe me anything for that. I wouldn't have been able to live with myself if I'd lost you."

The connection between us grows even stronger. It's not as if I could deny it before, but now it feels like a living, growing entity tying us together. The gravity of the situation begins to set in for Saban, and his longing to hear me say the words hits a fever pitch, but he doesn't want to feel as if he's forcing me.

But, honestly, he's not pressuring me at all. He's been

the most patient man I could've hoped to call mine. I've resisted the feelings I've had for him since the moment we met. Every minute we've spent together has only confirmed we are destined to be together. My own stubbornness has kept us at arm's length.

But no more.

"It's almost as if we're meant to be together, isn't it?" I trace small circles on his chest with my finger, excited and scared about what's to come next.

He grabs my hand, stilling my movements, and moves us to sit up so we're facing each other. "Sara, what are you saying?"

"I'm saying I love you, Saban. You're my soul mate—my only one. I've known since the moment we met, but I've resisted because those feelings scared me. But not now, not anymore. I'm giving you all the ammunition to destroy me. I'm trusting you with all of my heart. Please don't let me down."

"Never. I will never hurt you, never leave you. I love you so much. I can't even measure it, there's nothing to compare it to. But I promise to make you the happiest woman in Covis Realm. I'll never give you a reason to regret giving your love to me."

He cups my face with his hands and covers my mouth with his. What was meant to be a kiss of happiness instantly escalates into a fiery passion that consumes both of us. He leans toward me, pushing my back to the mattress, and covers my body with his. His mouth moves down my neck, nipping and licking at the sensitive skin.

He grips the hem of my shirt and slowly moves it up, giving me plenty of time to stop his advancement. But I have no intention of stopping now. I lift my arms in the most obvious signal I can give. He pulls his head back and watches my face as he removes the shirt. Then, when he can no longer stand it, he drops his eyes to my chest. His mouth immediately follows, closing around the pebbled bud of my nipple, laving it with the warmth of his tongue. My toes curl and my fingers grip his hair, tugging on it without even realizing I'm doing it.

"You are my dream come true." He murmurs against my skin between lavishing attention on my body. His hands slide down to the drawstring on my pants. "I dreamed of you, Sara. I couldn't see your face, but the magic of your love saved me from dying."

I can't confirm how close to the mark he is with that statement.

"My heart, my mind, and my body are yours—and always will be, princess."

He tugs on the string, and it comes undone under his touch, the same way my body does. I'm on the verge of spontaneous combustion. I lift my bottom off the bed and help push the pants down my legs. Now I'm laid bare to him and unafraid. I'm ready to become his and only his.

"Are you sure? We don't have to rush into this."

The best part is, he means every word of it. He would wait for me as long as I needed.

"I've never been more ready for anything in my life, Saban."

In a flash, he sheds his clothes and settles between my legs, the thick head of his erection poised at my entrance. I bite my tongue, waiting for the moment of pain when he thrusts inside me. But, true to my Saban, he moves gently at first, working his way inside and giving my body time to adjust to his size.

With the initial sting minimized, I can relax and let him show me how to move with him. Our bodies and movements are in perfect tune. Hands, mouths, and tongues roam with free will. We're slick with each other's sweat and winded from exertion. He murmurs sweet nothings in my ear, sending chills down my spine and goose bumps across my skin.

"That's my girl. You feel so good, baby. I can't get enough of you."

He grips my leg behind my knee and pushes it toward me, deepening his sensual assault on my body. The intense sensation spreads all over my body. My fingers dig into the skin of his back. He drives harder now that our bodies are in sync, playing me like a fine instrument only meant for him until the dam building low in my belly breaks. I cry out in complete ecstasy, and he tumbles over the edge right behind me.

He rolls over to my side and positions me so that his chest is firmly pressed against my back. His arm is draped over me protectively, and his lips are close to my ear.

"You make me feel invincible, princess. All my love will always be yours. I'll follow you anywhere. Whatever you need me to be, I'll be. There's nothing you could ever do that would change how I feel about you." He kisses the back of my head, and within seconds, his rhythmic breathing tells me he's dozed off.

Hold on to that promise, Saban, because I really need you to keep it in the near future.

CHAPTER 20

"How do you feel?" I gently rub my fingers over his bandaged head while we wait for our clothes to dry. After a hot shower and a long nap, we both feel refreshed.

"I'm fine, princess. It's a good thing I'm so hardheaded." He grins and taps on his skull with his knuckles. "I'm not going to the hospital. I feel fine."

"Saban, you drowned. You could still get an infection from the water getting into your lungs."

"Nah, not that water. It's clean and clear. If we'd been in murky water, I'd let you force me into going to the doctor. But I promise if I start to feel bad in any way, I'll go immediately. You can even take me and make me comply with whatever the doctor says. Deal?"

"Fine. But if you fall over dead at dinner tonight, don't blame me."

"I'll keep that in mind…if I die during dinner, I won't hold you responsible."

I'm speechless for a moment because someone in this world finally understands my sarcastic humor and can throw it back at me with ease. These seemingly insignificant moments between us only solidify my belief we actually do belong together. There's no way the little things are simply coincidences.

"It would make dinner with your sister a little more awkward, too. You really need to think more about my needs in this scenario."

"Princess, I am more than happy to take care of any and all of your needs." His eyes darken as he slides his hands around my waist. He bends his knees to put us at eye level. "When we get back to the palace, I want you to seriously think about moving in to my room with me. I know you've been working with Addilyn and you seem to enjoy it, but you'll be in a diplomatic relations position when we announce our bond to the other kingdoms."

"Diplomatic relations? Does that mean I'll work with representatives from each of the kingdoms on issues that impact the whole realm?"

"That's exactly what it means. You'll join me at the council meetings, and you'll attend separate subcommittee meetings. There's a lot of red tape that makes it difficult to make any progress. Plus, everyone has their own ideas of the best course of action—and those ideas usually only favor that one kingdom. It's maddening at times, but when we are able to work together on what's best for the realm, it's a beautiful thing. I realize I'm not making this sound very appealing."

"No, actually, I think it's all fascinating. Working with Addi every day has been great, and I'll miss seeing her so often. But the chance to help the whole kingdom and the realm is an opportunity of a lifetime. I'm ready to roll up my sleeves and get to work."

The chime on the dryer rings, and Saban walks off to grab our freshly laundered clothes. My mind races with possibilities of being included in their government meetings. I've held my own during persuasive debates in my high school back home, though I'm aware this is on an entirely new level. But my ultimate goal is to bring awareness to the undue suffering the prejudice against mages puts on the entire population of Covis Realm. If I can convince the others to listen to reason, we can unite against the dark forces trying to pull this world under its grip.

If I can manage to make a respectable first impression, maybe I'll stand a chance of persuading the leaders to take the threat seriously and protect the mages who just want to live freely.

"Good as new." Saban hands me my clothes so I can change before we fly back to the palace. He's right—there's not a single sign of the blood that stained my shirt just a few hours ago.

"Thank you. I'm sure my current attire would raise eyebrows in the castle." I giggle as I walk toward the bedroom, holding up my pants in one hand and my change of clothes in the other.

"You never know. Maybe you'd set a whole new fashion trend." He chuckles and follows behind me.

"What's the plan for tonight, then? Where are we going?"

"The four of us have dinner reservations at a four-star restaurant in the city, then we're going to the observatory for some romantic stargazing. But don't tell Isla I told you. She wanted that part to be a surprise."

"I promise to act as if I've never heard of it." Shouldn't be too hard to pull that off.

We walk out of the little slice of heaven cottage together and climb on the horse. During the ride back, the events of the day replay in my mind over and over. From seeing that beautiful place for the first time, meeting Fadryth, to finally realizing what I have and nearly lost because I allowed the fear of the unknown to keep me locked in an invisible prison. Giving him my heart was the right decision, I'm sure of it. But Talia's words still echo in the back of my mind.

All is not as it seems with him, and you'll need all your wits and cleverness when the time comes.

Though I can't let her prediction rule my life, I'd be a fool not to consider the warning involves my eventual confession. Will he assume the worst about me when that time comes?

With the horse stabled, Saban and I start walking toward the palace when he stops me just out of earshot of any of the workers. He seems unsure of himself, though he tries his best to mask it.

"Have you thought any more about moving in to the other wing…with me?"

"Yes, I have, and I accept your invitation. It'll be much easier than one of us sneaking back and forth between our rooms in the middle of the night."

We turn together and continue walking toward the front entrance. That panty-melting smile of his is back. He has a little more swagger in his step. His chest may be puffed out a little more. The emotions emanating from him are pure happiness, something I haven't felt in him before now. He's had moments of joy and contentment, but never to this degree.

Before we reach the front steps, the door swings open and Giselli marches out onto the terrace. Her gaze lands on us then drops to our entwined hands. A chill wafts over the warm late afternoon air from her icy glare. Apparently, I was good enough to attend the engagement party with Saban, but not quite up to par to be joined with him.

"Saban, you and I need to speak. Right now. Privately." She turns on her heel and stomps back inside after issuing her order, leaving both of us puzzled and annoyed by her rudeness. This woman's abrupt changes in mood and manners baffle me.

"Sara, you go ahead and get ready for our double date. I'll see what Mother wants and have the staff move your belongings while we're away. By the time we return home tonight, your new home will be with me." He kisses me on the forehead before rushing off in the direction Giselli went.

I scurry to my room in the servants' wing, where I know I won't be interrupted. I can multitask with the best of them—dress and listen in on their conversation at the same time. I'm well aware that one day I need to learn the difference between the need to intrude and wanting to eavesdrop, but today is not that day. Obviously, I have a bad feeling about what's happening in their conversation, but I'm also concerned about my safety. If anyone has learned who I am, I need to know with as much advance notice as possible.

"She's a very nice girl, Saban, and you know I'm fond of her. But not as a daughter-in-law. I thought you brought her to the engagement party because of what happened with the elves that day. As a way to calm her nerves and give her a place to live and work here in the palace."

"I invited her to the engagement party because she's different from every other girl who has tried to turn my head since I was thirteen years old. From the first moment our eyes met, I knew she was the one for me. She's my soul mate, Mother. We've pledged ourselves to each other and will make it official to the kingdom." Saban keeps his tone controlled, but I feel the anger bubbling below the surface, like hot magma about to erupt in a spectacular show.

"I understand you believe that, son, and it may very

well be true. But you're destined to be royalty, and as of right now, the only way that can happen is if you join with someone of noble blood. Then the other kingdoms will be more likely to approve your petition to be named king of Easthaven Crest. I'm sorry, son, but for you to be king, you can't be joined with Sara. Your wife has already been chosen."

Giselli at least has the decency to sound heartbroken for her son rather than like the heartless robot she was after Sagran died. But I'll never understand how some parents can put such blatant blind ambition before the happiness of their children. Though I know what he's promised me, and he's shown how much he cares about me, I wait with bated breath for his answer.

Will he choose me or the crown?

He scrapes his hand over his face and releases a long, pained sigh. "Mom…"

"I'm sorry, Saban. I really am. Had I known your relationship was progressing so quickly, I would've brought this to you much sooner. Isla mentioned a double date tonight, so naturally I had a lot of questions about it. Sara lives in our servants' quarters, Saban. Think about how that would look if the other kingdoms were to find out. They'd laugh you out of the council." Giselli paces across the room, her mind filled with regret over the decision her son has to make.

"Sara pledged herself to me today, Mom. She gave herself to me. She even saved my life—I told you what happened to my head on the way in here. How am I supposed to tell her I'm marrying someone else now?"

"The best thing you can do is tell her the truth—blunt and honest, even though it will hurt her. Then she'll understand it's not a matter of you rejecting her. It's what's best for the kingdom, it's your duty to your station, and it's a sacrifice you're willing to make to serve your people as the king." She puts her hand on his arm as a small sign of understanding. "Shall I contact Lord Renfry and inform him the union with his daughter is on?"

Saban nods his head, indicating his agreement and consent to her plan.

A million shards of glass stab me from the inside out in the space where my heart once beat. His promises were spoiled before they left his lips. His vow of eternal love was barely spoken before he broke it. The turmoil welling up inside him is minuscule compared to the pain and embarrassment that grip me. He's dreading telling me the truth, and I'm fighting the urge to tear him apart with my physical and magical strength.

I want to break the connection between us. I don't want his feelings mixed with mine anymore. His are all sorrow and remorse. Mine are all pain and anger—and I really want to focus my energy on the anger part. But I can't seem to break free from the hold his thoughts have on me.

"What's wrong with you, big brother? You look as if you've lost your best friend." Isla meets him in the hallway outside his wing.

"Worse. I've lost the other half of my soul." He hangs his head so low, his chin nearly touches his chest.

"What? Where did she go? Did she reject the bond?" The pitch of her voice rises with each word.

"No. It's not her fault. She pledged herself to me—gave me her heart. But I just had a talk with our mother, and she has made vastly different plans for me." He relays the entire conversation to Isla, and I relive each word of it as if it's the first time I've heard it.

"There must be something else you can do." Isla tries to offer some hope and solace, but her tone lacks conviction. She doesn't believe there's a snowball's chance in hell this will work out any more than he does.

Any more than I do.

"I'll cancel our reservations for tonight. You're in no shape to pretend anything's the same after this."

"No, sis, don't cancel. Give me one last night with her. I know it's selfish, but I can't tell her yet."

Exactly how am I supposed to play along as the doting girlfriend knowing what I know?

He made his choice, and it wasn't me. He chose to roll the dice on the slim-to-none odds of gaining a crown. Breaking every promise he made to me, not even half a day after swearing the oaths. There's no way I can go through with tonight.

I'm not that good at pretending.

My only recourse is to confront him and end this charade immediately.

CHAPTER 21

Dressed in my standard attire, nothing that would indicate I have evening plans with the love of my life, I march right up to his bedroom door and knock as loudly as my fist will allow. It only takes a moment for the door to swing wide open since he undoubtedly questioned who would be so bold.

Me. I would be so bold and then some.

His angry expression quickly changes to one of bewilderment before grief mars his perfectly handsome face.

Join the club, buddy. We have jackets.

"Sara, what are you doing—?"

"What did your mother have to say?" I drive straight to the point. There's no need to sugarcoat anything now.

"Oh, she just wanted to talk about some political stuff." At least he has the decency to avoid making eye contact when he lies straight to my face. Actually, it's not entirely a lie. It is all very political.

"Saban, tell me." If I had the ability to shoot lasers from my eyes, he would be a pile of ashes right now.

"I'd rather not. I don't want to ruin our evening." He glances at my clothes and realizes his plans to spend one last night with me just disintegrated.

"I'm not stupid, Saban. It doesn't take a genius to figure out what's going on. I have a few things to say to you before I leave. You will regret this decision for the rest of your life. I never would've betrayed you like this. At the first test of your honor, you abandoned me after whispering so many words of love in my ear. Even now, you stand here in front of my face, unable to tell me the truth of your own volition. You're not at all the man I thought you were. The truth is, you're still a scared little boy who's seeking parental approval."

I don't wait for a reply before turning to leave him standing in the doorway, slack-jawed and wounded. There's nothing he can say now to soothe my raw emotions. But there is one more thing I have to say before I leave the palace. I stop halfway down the hall and look back over my shoulder. He's watching me, on the verge of chasing after me.

But it's too late. His treachery has been revealed.

"And by the way, what kind of leader takes orders from his mommy? That's not quite the makings of a true king, is it? I'd say your subjects and fellow kings would question your ability to rule if they knew that."

His fingers curl around the doorframe, his knuckles turning white from his tight grip. A thin line forms where his lush lips once were. A deep red tinge fills his face. But his feet are rooted to the floor, and he does not attempt to speak. He knows what I've said is true, no matter how blunt or harsh my words are.

Sometimes, the truth hurts. Now we've both learned that lesson.

When I turn the corner, headed back to my room, Gerard steps out of his room and immediately stops when he sees the stern expression on my face.

"Is something wrong, Sara?" He's polite—but he already knows my world has changed. Whether I want to talk about it is another matter.

"Yes, Gerard, something is very wrong. I've just learned Giselli has other plans for Saban's mate, and he picked her over me. I'm afraid I'll have to decline our double date for tonight. Perhaps Saban can take his new mate instead. Thank you for the invitation, but I'll take my leave now." Before he can say anything in response, I scurry away. I'm on the very edge of breaking down, and I don't want to do it in front of anyone here.

It takes me only a few minutes to pack my meager belongings in a backpack and clear out of the servants' quarters of the palace. Rather than leave through the front door where everyone who's anyone will be watching, I make my way to the kitchen and out the back door. I'll be able to find somewhere to stay in the Veil, where I can practice my magic and learn from other mages. Where I'll be with my kind, who already accept me for who I am and don't expect me to pretend to be something I'm not.

Addi's previous words ring in my mind as I walk away from the palace. From Saban. From our life together.

I'll never fully be happy while I'm separated from my soul mate.

The only solace I have is knowing he'll never fully be happy with whomever he's betrothed to now.

Darkness has settled in by the time I reach the outer border of the Veil. My steps grew slower and my heart grew heavier the farther I roamed from him. Tears that stung the backs of my eyes flow freely when I reach the tree line, far away from prying eyes.

Ginevra waits for me underneath an old oak tree. Her eyes are full of compassion and understanding. She opens her arms, and I rush into them without question or hesitation.

"It'll be okay, sweet girl."

"It hurts so bad, Ginevra. How could he do this to me?"

"The quest for power drives men to perform all kinds of acts they'd never even consider otherwise. Come on, let's get you settled in for the night. Tomorrow, we'll get you a job in the city. Saban will be looking for you before long, and if you completely disappear, it'll raise too many questions. Plus, you need your own money, maybe a place of your own that's not in a tree, and a way to feel like a normal person."

I nod, deferring to her judgment for tonight. I can't make any more decisions today.

Inside the tree house, the familiar sounds of the forest bring little consolation. My body is tired, ready for a night of deep sleep to take over. But my heart and my mind are too conflicted to rest. All the events of the day haunt me… every single one. The instant replay is on a constant loop, each image so vivid, I think I could reach out and touch it.

Too many hours pass before I realize it's not only my memories I'm seeing, but Saban's as well. I'm still so intimately connected to him that his thoughts are mixed with mine despite the distance separating us. He's suffering every bit as much as I am, maybe even more. His regrets consume him, and his misery is intense, but I can't help him. I won't help ease his pain after he's caused me so much.

Then I realize I can use our link to my advantage. He was so cavalier with my feelings, so I decide to see how he handles having my pain heaped on top of his own. I close my eyes and channel my feelings through the light, letting it flow from me directly to him. I can't hurt more than I already do, carrying both of our wounds in my chest, but now he has a glimpse of how I feel.

For a few moments, I transferred all of it to him—the heartbreak, humiliation, rejection, and betrayal.

For those few moments, I was able to breathe again, but the weight on his chest felt as though it would crush him.

Welcome to my world, Saban.

The remaining hours of the night bring only fitful sleep, broken by recurring dreams that could've been mine as easily as they could've been his. All I know is I can't spend a lifetime like this. It's enough to drive anyone mad, especially after he's married to someone else. I'm strong-willed but watching him with her is not something I can take.

I rise and dress when the others in the Veil begin to stir but decline their generous offer of breakfast. Nothing I eat would stay down right now, so there's no use in trying. As promised, a couple of the mages take me into the city with them and put in a good word with their manager. Within the hour, I have a new job in the premiere clothing store servicing the entire realm.

My only qualm is who may show up here for an impromptu shopping spree.

But I'll cross that bridge when I come to it. For now, I'm learning how to work the computer, charge the items, and finalize the inventory sheets. Mindless work I can do in my sleep after helping Nana run our store back in Montana, but it keeps me busy and I desperately need that.

As each customer leaves, I catch myself staring at the door, waiting for someone—anyone—to walk in. With each chime of the door alert, my heart beats a little faster, simultaneously hoping it is Saban and that it's not him. By the end of my shift, I'm so far beyond exhausted, mentally and physically. When I make it back to the Veil, I climb into my guest tree house and crash.

The upside of being so completely worn-out is it keeps the dreams away. My brain finally shuts down along with my body, and I sleep until late morning. When I join the others around the table, a few pieces of toast are left, so I grab one to eat on the way to my new job. My shifts are set for the next two weeks, but I've made it clear I'm willing to cover for anyone who may be out unexpectedly. They can give me all the hours and keep me there around the clock for all I care.

When I walk in, my best friend in Covis Realm is there waiting for me.

"Hi, Addi." I walk directly to her and hug her. I've missed her, but I couldn't go back to tell her what happened.

"I already know everything. I'm so sorry, sweetheart. If I could cast a spell to remove his balls without serious repercussions, I would do it in a split second."

I chuckle, the mental picture firmly implanted into my brain now. "Thanks for the super idea. I may take the chance and do that spell myself."

We catch up on other non-Saban-related topics before Addi has to get back to work herself. I make it through another day, working on my feet all day, perusing the clothes and shoes for myself, and taking advantage of the employee discount. When I return to the Veil after work, the mages are having a meeting to discuss the upcoming vote on our rights, so I pull up a stump and listen to all the pros and cons they debate.

This information would've been beneficial if the job Saban told me I'd be doing had panned out.

Best-laid plans and all that.

THE DAYS BLEED TOGETHER, WORKING AT THE STORE, helping out in the Veil, and getting very little sleep at night, until a full week has passed. A week apart from Saban, without hearing his voice, seeing his face, or spending one minute with him. I'd like to say each day is getting easier, but that's not entirely true. I think I'm just adapting to the constant aching in my heart and coping with the fact that I have to move on. For my own sanity. For my own peace of mind. For myself.

On my lunch break, I take a stroll through the city. Over the last few days, I've been a hermit, avoiding all human contact when my job doesn't absolutely require it. Today, I'm going to sit in the park and do a little people watching. At least it's a first step to rejoining the world. After I grab a sandwich from the small bakery, I find a shady spot near the creek flowing through the park.

The footbridge crossing the creek is empty, so I find a spot near the middle and settle in to nibble on my sandwich. With my sandals off, I dangle my feet in the blue water and watch the mothers with their children playing in the adjacent clearing. Their laughter drifts across the field to me, and the bright smiles on their innocent little faces lift my spirits. I'm so focused on their activities that I don't notice what's swimming directly underneath me.

I should say *who* instead of *what*.

My eyes automatically jerk in the direction of a loud splash. In an instant, a handsome, muscular merman is in my face. His arms are on either side of me, caging me in, and his powerful tail fin holds him upright out of the water.

"I can make you forget all about him if you give me a chance." The brilliant jade color of his eyes glistens with mischief and lascivious promises. "You're much too stunning to pine over someone who doesn't appreciate you. You look so delicious, I could eat you up."

"That's a very tempting offer. There are a couple of problems with it, though." His gaze is mesmerizing me; I feel the powerful lure trying to ensnare me along with an odd sensation of wanting to be caught.

"Do tell. I'm sure we can work through them."

"For starters, I don't even know your name." I quirk one eyebrow while mentally pushing his influence away from my mind. Surprise registers on his handsome face.

"My name is Rio. And you are?"

"I'm Sara."

"Hello, Sara. Now that we've been officially introduced, the other reason should be easy to rectify."

"The other reason is actually slightly more difficult. You see, I've heard the stories about the siren's song. How they lure fishermen to their deaths, crashing the boats on the rocks and taking their bodies to the bottom of the ocean to feast on their bones. So, while I'm very tempted by your stunning good looks, charming personality, and captivating eyes, I'm afraid I'll have to pass on being eaten alive."

His stunned expression quickly morphs into a full smile. He throws back his head in roaring laughter before nodding in understanding. "You are everything I've heard and more, Sara. I know Talia very well, and she told me about your chat on the shoreline. She's very fond of you after one conversation, and I can assure you that doesn't happen with her. Ever. Naturally, I wanted to meet you for myself.

"Now that I have, I have to admit her assessment of you couldn't be more spot-on. You are different from every other human we've encountered. For the record, my offer still stands. I know what Saban did to you—news travels fast in the mage and wizard community—and I can help you forget him. It'll be as if he's no more than someone you used to know."

"I appreciate the offer, Rio, but I need more information first. What would you do to make me forget him?"

"There are a couple of ways we can do it. One way involves removing the bond you have with him from your psyche. Once that's done, you'll remember how you used to feel, but it'll be diminished. The other way is if I take him to the bottom of the ocean and feast on his bones." When he smiles, a dimple appears in his right cheek, and I can't take my eyes off it.

"Can you give me time to think about it? I'm not sure which option is more appealing at the moment."

He chuckles again, but this time, his laughter is contagious. I find myself giggling for the first time since that awful day. It feels good to release the emotions bottled up inside me—both good and bad.

"You take all the time you need. I'll wait for your word.

You should also know, the moment that bond with him is broken, my plan is to make you fall madly in love with me. Not to feast on your bones, though. There are other ways to eat you alive." He waggles his eyebrows suggestively. "All you have to do is step in the water and call my name. I'll be there."

With that, Rio lowers himself into the creek and swims away with a simple goodbye wave. I'm left with all kinds of conflicting sensations about my predicament. I don't want Saban dead; that's obvious. But the "removing the bond" option is very appealing. When Saban moves on with his new mate, I'll take Rio up on his offer. For the time being, I think it's essential for me to learn how to live with disappointment and anguish.

Something tells me this won't be the last time I'll face it.

My lunch break ends, and I return to the store, back to the work I know how to do. The familiarity of it is comforting. While I'm restocking the shelves and updating the store inventory database in the last few minutes before my shift ends, I lose myself in the menial tasks and momentarily forget about Saban, my broken heart, and the constant threat hanging over my head.

"Sara? Um…can we talk? Please?"

I'd know that voice anywhere. It haunts me in my sleep. It follows me during the day. It reverberates through my mind. It cries out my name in the dead of night. It soothes me and irritates me at the same time. It crushes my spirit and sends my soul soaring.

It belongs to him.

I slowly turn to face him, and I'm surprised to see the gaunt face staring back at me. He's lost weight in the last week apart. The vibrant man I knew, who was always so full of life, seems more like a dull black-and-white cartoon version of his previous self. There are dark rings under his eyes, his cheeks are more sunken in, and there's no sparkle in those gray eyes of his. The color is muted and lackluster, a ghost of what they once were.

"No, we can't. I have nothing more to say to you."

CHAPTER 22

"Then you can listen because I have plenty to say to you." He turns to follow me from the storefront to the employee break room, where I clock out with an eye scan. I grab my bag from my designated locker and continue to avoid eye contact with him. "I don't want to chase you down the street, yelling to make sure you hear me, but that's exactly what I'll do if I'm forced. We're not going one more day without settling this once and for all."

"You settled it 'once and for all' when you made your decision, Saban. As far as I'm concerned, that was the end of you and me. Whatever bond we had between us is broken beyond repair. If I think about it, why would I want to repair it now? Your promises are bullshit. You've already proven that. Why should I bother listening to a single word that comes out of your mouth?" I march out of the store and onto the sidewalk. The problem is, I can't walk toward the Veil with Saban following on my heels, so I turn the opposite way and go back to the park.

"Because I love you, Sara. I love you like I've never loved anyone in my entire life. But it's also more profound than that. We are linked together in this life and the next. We are not over, princess. We can't be. I still feel you in my arms. I still hear you in my head. You're a part of me now. Our love story will never end."

"That's a very touching sentiment, Saban. But words are worthless. Your actions showed me everything I need to know about you."

"Look, I know I've made a mess of things. I know I hurt you, and I'll regret that for the rest of my life. But I can't live without you, Sara. Believe me, I've tried and failed miserably. This past week has been pure hell. There were days I didn't know how I'd live through the next minute because the pain of losing you was so fucking bad. What can I do to make it up to you? How can I prove you can trust me?"

I stop walking, reach into my bag for a piece of paper, and hold it up for him to see. "This paper represents trust, Saban." I wad it up into a tight ball. Then I shove it into his hand. "That crinkled piece of trash is still paper. It can still be used. But it'll never be like new again. No matter what you do, you can't change the damage that's been done to it. When you can restore that paper to new, then maybe you've found a way to change what you've done to me."

"But I love you, princess. Not knowing where you are,

if you're safe, or if you need anything is killing me." His plea passes over his lips as a wounded whisper.

"I'm not yours to worry about anymore, Saban. I gave you all of me—my love, my body, my trust—and you threw it all away like it was yesterday's trash. I'm not giving you another chance to do that again. Don't come to where I work anymore. Stop looking for me. Go back and live your own life. Goodbye."

He stands still, staring at the crumpled paper in his hand, and I walk away, choking on my pride. When I'm far enough away, lost in the crowd, I circle the block and double back to head toward the Veil. The grief is overwhelming, almost to the point of making me lose control. I need somewhere I can be completely alone, to have time to think through the events of the past few weeks and decide what I should do next. A safe place to bawl my eyes out, scream until all the anguish escapes, and let it all go.

My focus should be on what happens when the cloak is lifted on my upcoming birthday, staking my claim to the throne, and saving my grandmother. Instead, I can't concentrate on anything except him.

He's your destiny, Saraya.

What am I supposed to do, Nana? Forgive him after he hurt me so much? Take him back after he humiliated me?

I swear I never realized how unfair life could be before now.

Yes, sweetheart. Have you ever needed forgiveness from someone you cared about?

Yes, of course I have. But this really feels different.

This is no different, Saraya. Remember how you felt when you'd hurt a friend? You would've done anything just to make your relationship right again. No relationship is perfect, my dear. They all take work and forgiving the other every day to make it work. Just because he's your soul mate doesn't mean you'll never have problems.

I'm not ready to forgive him yet.

I understand. You want to stay mad for a while longer, make him continue to pay for what he did. Just remember, we're not promised to our next breath. Don't wait so long that you end up regretting it.

Nana's advice is on repeat in my mind. To be alone, I walk to the clearing on the far side of the Veil, to the isolated spot where Aris took me to train with A.M., the Artificial Mage robot. With my back against an enormous cedar tree, I drop my head and let the tears flow and fall wherever they land.

I've stood firm for as long as I can, physically and mentally. I've tried not to feel sorry for myself after what happened to Nana, being thrust into a world I'm not familiar with, and learning my parents were murdered because they were magical like me.

But now I've hit the wall, and I need a break from reality.

Whiskers tickle my cheek, and a furry face rubs against mine. I open my eyes to find Laurelai curling up next to me.

"I've missed you so much. It feels like it's been weeks since I saw you last." I stroke her fur, and her purring engine starts automatically.

I've missed you too. But I'm more worried about you than anything. I felt your pain from across the forest. She peers up at me with those huge, gold eyes, silently asking me how she can help. She already knows why I'm hurt.

"I'll be okay. I'm just wallowing in my self-pity away from everyone else. When I'm done, I'll pick myself up, dust myself off, and get back to work." I smile through the tears, grateful to have such a loyal companion.

My offer still stands. Even though he's your true mate, his neck still looks very tasty to me. I swear she waggles her eyebrows, and that action makes me laugh again. *I know you're conflicted, but it seems to me that you want to forgive him but won't let yourself. Forgiving someone who hurt you doesn't make you weak, Saraya. It takes a lot of strength to give a second chance. Only the strongest are capable of doing that.*

"You're right, of course. Nana always said the same thing. She also said I was too proud for my own good, and it would be the death of me one day."

Those words stir a memory deep in my subconscious…Nana's warning about pride…a faraway princess hardened her heart and plunged the world deeper into darkness because of her unwillingness to show mercy to someone who displayed genuine remorse for their actions.

One of Nana's alien world stories.

Keep digging, Saraya. It'll come back to you. Laurelai's encouragement gives me the extra shove I need.

"She didn't read it to me before bedtime. That's why I

didn't connect the dots. I was young, seven or eight maybe, and I was playing with one of the kids after school behind Nana's store. The little girl broke one of my favorite toys. It was an accident, but I was so young, it didn't matter. My feelings were hurt, and I was mad at her for making a simple mistake.

"Nana pulled me inside and told me the story of a young princess in my favorite fantasy world. Her friend hurt her, but it wasn't his fault. He tried to apologize and explain what happened, but the princess wouldn't hear him out. The longer she held on to the anger, the harder it was for her to let it go. Eventually, it consumed her, and she turned into an evil witch, bent on destroying the land she'd once loved.

"Nana said the moral of the story was to remember everyone makes mistakes, people will hurt me even when I don't deserve it, but I must never let the bitterness control my heart. Like I've done for the past week. I was determined to hold on to it forever to avoid being hurt again."

It sounds like you have your answer, Saraya. You love him. Besides, you're linked to him until death.

"A merman offered to break the link. Do you know anything about that?"

I know that has been done before, but it doesn't always work. Even if it does, most still feel as if they've lost a part of themselves, never whole again. Finding your soul mate is old magic, Saraya. That's not something you should tamper with lightly. It can be very dangerous.

She and I settle into a relaxing silence, just enjoying the company and assurance we give each other. The sun is low in the sky, and most of the animals have settled in for the evening. The nocturnal ones are just starting to rouse from their daytime slumber, moving about in search of food. Listening to the natural sounds of the forest comforts me. With my jumbled mind settled, I can make more logical decisions instead of letting my emotions rule me.

Laurelai and I hear the faint, distant noise at the same time. Her head jerks up from its resting place on my lap, and I sit up straight, straining my ears and eyes to locate the out-of-place creature. Our eyes zero in on one specific path at the tree line as the sound of footfalls grows louder to our enhanced hearing.

Laurelai leaps to her feet, instantly on guard and ready to attack, and I quickly follow suit. But the face that steps out of the woods stuns me, rendering me utterly mute for a moment.

Do you know him? She sounds surprised and even slightly appalled.

"I do. Don't kill him yet."

Saraya, he's already dead. She emphasizes each word, but it takes a couple of seconds for her meaning to sink in.

"No freaking wonder I couldn't read his mind. Of course. It makes sense now. Vale is a vampire."

He approaches us slowly, keeping a close watch on Laurelai and trying to determine how much of a threat she poses. I don't need to read his mind to see the apprehension on his face.

"Hi, Sara. How are you?" His nonchalant greeting doesn't fool me. He knows I'd only be here, in the Veil, for one reason.

"Hello, Valerian. I've been better, to be honest, but I'm working on it. What brings you out here? You're a long way from the Nightside Mountains, aren't you?"

"I am, yes. You obviously know what I am, and I know what you are. But I assure you, I pose no threat. Your secret is safe with me. I'm actually just passing through here on my way to talk to the mage council meeting."

"You'll have to forgive me if I don't take your word for it. I've developed trust issues recently." I cross my arms over my chest while drawing all the white light into me. Just in case I need extra defensive powers.

He nods, a troubling realization flashes across his face, and he releases a deep breath. Then I watch as he draws the white energy into his body, and I instantly understand. Only those of us with magical powers can see the flow of energy. He saw mine as clearly as I see his.

"That's right. I'm a vampire and a wizard, though I admit it's a strange combination. Before you ask, Saban doesn't know about my magical abilities either. If his family found out, my vampiric alive-or-dead status wouldn't matter. They'd burn me at the stake for hiding my magical abilities all these years."

"His family?" I'm already not very fond of his mother. I don't need another reason not to like her.

"Yes, his mother is notoriously anti-magic, and she's very vocal about it at public events. Isla is following right along in her mother's footsteps. Sagran was the same way when he was alive. Saban seems to be the only one with a level head on his shoulders."

"That part remains to be seen, on many levels. We don't know how he'll react when he finds out about us."

"Why would he find out?" Vale seems genuinely clueless. Even Laurelai doesn't detect any dishonesty in him.

He is part of the white light. You can tell him. I glance down at Laurelai, and she nods, urging me to share my secret.

"Because on my next birthday, the powerful cloaking spell currently shielding me will dissolve, and everyone will know who I am. My parents were King Taerel and Queen Wren. I'm Saraya Nemertes, the heir to the East-haven Crest throne...and a mage."

He stares blankly at me for several heartbeats, possibly waiting for me to assure him it's only a terrible joke, but that never comes. Then his jaw goes slack, his eyes grow wide, and his hand flies up to cover his mouth. He begins shaking his head slowly at first, then increases the speed and intensity.

"No, Sara, she'll kill you. She knows about the prophecy too. She'll never allow it to come to pass. That's why she and Sagran killed your parents when you were a toddler—they were trying to get to you."

I stumble backward at his words. "What...what are you

saying? Giselli and Sagran, Saban's parents, were behind the killing of my parents?"

"You didn't know?" Regret mars his features, and empathy fills his eyes.

"No, I didn't. I was told no one knew who instigated the attacks."

"No, we don't know who the warlock is that instigated everything. But I'm not surprised you didn't know his parents' part in the attack on your parents. It's not widely known, especially since so many mages were killed during that time. But those of us who are part of the tight-knit political circuit are aware. There have been a lot of rumors over the years, but this one has merit. They were incensed when your grandmother got out of the palace with you."

The hits just keep coming.

Part of me wants to ask about the prophecy—what it is, who it came from, and what it has to do with me—but I'm not ready. Too much has happened in a short time. I haven't stopped reeling from one setback when another one slams into me out of thin air. If the prophecy is all doom and gloom with only a slight chance for a happy ending, I'm not ready to deal with it just yet.

"I can't stop the cloak from lifting. It'll happen whether I want it to or not. There's a warlock working behind the scenes, and when I'm no longer shielded, he'll come for me. Now you're telling me Giselli and Isla will too. I have no idea if I should trust Saban with anything after the last week."

"All I can tell you about that is he stood up to his mother. He put his foot down and said he's not living his life without his soul mate. He vowed to do whatever it takes to win back your trust. They had a rather heated discussion with one shouting over the other, but Giselli ended up stomping out of the room when Saban wouldn't back down.

"I have no idea what will happen when he realizes the throne belongs to you by birthright. But learning you're a mage on top of that? I wouldn't even attempt to venture a guess about that. He loves you, he's miserable without you, and every day you're away only makes it worse. But the quest for the throne has driven many men crazy."

I'm aware…and I'm doing my best not to be counted as one of them.

"When we have more time, I'd love to pick your brain with a million questions about vampires. I wondered why I wasn't able to read your mind when we first met. I'm guessing that's why."

"No, I keep it shielded, but I've found methods of hiding my shields so they seem more natural. I've had run-ins with warlocks and witches myself, especially roaming in the woods at night. I prefer to keep my gifts hidden. As far as that sit-down to talk about my people, your invitation to the Nightside Mountains is open-ended. Our door is always open to you."

Laurelai and I watch after he says goodbye and continues his trek toward the heart of the Veil. Maybe he was telling the truth about his meeting with the mage council, but I'm in no mood to eavesdrop tonight. When the sun disappears and the only light in the forest is from the flora and fauna, I give Laurelai a hug goodnight and head to my tree house to crash until morning.

CHAPTER 23

My manager has already opened the store and is chatting with some of the other salespeople when I arrive at work in the morning. She notices me walking in and flashes a smile that screams conspiracy if I've ever seen one.

"Sara, a very handsome young man came by as soon as we opened this morning and left this envelope for you. Whatever he's asking you to do, my suggestion is you reply with an emphatic yes, then marry him before someone else snatches him away from you." She hands me the envelope, and I immediately know it's from Saban. Instead of putting my name on the outside, it simply reads "Princess."

"Thank you, Cadence. I'll keep your advice in mind." I smile as I continue to the back to clock in. I can't deny I'm simultaneously dying to read the letter and considering shredding it before I even open it, especially after everything I learned last night.

But my curiosity gets the best of me, and I tear it open as if it contains the cure to every disease known to man.

Sara,

This paper may look familiar to you. It's the same one you challenged me to make as good as new again. So that's what I did all night, to the point of obsession and desperation. I tried misting it with water then steaming the wrinkles out of it. I tried pressing it between the pages of the heaviest book I could find in the library. Nothing worked.

I was tempted to tear it into a million tiny pieces and burn it until only ashes remained. Despite my frustration, I couldn't bring myself to actually do that. This piece of paper was the only hope I had left to win back your love.

Then the solution came to me from out of nowhere.

We'd sent this paper through hell and back. It has been crushed, drowned, put through the fire, and had the weight of the world on it...yet, it has endured. Sure, it has a few bumps and bruises on it. But who doesn't? The scars give it character and show its strength. After everything it has endured, it still carries all my love to you as if it's as good as new...

To most anyone else, this paper is a worthless scrap, no longer good for anything more than kindling for a fire. But I don't believe that for a second. It's the only object in the entire realm that can prove to you our love can endure anything. We only have to fight for it—together. Every single day, if that's what it takes.

I'm willing to do that and more. Are you?

When you get off work today, I'll be waiting for you in the park where I last saw you. If you don't show, I'll know your heart is no longer mine, and I'll respect your wishes to stay away.

Saving all my love for you,
Saban

I TURN THE LETTER OVER TO LOOK ON THE BACK, BUT there's nothing there. He made no mention of the argument with his mother or the rift it must have caused them. I know her well enough to say he didn't walk away unscathed. She'd retaliate against him for his defiance by withholding her love and affection. I've witnessed that firsthand already.

His only concern is restoring what was between us.

I have so many concerns, it's getting hard to keep them all straight.

And to keep them to myself.

The secrets are killing me. I want to tell him everything, to talk through what I know, and see his reaction right now. Waiting until we've meshed even more into one seems so unfair to him and me. Any one of my many secrets could be a deal-breaker for our relationship. I don't want to be eyeball-deep in love, only to have it yanked away from me again.

But I have to face the simple fact that I'm already in love way over my head. And a few more weeks with him will make it harder to walk away a second time if he can't accept that I'm a mage.

I fell through a door from another world.

He saved me from Rycan, assuming I was from the orphanage, and I didn't correct him.

He gave me a place to live and work out of the goodness of his heart.

I'm the rightful heir to the throne he so desperately wants.

His parents conspired with a dark warlock to murder mine.

His mom and sister will help kill me when they realize who I am.

Certain members of the realm have heard a prophecy about me.

My nana was taken from my hometown by the people who want me gone, and I now highly suspect his mother.

I've been sneaking off every day to learn more about the illegal magic inside me so I can use it to assert my claim at the right time.

I eavesdropped on his thoughts to be privy to the conversation with his mother.

Vale is a vampire and a wizard.

I've known all of this and didn't tell Saban, even though I know he's my soul mate.

And yet, he's the one begging me to take him back, to forgive him, to give him another chance.

My guilt over everything I'm hiding from him has kept me away from him more than anything he's done. His not choosing me when his mother gave him the ultimatum deeply hurt, no doubt. But what would I do in the same situation?

The minutes of my all-day shift drag by, with me looking at the clock every few seconds. I try to stay busy, continually flitting around the store and helping others with their assigned chores, but time stands still for sheer spite. The note he wrote is burning a hole in my pocket. I'm surprised I haven't worn a hole in the paper by reading it so many times today. When it's finally time for me to leave, I rush through the clocking-out process and down the street to the park.

My feet slow as I approach the entrance. Then when I reach the threshold, I stop, unsure if I should take the next step. Do I resume this relationship without spilling everything I know and trusting him with the entire truth?

Stick to the plan, Saraya. Trust me. You can't tell him secrets that put others in jeopardy.

Even when I can't trust my own rationale, I know I can trust Nana's. She's never steered me wrong before, even when I didn't want to hear what she thought. Especially when she gave me advice that went contrary to what I wanted to do. She's always had my best interests at heart, so I force my feet to move forward.

When I approach the spot where I last saw Saban, my

heart starts thumping against the inside of my chest so hard, I can see my shirt moving. He's sitting on a park bench with his elbows on his knees, staring at the ground between his feet. My heart leaps into my throat. Even if my head still argues against this move, my heart knows what it wants.

I walk straight up to him, stopping when my feet are in his line of sight. He suddenly jerks to sit up straight, and his eyes lift to meet mine. Shock and disbelief are quickly replaced by relief and gratefulness. He jumps to his feet and wraps his arms around my waist, lifting me off the ground with his embrace. My arms slink around his neck, my face fits in the crook of his neck, and I inhale a lungful of his unique scent.

Despite the unspoken words, I feel whole again. Laurelai's insight was unequivocally correct. If I'd tried to have a link this strong removed, I'd walk around with a significant piece of myself missing for the rest of my life.

He turns his head to kiss the side of mine. "I've been dying without you, Sara. Literally dying. I never knew I was capable of loving anyone so fucking much. Now I know I'd rather die than try to live the rest of my life without you by my side. Promise me we'll never separate like that again for any reason."

"I don't want to be without you again either." I can't bring myself to make that promise. Not yet anyway.

"Are you ready to come back home?"

I hesitate to answer because I don't know what to expect from his family. The old adage to keep friends close and enemies closer comes to mind, and I decide that's not a bad strategy. "Are you sure that's a good idea?"

"Having you back where you belong is the only way I'll have it. Anyone who doesn't like it can move out. The palace is *our* home. Everyone else is only a guest there."

I use his phone to contact one of the girls from the Veil, Kate, who helped get me the job and ask her to meet me with my belongings. Her smile is evident in her voice when she assures me it's no problem. She also emphasizes I always have a home there if I ever need to return. I thank her, hoping it doesn't come to that again, but I keep the offer in the back of my mind anyway. Saban and I sit on the bench, chatting about my job and my temporary home with my friends when Kate approaches us with my backpack stuffed with clothes and shoes.

"Don't be a stranger. We still expect to see you every chance you get." She hugs me goodbye, and I thank her again for everything.

Saban waves goodbye to her then turns to me, love shining in his eyes, and throws my pack over his shoulder. "The first thing we're doing is getting you a phone of your own. Not being able to contact or find you for the past week has been a living hell.

"The second thing we're doing is barricading ourselves in the bedroom so we can talk without any interruptions. I don't want you to doubt my love or my loyalty to you, so I'll tell you everything and answer all your questions. After those two steps are finished, we'll do whatever you want. Is that all right with you, princess?"

"Yes, that's all right with me. Let's get it over with now so we don't have it hanging over our heads all night."

With his arm around my shoulders and his lips nearly glued to my head, we stroll down the street to pick out the phone before driving back to the palace in his vehicle. A stray thought occurs to me…I really should learn to drive. Maybe Saban can teach me in a few weeks if everything is still calm.

When we walk into the palace, I half expect a full-scale revolution over my presence. But everyone moves about as usual, barely taking notice of my reappearance. Giselli and Isla emerge from the large dining hall, having just finished supper, and greet me with such fake excitement, I can barely hold my tongue.

"Sara, it's so good to see you again. We've missed you around here." Giselli embraces me but quickly releases me when I don't return the gesture. "This probably isn't the appropriate time or place to say this, but I want to apologize for my part in this fiasco. I didn't fully realize the bond between such resilient soul mates. In all my years, I can't remember another couple who was so perfectly matched for each other. After you left, it was quite evident that Saban couldn't go through with an arranged marriage, so I explained the situation to the other family. They were very gracious about it all, so everything is back to normal now."

"I'm glad to hear it." I'm civil. That's almost more than I can muster at the moment.

"Mom, Sara and I haven't had an opportunity to talk

about all the intimate details of what happened yet. You were right when you said this isn't the appropriate time or place. In the future, I'll be the one who shares information with her so there's no misunderstanding later."

"Whatever you say, son. I'll take my leave now. Good night, you two."

"Good night, Mother."

I don't bother returning the sentiment.

Saban starts walking in the opposite direction, heading toward his wing of the palace, and motions with a slight jerk of his head for me to follow him. When we're behind the closed double doors of his living quarters, I feel as though I can breathe easier. Just being near Giselli and Isla is so much harder now than I could've imagined.

We sit facing each other on the large, overstuffed couch, our knees touching and our fingers linked. Maintaining the physical connection to him helps keep me grounded and clears my cluttered mind. When I'm able to tell him the entire truth, I'll make sure he understands why I couldn't share the details earlier. Anyone who doesn't have the power to shield their mind poses a threat to the entire magical community, across all the kingdoms.

"For the record, I was bringing you up here so we could discuss everything my mom just blurted out in private. I'm not sure where to start now or what to say, but I'll answer any questions you have. Or I'll start from the beginning and share every detail with you. It's completely your call." His earnest expression and open body language show me he's ready to take all the responsibility. I don't need to read his mind to know his intentions.

"I don't want to talk about what happened before. I want to talk about what will happen in the future. If your mom were to do something terrible in the future, as bad as forcing you to marry someone you don't love, how do I know you wouldn't go along with her? I mean, she's your mother. How could you not choose her over me again?"

"You made me realize something about myself during the past week we've been apart. Yes, that is a short time to have this great epiphany, but that's also what makes it so profound. The truth has been staring me straight in the face for years, but I managed to avoid facing it. When you confronted me about her plans, you faced it head on and with no fear. When you were hurt by my actions and had nowhere to live, you packed your things and walked out of here anyway. You do what's right, regardless of how hard it is or what the personal cost to you may be.

"I've never been that strong before, but then, I've never had to be. I was barely able to keep myself from begging you to take me back every single day. When I finally did, you stood firm and refused to back down from what you believed to be right. Your strong convictions put me to shame. That's when I realized I had to make a fundamental change because the man I'd been wasn't the man I wanted to be.

"I also realized I'd been seeking my family's approval my entire life, and I'd always fallen short in their eyes. But I don't need their approval. I don't need their input. I don't need their permission. All I need is you. As long as you're with me, I can conquer the world."

I want to believe him. I also want an ironclad guarantee he won't flip-flop on me again in the future. But his love for me radiates from deep inside him, reaching out and wrapping around me like a warm hug. There's no denying the way our souls instantly recognize each other or the stronghold we can't seem to break free from.

He is my refuge when the storm swirls inside my mind, leaving me lost and confused.

He's the only one who can make me soar to all-new heights or come tumbling down with a terrible crash and burn.

No one else can hurt me the way he can…or love me the way he does.

"I believe everyone should be given a second chance. No one is perfect. There's no way around it—we all have to ask for forgiveness. Everything isn't always so cut-and-dried. Sometimes we hurt the ones we love, even when that's the last thing we'd ever want to do." I reach up and stroke the stubble along his jaw.

The spark of desire in his eyes ignites the flame deep inside me, and we're instantly caught in a raging inferno. It's more than just the days we spent apart. It's an overwhelming need to reestablish the bond that was broken and repair the damage to both of us. Our movements are synchronized without conscious thought. When he reaches for me, I'm already moving into his embrace.

My legs straddle his, and our mouths clash in a frenzied flurry of kisses. The silky-smooth sensation of his tongue gliding across mine sends goose bumps fanning out across the skin on my arms. I'm close to going up in flames from the level of heat building inside my body. Our lips barely separate as we remove our clothes with a hurried tempo.

Feeling bold, I reach between us and grasp him, gently stroking up and down the length of his hardness. During our first time, I let him take the lead since I wasn't sure what he expected. But this time, I'm taking a more active part. He drops his head back against the couch but keeps his hungry eyes fixed on mine. Then he wraps his big hand around mine, squeezes harder, and increases the speed. His hips buck involuntarily underneath me, and he grits his teeth, the muscles in his cheeks jumping from the force.

With his chest still heaving with heavy breathing, he loosens his grip and slows down again. I feel his muscles relax when he brings himself under control again. When he releases his hold on my hand, he slides his hand between my legs. I watch him with rapt attention and hooded eyes, then his finger disappears deep inside me. A needful whimper escapes from my lips at the sudden intrusion. When he adds a second finger, I nearly come undone.

I grip his shoulder. My fingernails dig into his skin as I hold my breath, the wave of heat starting deep in my abdomen and spreading quickly outward through my whole body. Then he presses his thumb against my clit, rubbing in small circles, and waves of pleasure radiate in pulsing beats outward until I scream his name.

"You are so sexy. I love it when you scream my name."

He sits up and pulls me closer to him until my core is aligned directly over him. With a measured pace, I lower myself onto him, letting my body adjust and stretch to take him until he's completely filled me. He grabs my hips and shows me how to move, then my body naturally takes control. The promise between us can never be broken, and we both know it beyond a shadow of a doubt.

The time we spent apart melts away with each passing minute. Our love seals us. Our bodies melding into one completes us and shows us how we should face every problem in the future. Together and as one person, one mind, one accord. This is precisely how I feel when we're together—that we can do anything we set our minds and hearts to do.

I know we can overcome any obstacle put in front of us because I love him with all I have. With all of me. This is a bond we'll never break. Without realizing what I'm doing, I start pouring out the thoughts and feelings I've kept bottled up for so long to him. With him deep inside me, giving me love in ways I've never experienced, the dam inside me overflows with the sincerest declarations I've wanted him to hear but was afraid to say or even to admit to myself.

I listed all the things about him I love and stressed how he completes the part of me that's been missing my entire life.

Then I confessed how much I need him and that I can't handle everything on my own. Maybe I'm not as strong as I once thought I was. Perhaps I need his strength to carry me through the hard times.

I finished my revelation with the fact that I will never let him go again. I can't do it, because being without him made me a different person, one I didn't like. One I don't want to be. He and I bring out the best in each other, and the only way to grow is to understand myself better.

The fact is, I can live without him, but I don't want to. Why put us through the misery when we're so perfectly matched?

Face-to-face and our eyes locked in sensory overload, we tumble over the edge of bliss together.

He wraps his arms around me, and I lay my head on his shoulder. We're both breathing as though we sprinted through an entire marathon. But after the intimacy we just shared, I wouldn't have it any other way.

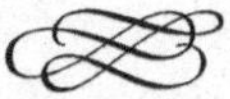

CHAPTER 24

Saban and I spent my first week back in the palace separated from his family for the most part. Every night, our bond grew tighter with our intimate moments. The way he worshiped every inch of my body hours at a time left me exhausted and elated, fully satiated yet longing for more, and deeper in love with him than the previous night. We fell asleep wrapped securely in each other's arms and woke each morning in the same position. He was desperate to fully restore our relationship, and I was anxious to put my fears to rest.

I managed to get in a little one-on-one time with Addi during the day when Saban was at work, even though my official position in the castle has changed. I opted to start my new role after the big wedding, while Isla and Gerard are off somewhere on their honeymoon, so I'll only have one of the Strydor women around to stab me in the back.

"Are you ready for the big day?" Addi grins, only a hint of facetiousness in her tone.

"You know, I actually am ready for it. I wish Giselli were getting married too so she'd leave on a whirlwind honeymoon to anywhere else in the cosmos. When the universe pairs two people, why can't it also make the family a match? His mom and sister are pains in my ass."

Addi laughs, but she knows what I'm saying is valid after the betrothal fiasco. "Well, I can tell you there was almost a war here after you left. Saban kind of lost his mind without you. Giselli pressured him to go meet the other woman, see how he felt about her after he'd seen her, but he wouldn't. They got into such a heated argument over it, he told his mother to pack her shit and leave. When she realized he was deadly serious, she changed her tune. She didn't want to lose her place here."

That insight makes me feel better about believing he'll choose me over his mother when the time comes. "Addi, I feel so bad about keeping all these secrets from him. I wish I could tell him every single detail about who and what I am. I'm afraid when it's finally time to share it with him, he'll be so mad at me, he'll never want to see me again."

"This has been bothering you for a while, hasn't it? I can tell because you don't usually talk about anything too personal when it comes to him. You know I can't tell the future, but you do know someone who has a glimpse into it." Addi raises her brows and gives me a sly sideways glance.

"Talia."

She nods. "But you should know it's not as if she can see every detail of what's to come. Merpeople get visions, but sometimes they only get feelings. They sense if something good or bad is coming. She won't sit down with a crystal ball and give you a play-by-play of what's going to happen."

Her phrasing surprises me. "You've been to the other world."

Panic replaces her usually calm demeanor, registering on her face before she can turn away from me. From her rigid stance, I can tell she's mentally kicking herself. With a resigned sigh, she nods her head. "Yes, I've spent time in the other world. Sometimes we need a break from everything in this realm, so we venture into the other world for a while. We have limited powers there, so most of us don't stay for long. As I'd told you before, that's how a lot of the tall tales and urban legends about witches, wizards, mermaids, and vampires got started."

"How do I get back there?"

She draws her eyebrows down and narrows her eyes at me before answering. "It's not exactly the best time for you to leave the realm right now. But it's not the right time of year for the portals to open anyway. It happens every sixteen weeks, so the next one isn't due for another four weeks."

"Wait…the last one was three months ago?"

"Yes, give or take a couple of days. Why?"

"Then how did I get here two and a half months ago if it wasn't time for the portal to open?"

"I don't know, Sara. That's a good question for you to ask Ginevra on your way back from Elderwater Basin. There's no way you're not going there to have a talk with Talia."

"I'm going there right now, as a matter of fact. Is there a way to get there that doesn't involve driving? I have no idea how to operate the vehicles here."

"Come on, I'll take you. With all the people here preparing the palace for the wedding, no one will notice I'm gone for a few hours."

Addi and I escape out the side door and drive away in her vehicle. She's right about the flurry of activities happening around the palace today. Tomorrow is Isla and Gerard's wedding, so I have to be back in time to dress for the rehearsal dinner tonight.

I'm lucky I arrived here when I did. The wedding party is already set, and there's no sense in adding me as an additional bridesmaid. Giselli, in a wholly disingenuous attempt to make me feel part of the family, suggested Isla should ask me to be one of the bridesmaids since I'm linked to Saban now. I quickly hit the brakes on that terrible idea, and Isla didn't argue.

Our chat on the drive to find Talia covers a broad range of topics from advice on leveling up my power to questions about how finding a real soul mate feels. A common thread between the two worlds can be summed up by one universal question. *How did you know he was the one?"* Love baffles everyone, without regard to place or time.

When we arrive at Elderwater Basin, I can't tear my eyes off the beautiful scenery all around me. The road dead-ends in front of an enormous waterfall with tropical foliage hanging off the rock wall behind it. The mountainside stretches for miles, with water cascading down the curves of the jagged rocks and collecting in the vast river below, creating a mammoth natural basin. The white sand beaches stretch along the riverside as far as the eye can see. On top of the waterfall, sitting astride the river, is an enormous castle adorned with statues of every sea creature imaginable, and a few I question because they're new to me. Trees dot the landscape on either side of the castle where it reaches the solid ground.

"How do we get up there?" I crane my neck and point toward the castle.

"We don't, not without the help of the merpeople. Most are leery of humans, so very few of us have seen the inside of that palace. I've heard stories of how beautiful it is inside. They say it outshines every other palace in the realm."

I remember when Rio offered his help, he said to step into the water and call his name. If that works with all merpeople, then Talia should hear me calling her name too. "Here goes nothing."

After I slip off my shoes, I wade into the clear water. "Talia, this is Sara. Can you hear me? Please, I need your help."

After several minutes, small ripples in the water drift toward me before growing larger and larger. Then Talia rises up out of the water in front of me with a dazzling smile covering her face. She seems genuinely glad to see me again.

"Hi, Sara. I'm surprised to see you here, but I'm glad you came. What can I do for you?" Her scales flitter and disappear, leaving regular legs instead and clothing matching the hues of her fin.

"I have questions about Saban, if you don't mind. I've been told you can see the future, and I have so many doubts about what I should and shouldn't do."

"Both of you can come up to the palace with me so we can talk in private. I'm happy to share what I know."

Talia walks to the dry land and motions for us to follow her down a narrow, winding path hidden by the fronds of the thick trees. At the end of the trail is an opening in the rock wall, nearly invisible to anyone who doesn't know it's there, that leads into a great room directly behind the waterfall.

A brook filled with brightly colored fish flows through the middle of the room, disappearing into the great mountain at the far wall. Crystal chandeliers hang from the ceiling on long lines, lighting the room with tiny rainbows from the sparkle of the clear prisms. The vaulted ceiling and all four walls are decorated with ornate gold trim that frames fresco paintings.

One painting is of the mighty Poseidon and his wife, Amphitrite. One arm holds her close, and the other hand holds his infamous trident. The next work of art is a detailed depiction of the lost city of Atlantis. Still another is of Triton, the son of Poseidon and Amphitrite, shown as a merman, with the upper body of a man and tail of a fish. Sometimes the truth is absolutely stranger than fiction.

I turn in circles as we walk through the grand hall, trying to commit every detail to memory since I may never come this way again. She waves her hand over a panel on the wall, and a door slides open. We step into an all-glass elevator, and I gasp loudly when my eyes land on the sight in front of us.

I expected the interior of the mountain to be solid rock, but I couldn't have been more wrong. From the mountain floor to its very peak, it's filled with clear water. Mermen and mermaids move with fluid grace among the various buildings. An entire underwater city is hidden inside the rock-lined face.

"This is amazing, Talia. Are those buildings apartments?"

"Some are, yes. Others are the same types of buildings you'd find in any other city. This is considered a suburb, of course. The main city is farther downstream and much farther under the surface. This area was built for the palace staff so they can have closer conveniences like those who work in the city do."

When the elevator stops at the top, we step into a ballroom bathed in deep blue, bright gold, and various hues of dark red. The furniture is arranged to create multiple seating areas throughout the expansive space.

At the far end of the room are two giant thrones positioned on an elevated platform. Matching curtains are draped on each side, completing the air of royalty as intended.

The three of us sit together in one of the more comfortable spaces. Servants descend on us immediately, leaving glasses, a tall pitcher of liquid libations, and a platter of snacks. Before they go, we each have a drink and a small plate of food placed in front of us. It's not until this moment that I realize the most obvious explanation.

Talia is part of the Elderwater Basin royal family.

That's how she knows Saban.

"What can I help you with, Sara?" Talia lifts her glass to her lips and takes a sip, but she doesn't move her eyes away from me.

"That day we met, you mentioned all was not as it seems with him, but you didn't have time to elaborate. What did you mean by that statement, exactly? Should I be afraid of him?"

She shakes her head and puts her drink back on the table. "I didn't get that impression from him. He's actually very much in love with you. But there's another part of him that's hidden behind a shroud. I can't tell if he did it himself, but it's concerning because it's deliberate. Usually when someone hides a specific part of themselves, it's for a very dark purpose."

"Does that mean he's a warlock?"

"No, he's definitely not magical. There's a mystery to him I haven't been able to solve yet. His deep feelings for you are a direct contradiction to everything that makes sense."

"Can you see my future? Can you tell me what happens?" I'm almost afraid to ask, but I'll kick myself later if I don't do it now.

"I have seen part of your future—several times—but it changes every time I have a vision. Your choices today directly influence and change what will happen tomorrow. For that reason, I don't share what I see unless it remains constant because you have to do what's right for you at the moment."

To say I'm disappointed in her reply is an understatement, but I understand her reasoning. She doesn't want to be the reason why I take one course over another. If she puts the idea in my head something specific will happen, I'm more likely to set myself up for exactly that and nothing more.

"Do you see me spending my life with Saban? Is he my true soul mate?"

"Yes, he is your true soul mate. There's no denying or changing that, even though my brother Rio is very taken with you. He told me he offered to make you forget Saban so he could make you fall for him instead." She shakes her head with a chuckle. "He would try his best to do just that, too."

"Yes, and as tempting as his offer was, I just couldn't go through with it. Also, he didn't mention he was your brother when he introduced himself."

"That's definitely Rio for you. As far as not removing

the bond, you made a wise decision. It's for the best, trust me. Your parents didn't want to leave you the way they did. They didn't choose it. You and Saban will have problems, like every other couple in the world. Just remember, you have to look past the surface, into his depths, and make decisions based on what you see there." Her kind smile reassures me, and I feel more at peace, trusting that Saban won't abandon me.

"Thank you, Talia. I'm sorry we barged in on you like this, but I appreciate your seeing us."

She shows us out of the palace and hugs both of us goodbye before she disappears below the water again.

"Did you get anything out of her advice that I missed?" Addi and I are back in the car, driving toward Easthaven Crest. I'm dissecting every word of the conversation with Talia.

"No, I didn't. Sorry. It sounded very specific to me. Basically, she said to try to understand why he is the way he is and why he does the things he does. That's true of anyone, though, isn't it?"

"Yes, it is. I was hoping I'd missed something more profound."

We make it back with plenty of time to spare before the rehearsal dinner, but I still shower and slip on an appropriate shell dress for the occasion. Thankfully, tonight is more low-key than tomorrow will be. With only the immediate family and the wedding party in attendance, the dinner is more intimate than I expected.

"You look beautiful tonight." Saban lifts my hand to his

lips and places soft kisses on the back of it.

"Thank you. You look very handsome yourself."

When the domes are lifted from our plates, I realize how famished I am from not eating all day. Addi and I were so busy, I didn't take time to grab anything. The first bite is delicious, and I moan in appreciation. Maybe a little too loudly. When I look around to see if anyone noticed my gaffe, the lurid expression in Gerard's eyes is definite confirmation. After a pointed glare, I return to my meal and ignore him for the rest of the evening.

If Saban sensed anything out of the ordinary with me and my moods, he never mentioned it. After the festivities wound down and all the guests left, he and I said our goodnights and retreated to our wing of the palace. The best feature it has is it's so far away from everyone else. It's almost as if we have our own home inside the palace, with all the amenities we could possibly need at our disposal.

He helped me undress and carried me to our bed in his strong arms. He never fails to show exactly how much I'm loved and appreciated, often rejecting my attempts to do the same. He claims he'd rather be the giver than the receiver, though I'm working on changing that mindset. It's better to give and receive as far as I'm concerned. But after the unpleasantness Gerard caused, I'm relieved to know our bedtime routine is the same as it has been every other night—falling asleep in each other's arms after we've spent every ounce of energy and we're drained of the ability to move.

CHAPTER 25

"I see you and Saban are back together again. You know, he was absolutely miserable without you. He was in such a bad mood, we almost couldn't stand to be around him. But all that changed the moment you came back here with him." Gerard leans against the doorframe, blocking the passage to the court-yard outside.

I feel trapped, but I'll never let him know. I get the sense he wants to knock me off-kilter with his faux concern about Saban's well-being. Isla must be the one who put him up to playing these stupid little mind games. She doesn't have the backbone to do it herself, but she is just devious enough to coerce her fiancé into doing it on her behalf.

Saban is busy with his family, getting dressed for the wedding and preparing to receive most of the kingdom in the spacious courtyard. I have to admit, the area is the perfect setting for a wedding. The collection of colorful flowers with their large blooms and aromatic fragrance is draped over the entire pergola. Long cascades overflow from all sides, creating curtains of living decorations. The light gold runner in the center aisle accentuates the royal red chairs on either side.

"I'm glad he's happy again." I keep my response short and to the point.

"As close as you two are, my guess is you'll be walking down the aisle before we know it. Have you talked about setting a date yet?"

I cut my eyes over at him with a glare, not trying to hide the fact that I don't want to talk to him. But he takes my disinterest as a challenge instead of accepting the hint. He also seems to have forgotten all his guests will begin arriving in about thirty minutes, so he really should go find his place to greet them.

"No, we haven't. It's still too soon for that."

"You know, I find that very interesting and telling. If you were certain he was your mate, I don't think you'd feel like that. I think, Sara, you'd be much more adamant about validating your relationship to the entire kingdom. People will start to question why you're hesitant to publicly claim him as yours." He pushes off the doorframe, completely blocking the passage now, and his eyes become predatory.

"That's an interesting theory, Gerard. But allow me to present an alternative one. First of all, I don't doubt my relationship with Saban in the least. I know exactly what I feel for him and what he feels for me. Secondly, I don't give a shit what anyone else thinks because no one else is in this relationship with us. If we want to wait a hundred years to get married, that's what we'll do. We're in this for us, not to appease anyone else. And lastly, the very fact that we're together is a public declaration of my claim on him. I don't feel the need to piss on his leg to mark my territory—and, in case you're wondering, he doesn't either."

"It's no wonder you have him caught in your spell. Your fiery side is mesmerizing. I have a proposition for you, Sara. Given the circumstances today, I admit it's highly inappropriate, but this feels like a now-or-never scenario."

I slowly arch one eyebrow as disgust fills me to my very core. He is not about to suggest what I think. A quick probe of his mind reveals nothing, which immediately puts me on guard. I've shaken hands with him before, but there was no recognition of a kindred magical spirit. For his mind to be blank to me now, he'd have to be…

"You and I should run away together. We're a much better fit than you and Saban or Isla and I are. We'll be happy, Sara. I'll take so much better care of you than he could, in every way imaginable. My family is very well-off, and I'm very well-endowed myself, as per my own financial assets." He smirks, thinking he's cute. He's not. "What do you say to that?"

"What do I say? I say there's absolutely no way that will ever happen. Even if I weren't in love with Saban, which I am, you would never be my choice for a mate. Let's forgo the entire discussion of all the other reasons why I'm not attracted to you and focus on the one at hand.

"Any man who would dump the woman he claims to love, *on their wedding day*, and proposition someone he barely knows, who happens to be in love with his soon-to-be brother-in-law, is not appealing at all. No, Gerard, you're not the kind of man I'd ever be interested in."

He's left speechless, and I turn on my heel to get as far away from him as I can. Saban is busy, but I can handle Gerard myself. I'm trying to be respectful and not cause a scene on their big day. As much as I'd love to reveal him for the type of man he really is, Isla and Giselli wouldn't believe my story. Not when it comes to his word against mine. But I have no doubt Saban would defend me, and that would only cause more division in his family.

Deep in my own thoughts, I don't hear Gerard come up behind me. Though the staff is buzzing about all around us, he stops way too close for comfort. He intentionally brushes the shell of my ear with his lips when he murmurs his ominous warning.

"Mark my words, my beauty. You will regret that decision one day soon."

When I turn to confront him, his long strides have already carried him too far away for me to respond privately. My temper gets the best of me, and every muscle in my body constricts as I ready myself to yell my reply across the large room.

Hold your tongue, Saraya. Don't do it yet. Your time will come.

I know she's right, as usual. But damn, it would feel so good to really give him a piece of my mind and get it all off my chest. Addi walks up just in time to save me from ignoring Nana's advice. One look at my face and she knows something is wrong. While we walk, I quietly explain the entire conversation to her, careful not to let the household staff overhear any part of it. I have no doubt the palace gossip already runs rampant about me. This juicy little tidbit would cause a fervor.

"He's so disgusting. I've heard he's propositioned several of the maids in the palace. They've all been told to keep their mouths shut about it so they don't upset darling Isla. If I were her, I'd want to know what he was doing so I could kick him out on his ass."

"Who is his family? He said they're rich and implied they're influential. I assume that's what he meant by I'd regret it one day." I stop walking when a menacing thought pops into my head. "Addi, do you think he'd try to use his family to take over the throne?"

"Hmm, I'm not sure about that. His family is very wealthy and holds a lot of clout in Easthaven Crest. They have a monopoly on our clean energy sources, so almost everyone in the realm is forced to go through them to buy it. If that's what he was after, why wouldn't he have already used his family to persuade the other kings? Why wait until now?"

Addi is as perplexed as I am, but I'm convinced my

theory is sound. There's a reason why he hasn't made a move yet. I mean, he's marrying into the family that's pushing their son to seek the throne for himself.

"Addi…he's waiting for me—the heir. If he'd made his move too soon, he would've had to abdicate his title if I came back for it. But my birthday is coming up quickly. If I don't assert my claim soon after, what happens?"

"It's open to whomever the other kings vote in." Her face looks a little paler now.

"And what do you think he'd do to his opponent after the vote?"

"I think any opposition would meet a suspicious and untimely death, but there wouldn't be any proof to link him to it." Addi chews on her thumbnail, looking for any holes in my theory. "Why would he marry Isla, though? If his parents can help get him on the throne, why would he need her?"

"My guess is she's his Plan B. If he couldn't get all the votes, who's next in line if something happens to Saban?"

"Gerard and Isla would be."

"You know, I could be way off base here, making up conspiracy theories where they don't exist. But something is off with him, besides the obvious." Now I regret not asking Talia who her vote would've gone to if she had to choose. I wonder if Gerard's family has already been promoting him to the other kingdoms.

"Excuse me, ma'am. The guests are starting to arrive, and your presence has been requested at the main door." One of the palace staff approaches cautiously, not wanting to interrupt our conversation but also needing to deliver an urgent message.

"Thank you. I'm on my way."

Saban had mentioned he wanted me at his side to help greet the kingdom residents as they arrived. He didn't say it in so many words, but I can read between the lines. If we welcome them into the palace together, our soul mate confirmation is implied without a formal announcement.

When I reach the entryway, my breath catches in my chest from how dashing and debonair he looks in his dress uniform. Every able-bodied male in the kingdom is required to serve two years in the royal armed forces in their youth. Saban extended his stint and continued in their version of the reserves. While I don't pretend to understand their rank structure, I've learned one vital piece of information.

I am a complete sucker for a man in uniform.

As if he feels me watching him, he turns his head directly toward me. The expression on my face must be a dead giveaway of my thoughts because his steel-gray eyes darken to almost charcoal. The air crackles with electricity as the current passes between us.

"This must be her now." The elderly man in the doorway is apparently amused with how we're lost in each other. His skin is weathered from years in the sun. His hands are wrinkled and worn, but the strength in his stature is still apparent. He worked hard in his younger days but has retained much of that vigor in his older years.

Saban clears his throat and regains his composure. "It is, indeed. Princess, come meet a longtime friend of the family."

I close the few feet between us and extend my hand to introduce myself. "Hello, I'm Sara."

When he takes my hand, the zing of magic surprises me, and I quickly school my features. "Hi, Sara. I'm Edel. It's nice to meet you."

"Nice to meet you too, Edel. It's a beautiful day for a wedding, isn't it?" Small talk is still not my forte.

"It certainly is. Seems there may be another wedding in the near future, if the way Saban looks at you is any indication."

"If I had any say in it at all, we'd already be married, Edel." Saban laughs good-naturedly, knowing I'm not quite ready for that step just yet. "Trust me, everyone will know when Sara says it's time."

"You're a smart man, Saban. Focus on making her happy, and you'll never go wrong. Take it from me, son. My wife and I were married more than two hundred years before I lost her. She was the only one for me, and I made every day with her count."

Edel still has my hand enclosed in both of his throughout the entire exchange. Had he been anyone else, I would've extracted mine long ago. But something about him won't let me. When I crack the armor in my shields, his thoughts flow to me, and I immediately fight against the tears stinging the backs of my eyes.

I worked for your parents when they were alive, Saraya.

Don't worry, Your Majesty. Your cloak is still intact, but I'd know your face anywhere. You spent a lot of time in the garden with my wife and me when you were a little thing. There's no mistaking your eyes, though. You have the same eye color as your mother.

Edel turns his gaze back to mine, his love for me shining brightly in his eyes. The slight nod of his head is a silent acknowledgment of the emotions welling up inside me.

"I still miss her, so I know you do, too. If there's anything I can ever do for you, all you have to do is say the word." Saban's offer warms my heart. It's refreshing to see compassion extended to others.

You were our gardener. Your wife's name was Fern, and you teased her about her name because she loved plants and flowers so much.

"Yes, my Fern was a wonderful woman. There will never be another one like her, and there will never be another one for me. But I have a feeling you already know exactly what I mean, Saban." Edel acknowledges my memory of them with his response to Saban, keeping our mutual secrets hidden.

"You are correct, sir. Sara owns me, heart and soul, and I'm not too proud to shout it from the mountaintops."

Edel releases my hand and moves through the already crowded vestibule toward the courtyard. I can't help but watch him walk away and wonder who else may have recognized me by my eye color but didn't say anything. With each additional guest and introduction, the question remains in the back of my mind. Many are older and could've known my parents.

They're naturally curious about me because I appeared on the scene seemingly from nowhere. The innocuous questions they ask about me aren't so harmless if they're able to put the pieces together the way Edel did. I'm dying to ask Ginevra how he saw through the cloak, but I can't take the chance of opening my shields with so many strangers here.

The staff begins ushering people through the palace and out the high archways leading to the courtyard. Hordes of people scurry to their seats, vying for the best views of the bride and groom. I take my place on the front row beside Giselli, not by choice but by assignment from the wedding planner since I'm "practically family."

When the music starts, everyone turns to look at the bridesmaids entering the courtyard, but I don't. I feel the weight of Gerard's eyes boring straight through me. One glance in his direction confirms my sense. His lips curl into a devious grin, and it's cold enough to chill my bones. The fighter in me flexes her muscles, and I see his smile and raise the stakes with an intentionally malevolent grin. His smile immediately falters, confusion taking its place.

If he thinks I'll just roll over and let him walk all over us, he's sadly mistaken. Any plans he has to harm Saban will be uncovered, and I'll expose him for the snake he is. In the meantime, I'll cover Saban with a protective spell and shield him with my magic from whatever Gerard is planning.

On cue, I feel the very second Saban steps into the area, pulling my attention away from Gerard. With Sagran gone, Isla asked Saban to walk her down the aisle. Being the thoughtful big brother, he couldn't deny her request. He stands tall and proud, his confident demeanor radiating from his mannerisms with his every step. I wish I could say the bride is radiant and only has eyes for the man waiting at the end of the aisle for her, but I can't tear my eyes away from Saban long enough to even glance at her. Not that I want to anyway.

After Saban gives her to Gerard, his ceremony duties are complete, and he moves to sit beside me. "I'm not pressuring you, but I want you to know that we'll have whatever kind of wedding you want. Big or small. Hell, I'll even run away with you and get married on horseback in the middle of the forest. As long as you're the bride and I'm the groom, the other details are irrelevant to me."

"I'll keep that in mind. Don't act all surprised if I choose something completely off the wall, though."

"I won't say one damn word about it, princess." His smile is contagious, and I forget about Gerard because I'm completely lost in Saban.

The reception is exactly as I expected—typical and boring. But while all the attention is on the bride and groom, the cutting of the cake, and the pictures with the wedding party, I'm able to work my way back to Edel. Since I can't ask Ginevra right now, maybe he can help me understand.

"I had a feeling you'd be back to see me." His eyes

sparkle with a hint of mischief. "You always were a curious one. What's on your mind?"

"I was told the cloak kept me hidden so no one would recognize me, but you did. How is that? That makes me question if others have too but didn't say anything."

"Most of the people who knew your mother are long gone, killed during the magic purge. Wren learned from a young age how to change her eye color so her distinctive feature wasn't so prominent. She only let her guard down when she was around other mages, so the humans never would've known the true shade. But to answer your question about the cloak, I recognized you because I knew you long before the spell was cast."

"What about the people who grabbed me and the others who stormed the castle? Wouldn't they know me now?"

"No, they may have seen you before, but they didn't know you, spend time with you. They also weren't magical beings. There's a difference, especially where magic is concerned."

"That makes me feel better."

Edel and I walk around to mingle with the other guests while Saban is still busy with his family. Edel introduces me to so many people, it's getting harder to keep their names straight. There's representation from every different kingdom present, making me think this ceremony is more of a political rally than a joyous occasion.

Then I see him. Long, blond hair that's straight as a board. Tall and muscular build with an inherent air of danger surrounding him. Sky-blue eyes that convey his every emotion. And pointy ears. His gaze swings in my direction, and our eyes lock. He instantly recognizes me and excuses himself from the ongoing conversation.

"We meet again." He stands a full head and shoulders taller than me. He is an intimidating figure, but at least this time, he's not hell-bent on killing me. "Allow me to introduce myself properly this time. I'm Rycan Zyldan, and it's a pleasure to meet you, Sara."

I nod, keeping my expression neutral. "It's nice to meet you too, Rycan. What brings you to this event—friend of the bride or the groom?"

"Neither. My father is the king of Elen Sevin and insisted I attend to help foster goodwill between the kingdoms. Perhaps my overreaction to your being on our land wasn't so helpful in promoting an alliance with the humans. I should apologize for my behavior that day."

I hold my tongue and don't point out that he, in fact, should apologize, but he still hasn't. Saying he recognizes the need for it seems to be as much as he's capable of doing. "I should apologize for accidentally wandering onto your land."

But I don't.

Realization flashes across his face and a smile attempts to break loose, but he regains his passive expression. "I've actually heard a lot about you since that day. My father speaks of you often, and that is completely unlike him. Do you have any idea why he would do that?"

"How would I know? Maybe you should ask him

directly."

He chuckles, but it's not a genuine laugh. There are secrets behind it—information he has that I don't. "If you knew my father, you wouldn't suggest that so lightly. He has less tolerance than I do."

"Well, that is saying something, then, isn't it?" I smile to let him know I'm joking and all is forgiven.

That elicits an actual laugh from him. "Yes, I suppose you're right. It's been a pleasure talking with you, Sara, but it's time for me to go. If you happen to stroll across the border onto elvish lands again, I promise not to hunt you down like an animal and try to kill you."

"I think that's the nicest thing you've ever said to me, Rycan."

I extend my hand to shake his before he leaves. He hesitates just long enough for me to know he doesn't typically touch humans, but he makes an exception for me. When our skin makes contact, we both feel the usual magical reaction, then it turns into something more entirely. In an instant, I'm able to penetrate the shields covering his thoughts, and he can access mine as well.

His eyes grow wide and his lips part before he jerks his hand away from mine. "You're half elf. How can this be?" His whisper is barely audible, but the thoughts swirling in his mind are screaming loudly. "Sara...Saraya. Now it all makes perfect sense. You know where to find me when you need my help—and you *will* need it. Those who seek power can't get enough of it. But you have our support. We never turn our backs on one of our own."

CHAPTER 26

Now that Isla and Gerard have been gone for a few days, life in the palace has returned to normal. I never realized how much unnecessary stress and strife they added to the atmosphere until they were completely out of it long enough to allow the rest of us to breathe freely. Even though there's plenty of space and places to be alone, I keep thinking about the cottage beside the lake and how appealing it is.

Today is my first meeting with the representatives from each kingdom. We agreed to meet here in Easthaven Castle for this round, then set up a schedule that includes visiting each nation to make it fair for all. While I'm looking forward to getting heavily involved in the push for mage rights, I'm also planning a private getaway for Saban and me. I haven't told him about Gerard's proposition yet, but I will soon. I've thought about it, and I would want to know if I were in his shoes.

The conference room is already full of delegates when I arrive a few minutes early. I greet each person individually, shaking hands for dual purposes, before taking my seat, though I already know almost all of the attendees. Princess Talia and Prince Rio represent Elderwater Basin, and both are magic-born. Prince Rycan is here for Elen Sevin, and obviously, he has elfish magic in him. Prince Vale volunteered for the vampires and dragons, though he said Fadryth sends her love. I already know he's a wizard. Kobi officially represents the fae, but I know she's also been delegated to speak for the mages who are too afraid of repercussions to attend on their own.

That leaves the one alpha male brooding in the corner. His keen eyes track each person in the room, suspicious of everyone and trusting of no outsiders. He's the only one with unknown magical abilities.

"Hi, I'm Sara. You must be Kenyon." I extend my hand, intent to learn whether the zing of kindred magic will spark. He lowers his eyes, looks at it with a half-snarled lip, and raises his gaze back to mine without accepting my gesture. "All right, then. You can have a seat at the table and make yourself at home."

I turn to walk to my seat when he grabs me from behind, wrapping his thick arm around my neck. A low voltage of electricity tickles my skin, and I instantly know he's attempted to cloak his powers. Everyone at the table jumps to their feet, ready to defend me, but I motion for them to sit.

"Never turn your back on anyone you're not one-hundred-percent certain doesn't mean you harm." His words have a distinctive growl to them. His voice is deep and masculine, leaving no room for discussion about who's really in charge.

"That's good advice. Thanks for the tip. Can I give you one now?"

His chuckle is dark and ominous. "Sure, little girl. If you think you can impart your vast wisdom to me, I'm all ears."

With the white energy already gathered inside me, I conjure a rope made of pure silver then command the light to tie him to his chair with it. His grip on me slips away easily when the light instantly deposits him in the chair at the end of the table and secures him with the silver rope.

I take my seat at the head of the table, directly across from Kenyon, and smile through the daggers he's hurtling at me with his eyes. "Never assume it's always the damsel who needs saving from the big bad wolf."

That earns me a genuine grin, and he visibly relaxes. "Okay, that was a good one. You win this round. I'm a big enough man to admit when someone gets the best of me."

With that, I drop the rope, and the rest of the table releases a sigh of relief. Kenyan puts his elbows on the table and directs his attention to me as I officially kick off the meeting. A few minutes with a wolf shifter revealed so much more about their character than any book I've found on their culture. He wanted to know the person he put his trust in could hold her own. When I proved my ability to him, I earned his loyalty and his faith, at least initially.

Now that all our cards are laid out on the table for the others to see, we're in a better position to get work done. Our discussions about mage rights are long but thorough. Though we're passionate about our cause, we try to understand and anticipate the opposition we'll encounter. We have a frank and respectful conversation about when and where magic could and should be allowed, even though we don't all agree with the suggestions. At the end of our first session, I believe we've made significant strides toward our overall objective of having a proposal ready to submit to the leaders.

Nothing will be implemented before my birthday. Knowing mages are still hidden at least until then gives me some comfort. We leave the meeting with a renewed sense of hope and a newfound set of friends. Even Kenyan thanked me for hosting the first meeting and said he looked forward to the next one.

"How was your day?" Saban asks when he walks into our wing.

"It was great. How was yours?"

"My day is great now." He wraps his arms around my waist and presses his lips to mine. "Everything before this moment was torture."

"I have an idea, if you're up for a little adventure."

"With you? Always. What's your idea?"

"Let's go back to the cottage for a few days. Just you, me, and the lake. Oh, and Fadryth, if she shows up. We can leave any other canoes you have behind the cottage and just swim this time. No more falling out and hitting your head."

"Hey, I only fell out because your pet dragon caused a tidal wave." He chuckles, but I can see the wheels turning in his mind. "That actually sounds like a little slice of heaven to me. Are you okay with leaving first thing in the morning?"

"Yes, I am more than okay with that. I'll pack our clothes tonight so we're ready to leave when we wake up. I'm so excited."

"We won't need too many clothes. Just enough to get us there and back. We won't wear any while we're there. I plan to keep you naked the entire time." He waggles his eyebrows suggestively. We laugh together over it, but I have zero objections to his request.

When the sun rises the next morning, Saban and I climb on the horse and fly to the secluded spot in the forest. The lake glistens in the early morning sun. Dewdrops still cover the grass surrounding the cottage. The silence is welcoming and serene, allowing us to drop our guard for the first time in weeks. We put down our backpacks inside and immediately set out for a hike around the lake.

"Look at the water. It's so clear and still, it's almost invisible." I kick off my shoes and wade into the shallow water, admiring the red and green pebbles that line the bottom. "Come on in. The water's fine."

Without hesitation, he takes off his shoes and joins me.

He inhales a deep breath of fresh air and closes his eyes. I watch the stress leave his face, and contentment takes its place. When he opens his eyes, he catches me during my obvious examination.

"What's on your mind, princess?"

"I'm thinking about how much happier you look here than in the palace."

"Well, this is my happy place, after all. Even more so now that you share it with me. It's the only place I feel like I can be myself and not have to put on a show for anyone else."

"What kind of show?"

"The political kind. When I always have to be 'on.' Say the right thing using the most impactful words, do the right thing, make the best decision. Every single time. No one knows how hard it is when half of the kingdom is thrilled with your choice, while the other half wants to skewer and roast your balls for it. There's no way to please everyone, but they all expect to be ecstatic. This job is exhausting and invigorating at the same time."

"You'll never be able to make everyone happy. Some people prefer to be miserable and spread their misery around like an incurable virus. All you can do is let your conscience help you make the best decision. If you were on the receiving end, would you be able to live with what was passed down to you? Will your decision cause unnecessary harm to anyone? Answer those questions, and you'll never go wrong."

"You excel at putting things into perspective for me. I think I'll keep you around a while longer."

"Oh yeah? How long is a while?"

"Only forever."

"As long as we're not talking forever and a day, I think I can handle it. That extra day would push me right over the edge, though."

"You think you're funny, don't you?" He's smiling, but his spirit energy changes from white to light red. I know he's not mad, but… "Don't you dare!"

My scream doesn't faze him in the least. He lunges toward me, snatches me up in his arms, and does a full-body flop into the deeper water. When we emerge, I'm sputtering and cursing, while he laughs ever so casually. As if he doesn't have a care in the world. His spirit feels as light as a feather floating on the wind. This place is his home, where his heart is, and he can be somewhat of a kid again. It brings out the best in him.

Since we're already wet from head to toe, we lay our clothes out on a rock to dry while we enjoy the freedom to skinny-dip. The water gliding across my bare body feels so good and is a natural aphrodisiac, as is the man swimming with me. Somehow, we manage to refrain from touching each other to dive down to the statues Saban hid in the lake.

It breaks my heart knowing I can't tell him he's the first person to show me a likeness of my parents. Obviously, Nana wasn't able to bring any pictures with her when she fled for our lives. She described them to me, from the angles of their faces, the slant of their noses, and the shape of their eyes, but my mental picture was always fuzzy. Even the memories I retrieved after the magical block was removed didn't give me full clarity for their faces.

Now, I have a detailed marble carving to help bring the rest of their features to life. I simply have to transpose the shade of their skin, the hue of their hair, and the tint of their eyes onto the statue, and I can see my parents in living color. This small favor means so much to me, and I hurt so badly, not being able to share this with the love of my life.

When we come up for air, I wrap my arms around his neck and my legs around his waist before placing kisses all over his face. I'm so grateful for him, and this is the only way I know to express my gratitude at the moment. He slides his hands under my bottom, holding me at first then kneading my flesh with his strong fingers. The grateful kisses become more demanding the longer our bodies are pressed together.

He slows the fervor and breaks our kiss. With his forehead against mine and our eyes locked, he gradually pushes inside me. He's taking his time, savoring every second and every sensation. The water around us sloshes and splashes when his hips surge against me. He pushes up, I push down, and we meet a state of pure bliss somewhere in the middle until neither of us can take any more.

While panting from our strenuous activity, Saban

decides to be funny. "You know, I think you may be the death of me. At least I'll die with a smile on my face."

"I don't think it's fair for you to put the blame on me. I'm like ninety-nine percent certain it's your fault and you'll be the death of me."

"Let's make a promise to each other right now. You ready?"

"What is it?"

"Neither of us is allowed to die without the other. We go together, or we don't go at all. Promise me."

"I promise, we go together or not at all. Though, I prefer the latter if you're taking requests. Now, you say it."

"You have my word. If I lose you, I have no reason to live."

"That's not exactly the same as what you originally said."

He shrugs. "It's how I feel, though. Enough of the sad stuff. We're here to have fun and relax from all the stress at home. Our clothes should be dry enough to wear now. Let's go for a walk in the woods."

"Sounds good to me. I'll race you."

I jump out of his arms and try to run through the water. His laughter is immediately behind me, almost breathing down my neck. He can take much longer strides than I can, but he's a complete gentleman…while we run in the water…completely naked. I clearly didn't take any of this into consideration before issuing my dare.

When we reach the rock where our clothes are drying, he looks back and forth at our soaking wet bodies and still damp garments. "This may be a little harder than I thought. We're putting semi-wet clothes on completely wet skin."

With minimal effort, I call on the elements to give us a hand. The soft breeze picks up speed, bringing a gust of warm air that swirls around us and dries the remaining water droplets. Bonus points to the wind for the extra burst of air to our clothes.

Now that we're dressed and hiking through the forest, I decide to bring up the issue with Gerard. "Saban, there's something serious I need to talk to you about. It's also potentially upsetting. I don't want it to ruin the rest of our time here, but I also don't want to wait any longer to talk to you about it."

He stops walking, takes a seat on a large boulder, and pats the spot next to him. "You have my undivided attention, princess. What's this about?"

"It's about Gerard. I haven't said anything until now for a few reasons. First, it was their wedding day, and I wasn't going to be responsible for ruining it. Second, I knew you'd believe me, and it would cause more problems with your mom and sister. And lastly, I've gone back and forth over whether I should say anything at all, but I finally realized I'd want you to tell me if the tables were turned. So, I'm trusting you right now."

"I won't let you down. You can tell me anything."

My heart cringes. I wish that were true.

Instead, I tell him the entire story of what transpired with Gerard. He listens without interrupting, though I can't miss the way he works his jaw while grinding his teeth in anger. Or the way the red tinge starts on his chest, works its way up his neck, and finally fills his face while his fingers repeatedly curl into hard fists then flex straight again.

"That's everything—the entire conversation. Tell me what you're thinking."

"I'm glad you told me." His voice is strained, and he barely contains the fury inside. "Now I'm going to kill him when he gets back from his honeymoon. My sister will be a widow, but she's young, so she can marry again one day."

"He's not worth all that, Saban. My more immediate concern is what he meant when he said I'll regret my decision one day soon. This may be really farfetched, but if I'm right, I'd never forgive myself for not telling you what I think." I'm not afraid of Saban, but this is a lot to digest and I've just word-vomited all over him. I'd like to give him a chance to catch his breath before I continue.

"I'm listening, princess. I appreciate your concern for my mental state, but I promise I'm still sane."

"It's a good thing one of us is, then, because you may think I'm completely crazy when I share my theory." As I did with Addi, I walk through the entire scenario with Saban—minus the part where I'm the heir—and explain why I think his life is in more imminent danger than mine.

"So, you took it as a literal threat and not a 'you'll wish you had me when it's too late' remark?" He tilts his head to the side and rubs his chin with his finger and thumb.

"Yes, I did. And I know how crazy that sounds, but I can't help it. I'm telling you this so you'll be careful around him and analyze his actions more. I don't want anything to happen to you."

"Don't you worry, princess. I will watch my new brother-in-law like a hawk now."

"Thank you for listening and not getting angry with me. Like I said, I've agonized over whether I should say anything at all. It's his word against mine. Even if he admitted it, he could say it was all a big joke and I don't have a sense of humor. But you listened to me and you understood why this was such a hard decision, and I love you even more for it."

"Sara, I will always take care of you. No matter what, you're my first priority."

I was so sure my confession would ruin the rest of our time together at the cottage, but I was wrong. The trust I put in him only made our bond tighter and the time we spent together sweeter. Hiking, swimming, cooking over the fire, counting stars, and making love countless times are our stress relievers. We left our little hideaway more secure in our love and more certain fate brought us together. On the ride back, I wore a smile the entire way, even past the point when my cheeks began to hurt.

"I just remembered something." Saban closes the latch on the stall and turns to me. "You were supposed to ride your own horse this time. I forgot all about that."

"I didn't. I thought about it, but I just wanted to be close to you, so I kept my mouth shut."

"Hmm. You're lucky you're cute." After a light peck, he slides his hand into mine, and we stroll down memory lane on our way up to the palace.

Déjà vu hits hard when Giselli jerks open the front door, steps out onto the veranda, and shoots us a nasty look. "Where have you been? I've been calling you for days. The whole kingdom is falling apart, and you ran away without leaving word of how to find you with anyone."

Saban drops my hand and rushes inside after her.

I step inside the palace, and everyone who's anyone in this kingdom is already there. Most of the council aides are rushing back and forth between critical decision-makers, chattering on their phones about the number of deaths, the concentrated police presence, and the urgent need to retaliate.

Then I hear one of the council members on his phone. "Yes, Saban just now returned from wherever the hell he's been hiding. I'll get back to you when he makes a decision."

My stomach drops, and bile churns inside my throat. Whatever happened while we were away is bad.

Very, very bad.

CHAPTER 27

"Talk to me." Saban is pacing back and forth in the council chamber. "Tell me every detail. Leave nothing out."

Every chair around the table is taken by his council members, and the wall is lined with their aides. I slip inside unnoticed, using my diplomatic relations position as a front for why I'm involved. For all I know, this conversation directly impacts me and everything in this room is need-to-know information for my role.

One of the older council members, Armand, stands to address Saban. "The first day you left without a word and none of us could reach you, a sixteen-year-old girl was walking to school and was attacked without provocation and without warning. That was the first case that morning. Then, one after another, humans were attacked all over the city, at all times of the day and night."

"Attacked how?" Saban turns his laser focus to Armand.

"At first, they pulled harmless pranks to scare people. They used their magic to lift people up in the air and hold them in front of vehicles, only to snatch them out of harm's way at the last second. They'd make people freeze in place, unable to walk or move. Or they'd make their belongings disappear and suddenly reappear. Stupid shit like that. But multiple attacks were happening simultaneously all over the city. Word spread quickly, and our citizens panicked. By the end of the workday, people were afraid to go outside at all.

"Early the next morning, the first body was found. There were no obvious wounds on the body, but the medical examiner found his heart had literally exploded in his chest. He was still in his driveway, sitting in his vehicle, when his wife found him. Then dead bodies started turning up every half hour, each more gruesome than the last. All the deaths were obviously caused by magical attacks. The mages basically left their signatures all over the bodies."

I'm frozen with panic over his recounting of the attacks. There's no way the mages and wizards I've met would've harmed anyone. They only want peace, but to live with the same freedoms all the races enjoy. There's only one explanation for what he's describing, but I can't speak up without giving anyone away, including myself.

Several other members chime in, throwing their fears and accusations at Saban for him to make a decision on what course of retaliation Easthaven Crest will take. All of their rage and fury is aimed solely at the mages, though. Not the wizards. Not the warlocks or witches.

It's as if no one understands or even knows the difference between the light and dark magical beings. I'm so confused, because if I know and have experienced all levels of it, then surely they have also. They've lived here their entire lives. They've experienced so many events I've only heard about from what I thought were fairy tales. But no one has acknowledged any other possibility for the violence.

The door bursts open, and a young man in a police uniform rushes into the room. He's out of breath, and his face is bright red. He searches the office until his gaze lands on Saban. A look of relief crosses his features, and he straightens his back before speaking.

"Sir, there's been another strike from the mages. This time, they murdered an entire family inside their home. We found it after a sudden storm started over the precinct. The rain turned to blood before the single cloud started moving on its own, leading us right to the crime scene. They *want* us to know what they're doing."

The panic that fills the room is nearly thick enough to suffocate all of us as it draws the oxygen from our lungs. The violence is escalating too quickly for anything but an all-out war to happen next. This is exactly what the dark forces of this realm want—more excuses to wreak their havoc in a world that's already had its fair share. With my birthday quickly approaching, the lines of which side I should be on blur more every day.

I've been straddling the fence since I got here, keeping both sides happy as I learn to navigate these unfamiliar waters. But my allegiance to the opposing sides puts me in a precarious position. Peace is the only option. Understanding is the only course of action that can save us all. Honesty is the only policy that will keep all my relationships intact.

I hope.

"Bring in every officer we have immediately. I'll come down to police headquarters and address them myself. We'll build a plan and get them out on the streets, going door-to-door if we have to. The people behind this will be found and brought to trial." I've never seen Saban with such a hard expression on his face before. The pure contempt radiating from him sours my stomach.

"Sir, the squad… Well, they…" The young officer stammers for the right words.

"They what, Hammers? Spit it out."

Saban's patience is prematurely wearing thin. If he's already losing his cool, he won't be able to handle what's coming. The witches and warlocks are creating as much fear and panic in the streets as they can muster. They're not doing this for nothing…it's leading to something big.

"They're afraid to face the mages, sir. The men don't want the mages to turn their powers on them. What if they wipe out our entire police force at once? After what we've seen, we know they're capable of anything. I mean, they killed women and children."

"Call in the entire department, Sergeant. We'll deal with one problem at a time." Saban crosses his arms over his chest and glares at the young man.

"Yes, sir." Hammers nods then closes the door behind him.

"What else does the council recommend?" Saban glances around the room, but the silence is deafening.

One man clears his throat. Another shuffles his weight nervously from one leg to the other. A chair leg scrapes the floor as someone shifts nervously in their seat. But no one has any suggestions.

"What if we request a meeting with the leader of the mages to figure out what's needed to come to a cease-fire? A diplomatic relations summit, of sorts." Suggesting this in front of the entire council is an underhanded move, but it's the best way to get the idea on the table.

Saban freezes in place and locks his gaze on me as others in the room voice their agreement. At the most inappropriate time, I think about how handsome he is. His jaw is hard set, the muscles ticking from his gritted teeth. His steel-gray eyes turn to coal-black, but definitely not from desire. The seething anger is only under control because of the broad audience. He flattens his hands on the table in front of him and leans over, his muscular arms holding him up while he continues glaring at me.

He knows he gave me this specific job. He can't prevent me from doing it and save face with his constituents, especially in this time of severe turmoil. When I return his glare with an innocent smile, he nearly loses his composure. Oblivious to our ongoing tiff, Armand addresses the room with a renewed sense of optimism.

"Sara, that is an excellent idea. So far, no one has made any demands or even claimed responsibility for these acts. This could be a small faction of their ranks that's causing trouble, but we automatically assume the worst-case scenario. Is there a way to get a message to them, let them know we're interested in peace talks?"

"Absolutely not." Saban slams down his fist on the table, keeping me squarely in his sights. He doesn't have to read my mind to know I'll be the one who volunteers to find a way.

"Saban, we have to try." Armand isn't backing down.

"Yes, there are ways. They obviously like the attention they're getting, so give them more. We can do news interviews, use the illuminated signs on the larger buildings in the city, and send notices out to all the residents, giving them a contact number. We can promise anyone who comes forward in good conscience will be held harmless."

"And who will handle these meetings? You?" Armand's elitist arrogance rears its ugly head.

"Yes, I will. Why wouldn't I? Diplomatic relations manager is literally my job, the one Saban assigned to me." Saban catches the sarcastic tone in my voice, but it goes right over Armand's bloated head.

"Wonderful. It's settled, then. We have at least an idea

of the next move to make." Armand barks out assignments to various people—arranging meetings with the most popular morning news programs, drafting messages for the scrolling boards, and crafting letters for the residents. Everything has to be worded perfectly to avoid more widespread panic than we've already seen.

"Sara, may I speak to you for a moment? Privately?" Saban's lips move, but his teeth remain glued together when he speaks.

"Of course." I understand he's concerned for my safety, but he's about to learn he doesn't control me.

We step into another room, and he locks the door behind us. When he turns toward me, his face is blood red, and his hands are shaking. But I'm no shrinking violet, so he'd better be prepared to get as good as he gives. I fold my arms across my chest, furrow my brow, and dare him to utter the wrong words.

One glance at me, and he knows this conversation will not be easy...and will not end in his favor. He inhales a deep, cleansing breath and releases it slowly. The red tinge to his skin begins to fade, and his eyes lighten to nearly their normal shade. My guard remains fully intact, though, because I'm dead set on this course of action. I can't send anyone else into the firing line, knowing I can defend myself.

I just can't explain that reasoning to him yet.

"Did you really have to do that in there?" His raw emotions bleed through his words, softening my heart and mind ever so slightly. "Do you think for one minute I can send you on this assignment and not completely break inside?"

"Yes, I really had to do that, my handsome caveman. I'm not afraid to do this. In fact, I'm the perfect person for the assignment, and I need you to trust me. I can handle myself. But if we don't get control of this soon, tensions will escalate even more, and we'll face a lot worse than we've already seen."

"If anything happens to you, I'll lose all sense of reason and end this war by killing them with my bare hands. I've told you before, but I don't know if you realized how serious I was at the time. So, I'm telling you again, from the bottom of my heart, I can't live without you. Losing you would be the worst form of torture anyone could inflict upon me, and I don't think I could stand under the weight of my grief. This is not me trying to manipulate you or control you. I just want you to realize how hard sending you into hostile territory is for me."

"I absolutely understand, because I would be no less worried about you. But if you felt strongly about being able to help, I would trust you to make the best decision for both of us. That's what I'm asking you to do for me now. This is happening whether you like it or not, but your support would mean the world to me."

He struggles with my request. One part of him wants to give his full support and watch me shine. He would relish the chance to brag on me to all his friends and colleagues. The other part of him wants to lock me in the highest tower for my own protection until this is over and behind us.

"No one has ever called me a handsome caveman before. Is it wrong that it kind of turns me on? I have visions of throwing you over my shoulder and carrying you off to my cave to have my way with you." He slides his hands around my waist, intentionally skimming along my skin underneath the hem of my shirt. "Then I'd chain you to the wall and keep you there as my personal sex slave, far away from the danger you enjoy putting yourself in."

The semi-serious expression on his face makes me burst out in laughter. "As appealing as you make cave life sound, I'm afraid I'll have to decline your invitation."

"You know, you're one of the few people here who understands sarcastic humor. I guess you picked up on it from people who frequently went to the other world. When you make those wisecracks that no one else gets, I feel like it's a private joke between us. I like it." One soft kiss from him makes my knees weak.

"Did you spend a lot of time in the other world?"

"Yeah, I spent a lot of time there before my dad died. It's a long story, but the gist of it is we were looking for someone who disappeared a long time ago. The story was she got into a lot of trouble here, then tried to dodge her punishment by staying away. I never found her, though— and believe me, I looked—so we had to let it go."

"Wow. What did she do that was so bad you'd still look for her after so long?" My mouth is so dry it feels as if I've packed my throat with cotton.

"She was the royal au pair, and she kidnapped our princess. She stole the baby from the king and queen and fled from our world. Since no one has been able to track her, both she and the princess were presumed dead many years ago, but we've never really given up our search for either of them."

"That's a fascinating story, and it brings up an interesting moral dilemma." I swallow hard, pushing the ball of emotion back down my throat before it suffocates me. "If the au pair had a good reason for doing what she did, do you think she should be forgiven and pardoned?"

"You never fail to keep me on my toes. Hmm. She would need one hell of a compelling reason. Her actions and deceit changed our way of life in this kingdom. An impact of that multitude isn't easily swept under the rug, but I'd be willing to listen to her."

"Hmm." I nod and remain calm on the outside while I'm sweating bullets on the inside.

"Did I pass?"

"Pass what?" I draw my brows down and crinkle my eyes in the corners.

"Your moral dilemma test. Did I give the answer you were looking for?" His eyes twinkle, knowing he's caught me unaware. And he did. I was so engrossed in his story I didn't even hear his thoughts.

"Did you mean it? Would you consider her side of it before passing judgment?"

"Absolutely."

"Then you passed."

I, however, am about to pass out. I'm not sure how I'm talking when I can't breathe, but my lungs are absolutely not working. For all this time, Saban has been looking for Nana and me. What would've happened if he'd found us? Would he have listened to her side and defended me? Would he have recognized me as his soul mate?

Don't worry, Saraya. Your soul mate will still love you when you tell him the truth about who you are.

Why am I not so sure?

CHAPTER 28

After a lot of arguments, threats, and negotiations, I finally convinced Saban I had to meet with the mage leader alone. Our campaign ran for more than two weeks before anyone stepped up and offered to meet with us. Going alone was the least I could do to make her feel safe and secure. Had I shown up with a full military escort, she would've disappeared.

That was my argument anyway.

The past two weeks have been pure hell.

The magical attacks on humans have increased in intensity and frequency. Day after day, the body count has increased, and the pressure from the kingdom residents landed solely on Saban's shoulders to resolve it. Many who had been staunch supporters turned on him overnight, calling for someone else to step up and fix the issues.

When the attacks started bleeding over into the neighboring kingdoms, I had a hell of a time calming those leaders. The more contentious the representatives were with me, the more protectively Saban responded on my behalf. I had to remind him, many times, our roles are diplomatic in nature, so we have to react tactfully rather than threatening.

Convincing Ginevra to meet with me on behalf of the mages was another miracle in itself. She was more than reluctant, understandably, because of how mages have been treated for the last eighteen years. But more than that, she was concerned about my safety in case we were seen together by the wrong people. The cloaking spell is still working, but it's obviously not foolproof.

We agreed on a secret location without announcing the meeting to anyone ahead of time. Having it in the Veil wasn't an option. When I take the information to the people, I want to be able to give specifics about our meeting to help reassure them. Everyone is on edge enough as it is and suspicious of everyone who crosses their path.

Now that I'm on my way to meet Ginevra, I have the distinct sensation I'm being watched. I don't know if Saban had someone follow me for my protection or if the warlocks and witches are up to their tricks, but the hairs on the back of my neck feel as if they are standing at attention and saluting a five-star general. A sidewalk bench up ahead catches my eye, so I hurry toward it and take a seat as if I belong there.

With my thoughts focused on who's following me, I

open my mind and let the inner expressions flow in from those around me. I've learned to filter out the noise more effectively so I can pinpoint exactly what I'm looking to find. Two familiar voices stand out, and I immediately know Saban sent men to follow me. I'm not mad since I know they're here for my protection, but I'm not thrilled with his overreach either.

When a taxi stops in front of me to drop off a fare, I slide into the back seat and give the driver an address close to the area where I'm meeting Ginevra. The two men on foot won't be able to keep up. Even if they're able to find out where the taxi drops me off, they'll be too late to find me.

After a short ride, the driver pulls over to the curb and looks at me over his shoulder. "Should I put this on Saban's account?"

My thoughts were on the men following me, so his question catches me off guard. My face must do all the talking for me because he immediately follows up.

"I recognized you from the news. You're working on the task force to stop the attacks. They also said you're Saban's mate, so I just assumed…"

"No, it's fine. It's my fault. I was lost in thought about other things and didn't even think about the fare. Yes, please put it on his account. Thank you."

When he drives away, I jog across the street and head toward our secret meeting place. Ginevra is already there waiting for me when I reach the plush hotel suite. After a long embrace, we move to the sitting area to talk.

"Do you have any news for me?" I'm hopeful, but I'm also a realist. If she'd learned anything urgent, she already would've contacted me.

"Nothing concrete. We know it's the dark element of this world, but what's still not clear is why they're blaming us. They've always been secretive about their coven and practices even toward other magical people, so these blatant attacks are out of character."

"But you have an idea."

"There's only one reason that fits. Only one motive that would make someone go to such extreme measures and act so out of character."

"Power. They're planning a power play against me. They'll reveal me and blame me for everything when I'm no longer cloaked."

"That's what I'm advising you to prepare for, yes. I'm sorry, sweet girl."

"Prepare for? The only way to prepare is to tell everyone now and beat them to the punch. The moment I do that, it'll be like opening Pandora's box—and all hell will rain down on everyone else."

"Start small. Tell Saban first. Then a couple more people. Then a few more. Let them react to the person they've come to know one-on-one instead of telling a roomful of people at once. An individual is smart and compassionate. A mob is angry and unreasonable. Whatever happens, happens. Don't worry about the rest of us. There's someone powerful, influential, and devious after you. We are not your primary concern at the moment."

"Ginevra, I don't know if I can do this—any of it. I grew up in Montana, in the middle of nowhere. The most exciting event in my life was the yearly homecoming dance. Now, my nana is missing, you've told me I'm supposed to step up as queen on my next birthday, and I have to tell everyone I'm a mage. Someone is out to kill me, Ginevra. I mean, I haven't even graduated from high school yet."

She takes my hands in hers, and tears swim in her eyes. "The hardest lesson to learn is just how unfair life is. Courage has nothing to do with not being afraid. It's about facing your fears and doing what needs to be done, regardless of how hard it is. It's about deciding what's right and what's wrong, then standing firm on your convictions. It's about helping those who can't help themselves.

"Yes, too much falls on your young shoulders. There are too many uncertain factors you have to face. But you have a lot of friends behind you, cheering you on, watching your back, and willing to defend you when the time comes. Remember us when you're feeling down."

What she doesn't say, but I feel the burden of anyway, is that those same people who have my back are also depending on me. They're waiting for me to pave the way so they can be free. They're counting on me to change the laws, sway the public opinion, and be the public face of the mage community. So, while her speech was moving and inspirational, her motives aren't entirely altruistic. She has a stake in this game, too.

But she is right about the people willing to help me when I need them.

Like my nana.

The only reason why I'm continuing this death wish of a quest.

She's still out there somewhere, and I will find her.

I push down the fear trying to take control of me and square my shoulders. If this is my destiny, I'll face it head on, whether I feel prepared to do this alone or with an army behind me. Regardless if I'm ready to be queen or mated or anything else that requires more of me than I'm prepared to give. When I think about what Nana gave up to save my life, I'm humbled and energized at the same time. If she could move to an entirely new world with a small child, with nothing to her name except the clothes on her back, and craft a life and a home for us, I can do this for the people of Easthaven Crest. For Nana. For myself.

"Okay. Moment of panic averted. Back to business. I'll go back and have a talk with Saban first. He deserves to hear it from me. I honestly don't know how he'll take it. His family has had their eyes set on the throne for years now. My showing up at the last minute and claiming heir status won't sit well with them. He may think I've been trying to trick him all along."

"Have faith in him, Saraya. He may surprise you."

"Fingers crossed." I shrug because there's nothing else I can do at the moment except hope for the best. "I'm heading back now to tell the council about the warlocks and witches, explain the difference between the dark and light, and try to persuade them to band with the mages and put their prejudices aside. Wish me luck."

"I believe you can do anything you set your mind to." She pats my cheek with a smile that doesn't reflect in her eyes. There's hope in them, but there's also an uneasiness brewing inside. I don't bother trying to read her mind, knowing her shields are firmly in place anyway.

WHEN I WALK INTO THE PALACE, THE EERIE SILENCE CAUSES shivers to run up and down my spine. Something is extremely off with this picture. There are always multiple people actively rushing back and forth, completing various tasks, and chattering in the hallways. Especially during regular business hours like now. Plus, Saban wouldn't simply disappear, knowing I was alone at a meeting with the leader of the mages.

I dash up the stairs and down the long corridor to his office area, but I already know he's not inside before I open the door. Nothing but silence greets me on the other side, and a terrible feeling sweeps over me.

What happened while I was in that meeting?

Though I haven't had a need to use it much since we're usually together, I still carry the phone Saban insisted on buying me. After calling his number several times and getting his voice mail on the first ring, I talk myself off the panic-induced ledge until I have concrete information.

I rush downstairs to find Addi, knowing if anyone has a clue about what's happening here, it would be her. She's in what we've affectionately dubbed "the closet" when I burst through the door.

"Addi, where is everyone? What's going on around here? I need to talk to Saban right now, but I can't find him." I blurt everything out as I move toward her, my eyes still glued to the phone in my hand as I continue to redial his number.

When she doesn't answer me, I look up at her and raise my hands palm up. She's staring straight at me but doesn't respond or move. "Can you help me out here, or what?"

"Sara?" She barely whispers my name. I don't think she even moved her lips.

"Yes. What is going on around here? What's wrong with you?" I rush to her side, thinking she's been put under a spell or something.

"You're alive." She reaches up and touches my face tentatively, as if she's afraid I'll evaporate into thin air.

"Am I not supposed to be? Talk to me, Addi. I'm completely out of the loop, and it's not a good feeling."

She pulls her phone out of her pocket, clicks on a news channel app, and plays the site's featured video. I watch in horror as Ginevra and I leave the hotel together and say goodbye. The moment I turn my back on her, moving toward the taxi, Ginevra lifts her hands and hurls a broad swath of black magic at me.

In an instant, my body is completely vaporized, disappearing into the breeze. Ginevra is left staring directly into the camera on her, sporting an evil grin and coal-black eyes that are as cold as ice. She cackles menacingly before twirling her hand over her head and disappearing into a cloud of black haze.

"I haven't been able to reach Ginevra by any means—natural or magical. Saban freaked when he saw this. There was no warning, no preamble leading up to what was about to air. This video simply started playing on every device. The electronics that were off all turned on at the same time. Whoever did it was hell-bent on everyone watching it at the same time."

"But Ginevra? You believed she would do something like that?"

"No, of course not. Witches and warlocks can change their appearance with their dark magic. It's unnatural and deceitful, so those spells are forbidden for us. But I'm afraid of what they've done to Ginevra if I can't reach her, and I believed with all my heart that they'd killed you because you didn't answer my calls either." She throws her arms around me and sobs on my shoulder, half in sorrow for Ginevra and half in relief for me. One hundred percent in frustration over the whole situation.

"Addi, where is Saban? What is he doing now?"

She sniffles and wipes the tears from her face. "He was inconsolable, Sara. Despite all the strong objections against it from everyone, including me, he took the king-dom's army to the place where you were last seen. I wasn't worried about him finding the Veil. That'll never happen. But I did try to warn him off because of the attacks. I pointed out how vulnerable he would be out there, but he didn't care. Seeing that video turned him into a crazy man."

"I have to get back to the city before a bunch of people are hurt or killed. His phone is going straight to voice mail. You can't reach Ginevra. I didn't hear anything from you—magical or otherwise. Do they have the power to block us, Addi? Is that a thing?"

"If anyone in their ranks has that level of power, we are all in deep trouble. The things someone like that could do are terrifying."

"Let's go stop Saban from starting an all-out war in the streets. I may need your help out there."

We take Addi's car and head toward the hotel where I met Ginevra. While she drives, I focus on Saban, trying to reach his mind. If I can project to him, speak to him through his thoughts and convince him I'm still alive, maybe the tensions will be dispelled before I reach him. I center my attention on him, straining every brain cell in my head, but I can barely break through the obstacles blocking my attempts.

With every drop of white light in me, I push harder and break through the barrier long enough to reach him.

"Saban, don't do this. I'm still alive."

An invisible force slams into me, knocking the breath out of me and breaking my connection to him. But my attempt succeeded—he and I both felt the unmistakable tie that binds us together for all time.

"Whoever's doing this is blocking me from reaching

Saban. There's definitely a series of brick walls between us, and they don't want me to get through a single one."

"That's more concerning than anything I've seen or heard so far. We're all in danger if that's the case. Everyone in the Veil…everyone living a secret life…and every other person in the realm."

There's nothing I can say to that sobering thought. How do I fight an unknown enemy with unimaginable powers and no convictions to stop him from crossing any line?

The size of the crowd surrounding the hotel is over-whelming. Addi wasn't kidding when she said Saban brought the entire army with him. I jump out of the car before Addi even puts it in park. Weaving through the soldiers dressed in full riot gear, I scan every face until I see Saban at last. He's barking out orders to a group of men, driving them to find me at any cost.

"She's alive. I know she is out there somewhere, and we're going to find her today. Right now. You have your orders. Move out!"

"Saban—I'm right here!"

When he hears my voice, he whirls around on his heel and stares in disbelief for a heartbeat before he rushes toward me. I run full speed to meet him halfway, leaping into his waiting arms.

"I thought I'd lost you, princess. When I saw that video… I just…"

"I know, my love. But it wasn't real. Someone played a cruel trick on us. No one hurt me, I promise. The woman

I met with wants nothing but peace. She didn't do this. Please tell the troops to stand down before more people get hurt. There are other ways to stop this—better ways."

He puts me down but keeps me close to his side as he dismisses the units with a sincere message of his gratitude. "I'm taking you home now, princess. Today went from bad to fucking unbearable in an instant. But now that I know you're okay, I can breathe again. I don't understand what's happening, though."

"Take me home, Saban. We'll have a long talk, and I'll explain everything. Just you and me. Okay?"

"Anything you say." He presses a firm kiss against my lips, full of the promise of love and passion, before carting me away to his vehicle.

I rehearse what I have to say the entire way back to the palace, but nothing sounds right. Every scenario I run through in my head ends badly, regardless of what I mean, how I say it, or what reassurances I make him about what I am. In the end, he never accepts me. His animosity toward mages overrules his rational mind. Years of conditioning under his family's thumb have hardwired his brain to distrust anyone who's not like him.

By the time we're back home, I've nearly talked myself out of telling him anything.

He needs to hear it from you, Saraya.

She's right. He deserves to know the truth. He has every right to see the real me before making a lifelong commitment. Even if that means I'll lose him.

He pulls me close to his side as we walk toward the

front door, our steps in sync. His lips are pressed against my head as he murmurs his gratefulness under his breath that I'm still alive. I wrap my arms around his waist and hold tightly, inhaling his scent and savoring what may be the last time I'm in his arms.

"I've never felt for anyone what I feel for you. This is more than love—it's truly a spiritual connection we can never break. No matter what happens, I hope you know I love you…and I need you." I look up at him, choking on the ball of emotions stuck in my throat. Dreading the inevitable conversation that will come next.

His puzzled expression gives way to gratefulness when he realizes how hard it is for me to admit I need anyone. Fiercely independent. Stubborn to a fault. Self-sufficient and driven to succeed. This is how I've been described my entire life. Needing someone is the opposite of who I've always been. But I'm finding that to be true about a lot of characteristics lately.

I've never felt this vulnerable before…and I don't like it one bit.

CHAPTER 29

Saban and I head straight to our wing of the palace for guaranteed privacy. There's too much to say to chance being interrupted, and the last thing I want is for any of his family to eavesdrop on our conversation. He's his own man, but anyone can be swayed under the influence of their family if the circumstances are right. In this case, the conditions are perfect.

The second we're behind closed doors, he scoops me up in his arms and buries his face in my hair. "I know it didn't seem like it, but I actually held my cool in front of my men compared to what I felt inside. Then, I swear, I heard your voice inside my head, telling me you were alive. For a minute there, I thought I was losing my mind. Then you appeared out of nowhere, and I thought the mages were messing with me."

"Saban, about them…"

"You can tell me all about them in a few minutes,

princess. Right now, this is all I care about. I need you in my arms, your body next to mine, feeling your heart pounding against my chest, to convince me you're alive. When I thought I'd lost you forever, the pain was so bad, I couldn't breathe. In those few moments, I questioned how I'd ever be happy again. But now you're here, and I can't let you go. Ever. We're conjoined twins now."

We chuckle together, but neither releases the other. When I rushed to him on the street, I felt his pain. It was crippling, and I know my reaction would be no less dramatic if the tables were turned. Which is why this discussion has to happen now.

"I'm well aware of that feeling. When you hit your head at the lake, I thought I'd lost you too. You don't doubt my love for you, do you?"

"Not at all. You saved my life that day, and you gave me a life I never knew I wanted when you agreed to be mine."

"I have a lot to tell you, Saban, and you won't like all of it. What I'm asking you to do is trust me and believe in us if you don't believe anything else."

"You never have to be afraid to share anything with me. Nothing can change my love for you. I'm yours forever."

I step back, take his hand, and lead him to the settee beside the window. Finding the best words to start this conversation is harder than I thought it would be. For all my rehearsing, every single word I had in mind has escaped me.

"I guess first I should tell you these attacks aren't being

committed by the mages or wizards. There are other factions that have broken off and are following their own rules now. They're the true witches and warlocks, the dark magical element. Mages are good and wouldn't hurt anyone unless they're defending themselves. No one knows for sure why the dark forces have started making themselves known since they've always preferred the shadows before now. There's a theory, but it's not confirmed yet."

I pause, letting him absorb everything I've just dumped in his lap. It's a lot to take in, and I'm asking him to trust my judgment based on my word and one meeting with the mage leader.

"This is what the woman you met today told you?"

"Her name is Ginevra. Yes, we talked about the witches and warlocks." I take a deep breath to calm my racing heart.

"Sara, what's the theory? What have you not told me?" He covers my hand with his, giving his reassurance without saying a word.

"The theory is they're trying to find me, Saban. I've had one run-in with them before, but they didn't recognize me. Almost no one here has, to be honest."

Tell him everything, Saraya.

"I'm originally from Easthaven Crest, but I grew up in the other world. I didn't even know about this place until the day I met you. I accidentally fell through a hole in the middle of nowhere and landed here. I'd only heard of this realm in fairy tales when I was little. To be honest, I can't even remember all of them right now. But what I do know is...I'm Saraya, the daughter of King Taerel and Queen Wren. And I'm also a mage."

He jerks his hand away from mine before he withdraws completely from me. His body language makes his thoughts clear enough that I don't need to peek inside his mind. The hard glare in his eyes and the firm set of his lips barely disguise his disgust. He stands abruptly and begins pacing, running his hand through his hair before scraping it over his face. All the while, I'm holding my breath, waiting for him to say something.

"What am I supposed to say to this, Sara? Or Saraya? Whoever the hell you are."

"Whoever the hell I am? Just a few seconds ago, I was the love of your life. Your soul mate. Now, you want to act like you don't know me, like you haven't spent every waking minute with me for months now. Make up your mind once and for all, Saban. Either we're in this together, or we're not in it at all. I'm not one to straddle the fence. If you love me, then you have to love all of me—even the parts you don't like."

He stops pacing, and his full attention is focused on me. "I'm sorry, Sara. Forgive me. That came out much harsher than I meant for it to. I'm just reeling over finding out you've been lying to me this entire time about who you are and who your family was. I think you can cut me some slack for my poor choice of words, considering."

"You're right—you're absolutely right. I completely understand why you're upset about that. I've felt terrible about keeping this from you. You don't know how many times I've almost told you. I can explain why I kept my identity hidden. I'm not trying to make excuses, and I know I can't change the past. But maybe you'll understand and can forgive me for not telling you sooner."

"Of course I forgive you. When I said nothing would change my love for you, I meant it. That means *forever*, Sara. Just give me a minute to deal with this."

He paces for several more minutes, walking from one end of the room to the other. When he finally stops to speak again, I can feel the weariness rolling off him. "You're the heir to the throne. My pet name for you isn't far off the mark, is it, princess? I suppose I'll have to change that to 'queen' now."

"I am the heir, yes. But I didn't know that when I met you. I didn't find out until much later. I couldn't tell you any of this because there are other mages I have to protect. Your family isn't exactly known for their great love of mages."

"What's that supposed to mean?" He puts his hands on his hips and furrows his brows.

"That means your mother and your sister openly revile mages to this day, and your parents were the ones who killed my mother for being a mage." His immediate crestfallen expression breaks my heart. "You didn't know?"

"No. I had no idea. Are you sure?"

"As sure as I can be. I never knew my parents. They died when I was very young. My father died protecting my mother when the kingdom turned on her for being a mage, but not before he sent me away to safety."

His knees buckle, and he barely makes it to the couch beside me. "Is that what my father meant when he used to say the sins of his past would catch up with him one day? Sara, I didn't know, I swear it."

"I believe you, and I don't hold the sins of your family against you. What I need to know is how you'll deal with this. Will this cause a rift between us? Will you be able to live with knowing I'm one of the people your family hates?"

He shakes his head. "I stand by my promise to you, my queen. I love you, no matter what. Can you start from the beginning and tell me everything? I think I missed parts when my blood was rushing through my veins and beating the bass drum in my ears."

"Yes, considering I've been in your shoes before and understand how unsettling this story is, I can do that."

He listens as I recount the story from the very beginning when my parents were the king and queen and the mysterious attacks began that frightened the humans, much like what's happening today. How Nana barely escaped with our lives and had to start over with nothing in the other world. He asks questions about my experiences there, interested in everything about me. His concern for my safety is visible when I tell him about Nana's disappearance and the cloaking spell that hides me from those who are still on the hunt.

We spend hours simply talking now that I can share

everything about my life and my abilities with him. His initial anger and distrust from my pretenses fade, replaced by empathy and acceptance. When he realizes all those hunting missions he and his father conducted in the other world were to find me, he visibly pales.

"What if we'd found you then? Would he have killed you?"

"I think that was exactly what he intended to do."

"You thought I'd be mad about the throne, didn't you? That it would be you sitting on it instead of me." He lightly strokes my cheek and searches my eyes.

"Yes, I did. You've had a lifetime of being pushed to take it, to lead the kingdom. I fell from the sky and inherited it without even knowing this place existed. Life isn't fair. I've learned that the hard way. But I didn't want you to think I'd planned any of this behind your back."

"If the thought crossed my mind, even for the briefest moment, I have no doubt about the day we met. Rycan intended to kill you for crossing the border onto his land. He wouldn't have done that if he'd known who you are… and you could've stopped him in his tracks if you'd announced your lineage. In fact, I was damn surprised he didn't catch you. Not many can evade his patrols. Even I would be hard-pressed to escape."

"I used the thick trees since the horses couldn't run full speed through them. That was my only saving grace. Until I met you."

His eyes darken with need as he threads his fingers through my hair. His sultry expression makes my temperature rise instantly. Without a word or a gesture, I'm completely under his spell. With a single touch, my body is in his charge. But when he looks at me like that, my heart races at the speed of light, and everything in the world disappears except him.

A slight tug on the back of my neck prompts me to straddle his lap. Our mouths clash with reckless abandon. He swirls his tongue around mine before nipping on my bottom lip. The feral growl from his chest is deep and dark, both dangerous and exciting, sending chills down my spine. We tear at our clothes, the urgency of the moment taking over.

"I want to feel you wrapped around me. I need to be inside you right now." The deep timbre of his voice and the way he murmurs the words against my ear drive me crazy.

"You know I can't resist you." I position myself over him, poised to take all he's offering.

"You have no idea how much I'm counting on that." His lips land on my outstretched neck. He bites and pulls my skin between his teeth as I lower myself onto him. "Mmm. You feel so fucking good."

I barely begin moving my hips when he suddenly stands. He grips my bottom in his hands, and he holds me up with his muscular arms with no effort. I wrap my legs around his waist and lock my arms around his neck. The wild expression in his eyes makes the butterflies in my stomach take flight. My back hits the wall, and he slides his arms to the bend of my knees, steepening the angle. He thrusts upward to the hilt, and sparks fly behind my eyelids. I curl my fingers, scraping his smooth skin, and my body shakes and shudders involuntarily from the waves of pleasure that repeatedly surge through me.

Our bodies are both slick with sweat, but he shows no signs of slowing. My body is nearly spent and dehydrated from the onslaught of repeated climaxes, but he's still going strong.

"I'm not through with you yet, princess." He walks to the bedroom and places me on the bed, then flips me onto my stomach. He grips my hips and pulls me backward until my feet touch the floor. "Hold on tight."

He barely issues his warning before he slams into me again. His punishing grip is so hard, I'm sure I'll have bruises. But at the moment, I couldn't care less. The way he loses control with me is both humbling and empowering. Each time we're together is better than the last. I'm in pure heaven when he finds his release. I melt into the bed, exhausted and satiated beyond belief. He collapses on top of me, his chest flush against my back, and kisses my hair.

"I didn't hurt you, did I?" He sounds sleepy. We've both had a long day.

"No, you didn't hurt me, my caveman. Just the opposite, actually."

He rolls to the side, curls his arm around my waist, and hoists me up toward the head of the bed. I turn to face him with a big, goofy smile on my face. "Good. You know I'd never intentionally hurt you, right? I get carried away with you and have to fight to keep my composure. But I want you to tell me if I ever go too far."

"I'm fine, I promise. But if I feel the need to stop you, you will definitely know."

When he moves his head to kiss me, he winces and grabs the back of his neck, massaging the obviously painful area. "I must've hurt myself. My neck is so sore."

"You probably got a crick in your neck from holding me up for so long. Roll onto your stomach, and I'll massage it for you." I begin kneading the knots and tight muscles in his neck, and he moans in appreciation. "All the stress you've been under hasn't helped this, you know."

"I know. It comes with the territory, though." He slightly lifts one shoulder before thinking better of it.

"You need an assistant or something. Someone to help shoulder the workload instead of— Wha...what is this on your neck, Saban? Is this some kind of tattoo?"

"I don't know what you're talking about. I don't have a tattoo. What does it look like?"

"It kind of looks like an eye with three dots over the top of it, but it's not very clear. If you didn't do it on purpose, how did it get here?"

"It's probably just an odd-shaped scratch from something during the day from hell I had. Or it could be from your fingernails digging into my skin."

"That's not from my fingernails, Saban, and you can't just dismiss it as nothing. Your neck is sore, and there's a visible mark on it from something. You need to get it checked out." I don't know enough about the medical implications in this realm to speak with any certainty, but I know when something is off.

"Who knows what happened? I'm fine, my love. But if it'll make you feel better, I promise to see the doctor tomorrow and get a clean bill of health to ease your mind. Deal?"

"Deal, but only because I don't have another choice at the moment." He chuckles at my pout.

"What I need right now is some sleep, nestled against your body all night. Come here." He spoons me from behind, all our limbs entwined like a pretzel, and we fall into a deep sleep together.

It's still dark out when I'm pulled out of the best sleep I've had in a while. The chilly air in the room washes over my bare back, making me shiver and search for Saban. His natural body heat is better than any blanket. I reach out for him, but he's not there. I lift up on my elbow and look around the room, waiting for my eyes to adjust to the dim light.

"Well, if the queen herself isn't finally awake. I was beginning to think maybe I'd fucked you into a coma." I recognize the voice, but not the menacing tone.

I quickly wrap the sheet around myself before turning on the bedside lamp. "Saban? What is it? What's wrong?"

"Absolutely nothing's wrong. I have you right where I

want you. Wrapped around my little finger. Naked and in my bed. Under my thumb and out of the public eye. You proved beyond a shadow of a doubt that you're too naïve and trusting to lead this kingdom. I gave you a little attention, a few orgasms, and you spilled all your secrets. I mean, everything I could use against you to usurp any claim to authority you could've had.

"You're a mage. You weren't even raised here, but you think I'll let you waltz in and take over what should be mine? No chance in hell that will happen. If any of your little mage friends see you again, it'll be in your next life."

His words are like knives stabbing my heart one at a time. I'm so hurt and confused, it's hard to think straight. But I do know I have to get away from him. His parents killed my parents…and he's just decided to get rid of me. I stand, gripping the sheet tightly around me with one hand and holding out the other in mock surrender, and step toward my clothes that are still on the settee.

"Saban, I don't understand why you would do this to me. We're soul mates. You love me. What happened to you in the last couple of hours?"

"Not a damn thing, Sara. Or Saraya. Whoever the hell you are. It doesn't matter what you call yourself now." His muscles tense in preparation to pounce on me.

I jump to the side when he lunges forward, and I scoop up my clothes off the settee with my free hand. With all the white energy I can muster, I create a protective barrier around me and push him backward.

But he breaks through it as if it wasn't even there. He

wraps his hand around my neck and squeezes. His eyes are black and devoid of anything remotely resembling the man I know. With both hands full, I can't fight back, so I drop the sheet and try to break his hold on me. But it's no use. He's too strong physically for me. I begin punching him in the face as hard as I can, ignoring the pain shooting through the bones in my hand.

He pulls me close to him so we're face-to-face and growls at me through gritted teeth. "I should've done this a long time ago."

My free hand randomly connects with his face and head, trying to find a vulnerable spot to give me a fighting chance. Even for a split second, just enough for me to get away from him. I wrap my fingers around his neck, determined to scratch his jugular out from under his skin if I have to.

That's when it happens.

Amid the foggy haze inside Saban's mind, I can barely make out the image of another man's face. His ugly sneer and cold, dead eyes frighten me more than the angry man I'm currently fighting. The stranger smiles at me, but it's an evil grin, full of hate and horror. *Now I can see you. I'm coming for you, Saraya.*

Then I hear a different voice scream loudly. A voice I'd recognize anywhere. *Run, Sara!*

Saban is stunned for a moment, and I break free from his grip. Coughing and sputtering, I make a mad dash for the balcony doors when the glass shatters, flying inside toward me, and a large, beautiful cat stands ready to kill.

"Laurelai!" My voice is hoarse and barely intelligible, but she senses how happy I am to see her. She snarls her lip up, baring her long teeth at Saban, then releases a loud roar. It's a clear warning that she will shred him to pieces if he makes a move toward me. She *wants* to kill him. I can feel the rage coursing through her veins. She craves the taste of his blood on her tongue. "We need to get out of here. Right now. Come on, girl."

The difference in gravity in this world comes to my rescue once again. I leap from the balcony with my spirit animal right behind me, and we put as much distance between Saban and us as we possibly can. I'm hidden behind a large tree in the dark shadows of the night, where I quickly dress in the clothes I wore earlier.

When I glance up at the window, I see Saban standing there, stock-still as if he's a statue. He's staring down at me with no expression. Lifeless. Dead. Unfeeling. When I look into his thoughts, there's nothing there but an ice-cold wall.

In a way, I envy him.

I wish I couldn't feel anything right now.

aurelai and I run the entire distance from the palace to the Veil, making sure no one is following us along the way. My throat is killing me, my neck is sore, and my heart is broken. But I think what he said to me and the way he said it hurts worse than my physical injuries.

Ginevra meets me with open arms on the path before we reach the community area. I rush into her embrace, thankful for a friendly face and an understanding ear. She pats me on the back in a soothing, grandmotherly way that makes me miss Nana even more. "Come inside, have a hot cup of tea, and tell me everything. We'll sort it out together."

I follow her to the tree grove, where Kobi sprinkles me with her dust before kissing my cheek. "Don't worry, Saraya. Everything will work out the way it's meant to be."

"You're sweet, Kobi. But right now, nothing feels like it'll ever be right again." My raspy voice is barely audible.

Inside the tree house, Ginevra starts the teakettle and takes her seat while the water heats. I suspect she could simply use her magic to conjure a ready-made drink, but she's purposely giving me time to calm down. She waits patiently for me to collect my thoughts and begin my lengthy narrative. With a heavy heart and a strained voice, I start from the beginning and share every humiliating detail, straining my vocal cords but wanting to get the full story out.

By the time I'm finished, we've each drunk two cups and my throat is beginning to feel better. Then the tears start, and I can't stop them. After the first one falls, it's quickly replaced by more and more until I finally quit fighting and let it all out. Ginevra offers her shoulder for me to lean on, then wraps her arm around my shoulder.

"You love him, Saraya. When we love someone, we give them everything we have. Sometimes they take that love for granted and we end up hurt. Sometimes they return our love and make us feel whole. Love given is never wasted, regardless of what happens. Anyone worth your love is worth a fight. My girl, you need to steel your nerves for the fight of your life."

"I just feel so stupid, Ginevra. I told him everything about me. My life in the other world, my powers...I gave him all the ammunition he needs to hurt me even more. How did I miss this? I've racked my brain, and I don't recall a single sign that this was coming. I fought the attraction to him for so long, not believing in the whole soul mate thing, unsure I was ready for that kind of commitment. I wasn't even sure I wanted to stay in this world. My original plan was to find Nana and go back to Montana.

"Then he almost died right in front of me, and I realized I would be devastated without him. That's when I stopped resisting my feelings for him. Was it all a game this whole time? Did he know about me? My parents? Was he just waiting to expose me as a mage?"

"I don't know, sweetie. I've tried to peer into his thoughts, but I can't get through the barrier to see what's really going on in there."

"The same happened to me when Laurelai and I were leaving. He was staring down at me with no emotion at all. I tried to see into his mind, but it was as if I were staring at an ice wall. I even felt the bitter coldness radiating off it. I've never experienced that before."

"You said you saw a man's face and he spoke to you. You didn't recognize him? You've never seen him before?"

"He seemed familiar, but I was dealing with so much at once, it was hard to focus on just his face. The image wasn't clear, and I was close to losing consciousness. But then Nana's voice broke through and stunned us both. She's the reason he let go of me. She told me to run, and I didn't waste time asking questions. Then Laurelai leaped through the window to protect me, and we got out of there together."

"Zu is a very powerful mage. I'm not surprised she

intervened when she did." Ginevra leans her head into her hand and rubs her forehead.

"She called me Sara." I sit up straight and wipe the tears from my face.

"So? What does that matter?"

"Every other time I've heard the voice in my head, she called me Saraya. I dismissed my initial doubts about it. But Nana never called me Saraya. The first time I heard that name was here in Easthaven Crest. She has *only* called me Sara my entire life.

"Her voice was distinct and clear this time, unlike the other times when it was so muffled, I couldn't tell if it was really her or not. What if it wasn't her any other time? What if it was the warlock telling me what to do so he could get to me? He's been looking for me this entire time, but he couldn't find me because of the cloak. He knew my mage name but not the one I go by now. But he saw my face through Saban tonight."

The blood drains from her face, and she grips my hand so hard her knuckles turn white. "If he knows who you are now…"

She jumps up and pulls me into the kitchen with her. She pulls an enormous leather book from a cupboard above the refrigerator and hurriedly flips through it until she finds the specific page she needs. She reads from the text, and though I don't recognize the language, I know it's a spell.

She stumbles backward until the backs of her knees hit the chair. She drops into the seat, her hand covering her mouth, and shakes her head with a panicked expression on her face.

"What? What is it?" She can't leave me hanging like this, not after the night I've had.

"The cloak is broken, Saraya. He found a way through it and broke our spell to hide you. Now that he's seen your face, he can find his way into your mind. You have to keep your thoughts shielded at all times, and you'll have to fortify the shields with extra measures." She stands and begins pacing and talking to herself more than to me. "We have more work to do. You need to strengthen your powers and learn our more advanced techniques. We should look into other places to hide you for your own protection."

I grab her shoulders to stop her kitchen parade and make her look at me. "I'm not going into hiding anywhere. I'm standing and fighting this, Ginevra. Look, I have no desire to be queen, but I'll be damned if I'll let him be king and rule this kingdom with an evil iron fist."

"Sweetheart, I hate to say this, but I don't think the people here will ever be ready for a mage queen. They just won't let it happen. You'll be in constant danger and fending off attacks from every direction."

"I may be young and naïve in many respects, but I know right from wrong, Ginevra. This isn't something I'm willing to concede. The very fact that the people are prejudiced against mages is enough reason why this has to be my course of action. As my parents' daughter, if I don't stand up for *all* the people, who will?"

"You may not want it, but you will be an amazing queen. Mage Queen Saraya. That has a nice ring to it, don't you think?"

"I'm fine with plain old Sara. But let's figure out how to stop him first. You said I need to level up my powers. I have an idea on that topic I've been thinking about for a while. My father was an elf, and they have natural powers. Ruvaen and Rycan both pledged to help me when I needed it, and they were positive I'd need it. Would learning how to better harness their powers strengthen mine more?"

"Yes, absolutely. That is a fantastic idea. If they shared their secrets with you, you'd be the most powerful mage our world has ever known. Some of the powers are innate because of the bloodline. But if you can access their academic abilities, that warlock wouldn't know what hit him. Oh, but wait…did you tell Saban your father was an elf? Does he know you're half elf?"

"No, actually, I didn't even think about that when we were talking. I mean, I don't know if people think that's a big deal in this world, but races mix all the time in my world."

"It's not normal practice in the realm. The merpeople are obviously distinct in their abilities to breathe underwater. That proves tricky when a man and woman of different races try to live together in their kingdom. The elves have their own family expectations about continuing their bloodlines and gifts. They tolerated your parents' union because your father had a unique situation. There aren't many elvish orphans. Shifters and vampires are more secretive, but I haven't heard of any intermixing in their races. It's sad now that I think about it, but our lives are lived very much separately."

"My plan is to change that completely. We still have a couple hours before the sun comes up. I'm going to try to get some rest then go visit Ruvaen to ask for his help. There may be a couple other people who would be willing to pitch in if we need them. I have a feeling this is much bigger than just taking over the Easthaven Crest throne."

"I think you're right."

WHEN I WAKE FROM MY FITFUL NAP, SEVERAL HOURS HAVE passed, but I don't feel any more rested than when I first lay down. But I have too much to do to try to sleep now. After a quick shower, I step in front of the mirror, and the dark black bruises in the shape of fingers serve as a stark reminder of the dangers waiting for me.

With my hands on the vanity for support, I lower my head and close my eyes. I've learned defensive and offensive magic to protect myself. But in the heat of the moment, I couldn't think straight to do anything except swat at him with my fists. That wasn't even part of the war—it was only a minor skirmish. If I'm going to survive the real conflict that's coming, I have to keep my cool and use the skills I've already mastered.

My hope is the elves will be able to help me learn that

control. Rycan doesn't seem to have any fear and is always in charge of the situation. I never pushed the topic before, but now I wonder what caused the rift between him and Saban. Should that have been a red flag to me before now?

As Ginevra tried to tell me, I can't keep second-guessing everything about Saban. Loving him wasn't wasted time at all. He spoke the words and carried out the acts, but I'm holding on to the possibility he wasn't responsible for any of it. If the warlock somehow possessed him, there's a chance Saban doesn't even realize what he did.

But can I ever trust him? How can I find out the truth?

"Those are problems for another day, Sara. Those are numbers 992 and 993 on your list. You're just now starting on number one."

After I dry my hair and pull it into a loose ponytail, I walk into the bedroom. A large duffel bag is on the bed, stuffed to the brim. When I open it, all my belongings from the palace are inside. I smile to myself, knowing only one person would've packed my clothes and shoes for me.

"Addi."

I rush out after dressing, hoping to catch her still in the Veil, but she's already left. More disappointment hits me in the center of my chest. I had so many questions for her...yes, mainly about Saban, but for strategic purposes as much as for personal reasons.

"She said to tell you Saban is acting very strangely. His personality flipped overnight, and even the council members are concerned about how dangerous he's becoming. One member asked where you were, and he told them you were dead." Ginevra stops talking when she sees what a mess my neck is. "After seeing this damage, I'd say he's lucky not to be the dead one."

"This is not the man I know, Ginevra. Can a warlock possess a human body?"

"I've never seen or heard of it, but this is a matter that needs to be brought to our mage council. There's something else you should know, and you won't like it."

"Okay, let's have it. No sugarcoating."

"I've been thinking about everything you told me. Processing it a little at a time because it's too overwhelming to take it all in at once. The warlock has been sending you mental messages, pretending to be Zu. That means he's holding her captive and using her knowledge of you to speak to you. She's been able to keep your identity hidden from him.

"Then you heard her voice, so she was able to reverse the magic flow and get a clear message to you. That tells me they're both somewhere close. To figure out where, you'd have to focus on the face you saw and locate him. But you'd have to lower your shields to do that. That is not a good idea, for the record, but he's been draining Zu's power to speak to you. We just don't know how much longer she can hold on under those conditions."

"Whether it's a good idea or not, I'll do whatever it takes to save her. I'm not sacrificing her to save myself."

"When you see Ruvaen, talk to him about it. Maybe he has a better solution or can help in some other way. Let's try all the resources we have before you become a sacrificial lamb yourself."

"Now, that is a good idea. Maybe they will know what to do. I'm off to Elen Sevin now. I'll be back as soon as I can." I kiss Ginevra on the cheek before I leave because I'm not confident I'll see her again. I want her to know how much I appreciate everything she's done to help me and all the risks she's taken on my behalf.

The trip to the elvish border is harder and takes longer than I anticipated. My face is on every billboard and street corner between the Veil and Elen Sevin. Enormous wanted posters calling for my immediate arrest and return to the palace for being a danger to society are everywhere. Residents are urged to call the palace police and not try to apprehend me themselves.

But we all know how the mob mentality works. Once one person becomes bold or greedy for a reward, others will quickly join in until the situation escalates beyond reason or control. Keeping my face hidden and avoiding others means I'm forced to take the long way, through quiet neighborhoods, through the tree line in backyards, and finally through the section of forest where the border lies.

When I finally cross into elvish lands, I breathe a sigh of relief. The worst I'll encounter here is Rycan and his band of angry elves on horseback. His father gave me the secret password, though, and I fully intend to use it, especially if Rycan isn't around. My legs burn as I climb the steep hill, but the elf king's palace is just over the other side.

As expected, my presence doesn't go unnoticed, and a large herd of horses gallops at full speed toward me. I stop in my tracks and wait for them to reach me, hoping standing still in an open field shows I mean them no harm. The riders' swords are drawn and ready to attack, the electricity humming and arcing off the tips with loud pops and crackles.

Rycan emerges from the center of the herd and sheaths his sword. His eyes change from pitch black to light blue in an instant. "You again? Did you not learn your lesson last time, Sara?"

There's a suspicious glint in his eye, but he's at least willing to give me a chance to speak before cutting off my head this time. Maybe our chat at the wedding softened him up more than I realized.

"Dryadalis qui sanctuarii."

His smirk fades and his lips part. A stunned speechless Rycan is a gorgeous being. I may never have the opportunity to enjoy this experience again. He regains his composure and nods once. "I see. Give me your hand, and I'll help you up on my horse. You can ride back to the palace with me."

He lifts me onto the enormous animal with one arm, and I throw my leg over the side. Sitting behind him, I wrap my arms around his waist and hold on tight. I've seen the way they ride—at full throttle. I don't want to be the one who bites the dust when I go flying off the back.

"You can relax your grip a little. I still need to breathe, you know." He glances over his shoulder at me with a genuine smile on his handsome face.

"Okay. But if you make me fall off, I'm telling your dad."

He responds with a loud bark of laughter, and all his men join in. "You have my word. I won't let you fall off. But I can already tell you'll be trouble around here."

"I prefer to call it fun instead of trouble. And in all fairness, you could use a little more fun around here. You're much too serious."

"Oh, Queen Saraya, I have a feeling you'll be the cause of a lot of 'fun' in the very near future. Maybe we should hold off on inviting more until we're sure we can handle what we already have."

"You may have a point there. I'll let you have this round. We're not finished, though."

"You are correct there, my queen. We're nowhere near finished." He nudges the horse with his heel, and we take off toward the palace. The other men surround us, giving us a full escort the entire way.

His words replay in my head, though. *My queen.*

I'm so confused.

I'm not his queen…

"GINEVRA, ARE YOU IN HERE? SORRY IT TOOK ME SO LONG with the elves. I hope I didn't worry you too much. We had a great conversation, and I can't wait to tell you all about it."

I step into the main living room and find her on the floor, curled in a fetal position. Her whole body shakes from her uncontrollable sobbing. I drop everything and rush to her side, kneeling over her and checking for wounds.

"Ginevra, what happened? Who hurt you? Please talk to me."

A long, pitiful moan escapes her throat. There's so much pain behind it, tears spring to my eyes, and I don't even know what's happened yet. She grips my hand, holding it as if it's her only lifeline.

"He killed her. He killed her." She just keeps saying the same three words over and over.

"Who are you talking about? Ginevra, I need you to calm down and tell me what's going on."

"Saban. Killed. Addi."

The room starts spinning, and I lose my balance. I fall to the side and catch myself with one hand. The other one covers my mouth as the tears flow unchecked over my cheeks, dropping onto the floor beneath me. "What? Why? When? How? What?"

I'm just muttering words because I have none that makes any sense. Nothing about this entire world makes sense to me now.

She sniffles and takes a deep breath. "He couldn't find you anywhere, and he knew you two were close."

"She died because of me? It's my fault Addi is gone?"

Tortured screams fill the tree house, so loud they echo off the walls and filter through the glass windows. "No! No, no, no, no, no!'

Then I realize the screams are mine. Sympathy flows to me from all over the Veil as the other mages and wizards share in my pain. There's no blame, though. No one holds me responsible…except me. And Saban.

Aren't we a pair?

I calmly stand and walk outside. Kobi doesn't argue; she simply helps me back down to the ground. Even though I notice the tear she wipes away, I don't stop walking. My mind is made up now that war has officially been declared.

My feet carry me through the darkness back to the castle I left not even eighteen hours before. The place that had been my home. Where I fell in love with the man who has now become a monster.

I stop at the same tree where I dressed after my dramatic exit from Saban's life. After we'd spent the evening talking, sharing intimate details about our lives, and making love until late in the night. Movement catches my attention, and I look up at the same balcony from where I made my escape earlier. Saban steps outside, searching the ground below as if he senses my presence.

So, I move out of the shadows and directly into the bright light of the full moon. Where we can see each other plainly. The crown rests upon his head as if he's the epitome of royalty. He looks directly at me, his lips parting as his grips the balcony railing with both hands.

The barrier around his thoughts is gone now, but they're jumbled and confused. I can't make sense of any of it. Maybe I'm the confused one after everything that's happened in the last few hours. Either way, there's one message I know I want him to hear loud and clear.

Enjoy your new chair while you can. I'm going to burn your world to the ground. You'll be lucky to find the ashes after I'm done.

I send the message straight to him with as much venom as I can muster. He stumbles backward a couple steps and grips his chest with one hand.

Yes, I hope that hurt more than he can stand.

In my peripheral vision, I see silver glimmering in the moonlight. When I glance over to see who's encroaching on my space, I feel as though a sledgehammer has been slammed into my chest from nowhere.

It's Addi…still bound to a stake on the front lawn… with a silver spike driven through her chest. They left her there to send a message to all mages—a visual threat of what's to come for them.

I drop to my knees and scream until I have no voice left to make a simple sound. My heart feels as if it's ripping in two inside my chest. He didn't just kill her—he tortured her. Visions of what she must've endured fill my mind. The fear, the realization I wasn't coming to save her after all the times she helped me, the pain she endured all alone.

It's too much. My warring feelings for Saban, Addi, Ginevra, Nana, and my life are all too much to handle.

The ground beneath me opens up, and the portal draws me inside, hurtling me through time and space, until I land with a thud back in the forest.

My forest.

Regular trees.

Natural wildlife.

I'm back in Aspen Springs, Montana.

What the hell am I doing here?

To be continued in Deceived...coming soon!

ABOUT THE AUTHOR

A.D. Justice is the USA Today bestselling author of the Steele Security Series (Wicked Games, Wicked Ties, Wicked Nights, Wicked Intentions, Wicked Shadows), the Crazy Series (Crazy Maybe, Crazy Baby), the Dominic Powers series (Her Dom, Her Dom's Lesson), the Immortal Obsessions series (Immortal Envy) and a few stand—alone romance novels, such as Saving Grace, Completely Captivated, Just One Summer, Mistletoe Not Required, and Intent.

When she's not writing, she's spending time with her own alpha male character in their North Georgia mountain home. She is also an avid reader of romance novels, a master at procrastination, a chocolate sommelier, a twister of words, and speaks fluent sarcasm. An avid animal lover, A.D. Justice has two horses, three cats, and two very spoiled dogs.

While the primary focus of her books has been romantic suspense, she has expanded into different sub—genres of romance. Stay tuned to read what she has in store for you!

Connect with her online!

Newsletter
Facebook Reader Group
Website

facebook.com/adjusticeauthor
instagram.com/authoradjustice
bookbub.com/authors/a-d-justice
amazon.com/author/adjustice
pinterest.com/adjusticeauthor

BOOKS BY A.D. JUSTICE

Steele Security Series

Wicked Games (Book 1)

Wicked Ties (Book 2)

Wicked Nights (Book 3)

Wicked Intentions (Book 4)

Wicked Shadows (Book 5)

Crossing Lines Series

Fine Line

Blurred Line

Hard Line

Covis Realm: Easthaven Crest

Cloaked, Book One

The Vault Series

Warning, Part One

Warning, Part Two

Warning, Part Three

The Crazy Series

Crazy Maybe (Book 1)

Crazy Baby (Book 2)

Crazy Love (Book 3, Free Short Story)

Dominic Powers Series

Her Dom (Book 1)

Her Dom's Lesson (Book 2)

Stand—alone Novels

Saving Grace

Completely Captivated

Intent

Mistletoe Not Required

Immortal Envy

Just One Summer

ACKNOWLEDGMENTS

Writing a book is no small feat, especially one that delves into a whole new world that's created from imagination. Speaking for myself, I put my heart and soul into the story, taking time away from family and friends to finish writing one more chapter. When I finally reach those two little magical words, a weight is lifted from my shoulders and I'm able to breathe again. Until I start the next book.

My writing journey includes conferring with several people I trust and admire to give feedback and suggestions. There are also people who encourage and support me along the way, taking a chance on a new type of book or a storyline outside the norm. Those who aren't afraid to step outside the box and give "different" a chance. These are my people—my tribe—whether they realize it or not.

Acknowledgments are hard to write because I never

want to leave anyone out or make anyone feel their place in my life isn't important. If you've ever read my books, you hold a special place in my heart. There are a few special people I want to recognize for helping make this book special to me.

First and foremost, I thank my Lord and Savior, Jesus Christ, for his unending love, mercy, and forgiveness of a sinner like me. Without Him, I am nothing. Yes, when I say I fall short, I realize I fall way short, but thankfully, there's no such thing as being too far from Him. He knows my heart.

Michelle Dare and T.K. Leigh, thank you for all your support—every single day. I'm so thankful for your friendship, your insights, and all your advice. You can never leave me...because I'd find you. Love you ladies with all my heart!

Victoria Renteria, thank you for being my alpha reader and putting up with my craziness throughout this entire process!

Lisa Hollett with Silently Correcting Your Grammar, my editor and my friend, thank you once again for working through this book with me, polishing it until it shines, and laughing with me along the way.

Jennifer Stevens, thank you for creating the map of my world to give readers the lay of the land. It's perfect!

And to my readers, whether you love, like, or hate this book, thank you for taking your time to read it. Thank you for your reviews, even if all you say is you liked it or not. Thank you for your support—you have no idea how much every little bit means to an author.

All my love to you,
Angel